Lightning STRIKES

LIGHTNING STRIKES SERIES 1

Roni Denholtz

Lightning Strikes, © 2020 Roni Paitchel Denholtz
Published by Roni Paitchel Denholtz
Cover and Interior Layout: www.formatting4U.com

For more information on the author and her works, please see www.ronidenholtz.com.

For a long moment, they regarded each other. The moment stretched, and spun out. Sabrina's breath caught, and then, Parker bent forward, and brushed his lips against hers.

Without thinking, she wrapped her hands around his neck, and pulled him closer.

His lips hardened against hers, the kiss going from tender to demanding in an instant.

She felt electrified, heat licking her nerves from her head down to her toes. Her heart accelerated, and she felt bursts of energy and desire throughout every cell.

He pressed her closer.

She could smell his lively aftershave, feel his springy hair by his neck. She could hear the quick breaths and feel the rapid beat of his heart against her body as he held her tightly in his arms.

She couldn't think; she could only feel these things, feel the acute awareness of being held by Parker, kissed by him.

DEDICATION

For My Friend

Judith Amy Sanger

You Introduced Me to the Book
"Hidden Channels of the Mind"
In 10th Grade…
Which Really Sparked My Interest
In the Paranormal.

This one is for you, Judy!

ACKNOWLEDGEMENTS

Thank you to my editor and formatter extraordinaire, Judi Fennell!

Thank you to the many people—too many to name—who shared their fascinating psychic experiences with me, especially Christina Lynn Whited and Christina Santoli.

Thank you to our daughter Amy who designed The Lightning Center's logo!

CHAPTER I

Did she really want to be here?

Sabrina swallowed and shifted in her chair, clutching her purse in her lap. The leather strap dug into her palm.

"So, I see from the form you filled out that you're healthy," the social worker sitting at the desk said, skimming the papers Sabrina had filled. She'd introduced herself as Meredith Costigan, and she seemed friendly. "And the nurse who just saw you said your blood pressure is normal to low—which is good—and everything else looks fine…"

As she continued, Sabrina tried to relax her hands, loosening her grip on the purse. She knew she shouldn't be nervous. But she felt the impulse to flee that she'd felt briefly in the waiting room. Did she really want to be at this place, The Lightning Center, participating in one of their studies?

She knew only a little about them. Her general physician, Dr. Hutchins, and her best friend Leanne had persuaded her to come here and take part in their studies.

The Lightning Center had been advertising on and off the last few months. They were looking for people who'd been struck by lightning, and developed, or had enhanced, ESP and other abilities. They wanted them to participate in research studies and help their staff to "learn more about these extra-ordinary abilities." Sabrina had always wanted to use her power to astral project for something good. She was also intrigued by their research. And, she also secretly hoped these studies would help her. Help with her crazy dreams and the results, which were increasingly interrupting her sleep.

Now she wasn't sure. She knew they'd have to examine her and do tests—but the brochure she'd read in the waiting room about all the cutting-edge research they were doing had unnerved her. She hoped those studies didn't bring back those feelings of being a freak, an outcast because she was "different."

"Studies of people struck by lightning, and the amazing abilities some have acquired…" was one phrase from the pamphlet which stuck in her brain.

"So…" the woman said, meeting Sabrina's eyes. "Tell me, about the day you were struck by lightning and how you actually discovered your ability."

Sabrina stared at the counselor. The woman was attractive, with long red hair, and appeared to be in her early 30s. Dr. Meredith Costigan, she'd introduced herself. The social worker here at The Lightning Center. She would interview Sabrina before she began seeing any doctors or having any tests.

Sabrina swallowed. The counselor was calm, her voice soothing, and she had tried to put Sabrina at ease. But Sabrina didn't feel completely comfortable. She switched her position, crossing her legs in front of her, and smoothing one hand on her jeans. She gazed around the office, painted a soothing sky blue.

2

"It's all right," Meredith said, as if sensing her discomfort. A subtle floral fragrance surrounded her. "Most people are a little nervous when they first come here. Some haven't let another soul know about their abilities. Everything you say here is confidential." She smiled suddenly. "Believe me, I understand. I've seen over one hundred people in the last three years, many of them feeling nervous the first few times they came in." She paused.

"I…" Sabrina hesitated. Meredith really did look like a nice person. Her face held an expression of sympathy and caring.

"I was never struck by lightning myself," Meredith continued. "But my own grandmother had dreams—many of which foretold future events—so I do understand the ramifications when people have ESP and other psychic abilities."

"Was your grandmother struck by lightning?" Sabrina asked, curious about this woman's family.

Meredith shook her head. "No—at least we don't know if she was. She's been gone for many years now, so we can't ask." She leaned forward slightly, regarding Sabrina across her wood desk, which was piled with folders and what looked like a few photos. "But my brother and sister—they're twins—were struck."

Sabrina opened her mouth to question Meredith, but then shut it. She wasn't here to discuss Meredith's family. She sighed, knowing she had to answer the question about how she was struck. Which was only the first of many, she guessed.

"It was eighteen years ago when I was struck," Sabrina began. "I was ten. I was playing in our backyard. My sister—she was almost eight—was

3

playing with the girl next door at her house. It was a nice fall day. My mother was inside with my brother—he was five—he was getting over a cold and he was watching cartoons. She was doing laundry. It was a Wednesday afternoon, and I had no homework." She paused, recalling the day. "I was on the swing. I had just finished a Nancy Drew book and was imagining I was solving mysteries too."

Meredith smiled. "Many of us did that when we were younger. Nancy's character was actually a good role model."

Sabrina focused on one of the many colorful landscapes hung around the room. She recognized Stonehenge in one photo. A mysterious place, in keeping with this institution which sounded a little spooky too.

"Go on," Meredith said simply.

Sabrina shifted in her chair again. It was hard to talk about that day, after all her mother's admonishments to keep it a secret. She was used to remaining silent about this aspect of herself. But Meredith had assured her that whatever was said at The Lightning Center, stayed here. Kind of Las Vegas. She smiled briefly at that thought.

Sabrina consciously tried to relax her hands, which were still gripping the brown straps of her shoulder bag.

"It was windy. I remember hearing thunder—but it seemed far away. I went back to thinking about how I could solve a mystery. Then I felt something, a stinging—like I was stung by a bee, only hotter and stronger. On my arm. Next thing I remember, I opened my eyes, and I was on the ground, and my mom was shrieking."

4

"And..." probed Meredith. She extended her hand, palm up, as though inviting more confidences. Her smile was gentle.

Sabrina shrugged. "Someone called 9-1-1, and they took me to the hospital. My dad met us there. The doctors checked me. I felt kind of dazed—but they said I was alright." She frowned. "We went home, and later I heard my father yelling at my mother that she should have told me to come in, there were reports of thunder and lightning in the area. I could have been killed. She yelled back that she didn't know about the bad weather. They hovered over me, though, for the next few days, so I knew they'd been scared. But I—I thought I was alright, and so did they." She leaned back in her chair. The cream colored- material was newer looking and the seat felt comfortably cushioned. She deliberately relaxed her body.

Meredith was nodding. "So everyone thought you had no effects from being struck by lightning."

"Yes." Sabrina paused again. After the last few years—keeping her secrets to herself—it was hard to talk about what her mother called the "weird results" of that accident now.

"Why don't you tell me about the first time you experienced astral projection," Meredith said quietly.

Sabrina uncrossed her legs. "I didn't know what it was."

"Of course. You were young."

"I was in bed but not asleep. It was about three or four weeks after I was struck. At dinner my parents were discussing this kid, Jake, from the neighborhood, who had run away. He was a teenager, and I didn't know him well, I'd just seen him around. Everyone

5

had been out looking for him that afternoon, and there were police all over the place."

Sabrina fell silent, remembering lying in bed with her covers drawn up around her.

"I started thinking about him..." she paused. Really, this was difficult. She hadn't told this tale for years. She bit her lip.

"And...?"

"And—suddenly I felt like—like I was floating. I could look down, and see my house. It was dark out, but the moon was shining—almost a full moon—and I could see clearly. I began moving, floating. It actually felt good." She felt herself smiling, remembering the sensation which was now all too familiar to her. "And I began to—kind of—fly. I was looking down into the woods that were right near our development. Suddenly, I could see where Jake was. He was huddled in the woods, with a blanket, and I knew he was cold. He was further away than the area they'd been searching, past some old camp grounds. I floated above him—I could see him!"

She stopped, remembering her excitement and amazement. Meredith was nodding, a smile on her face.

"I knew I had to let someone know," Sabrina continued. "I could feel myself going backwards, and then suddenly I was back in bed. I jumped up and ran downstairs to tell my parents." She paused, remembering their astonishment as she had described her experience. "They didn't believe me at first.

"And then my mother said to my father, 'we should at least call the police and tell them where to look. We'll tell everyone Sabrina dreamed about it'. My dad agreed. They called, and then they told me to go back to sleep.

The next morning, I was tired, but they told me Jake had been found by the police, right where I'd told them to look." She couldn't help the satisfied note that crept into her voice. She had helped someone.

"You certainly helped to rescue that boy," Meredith said. "How did your parents and everyone react to your finding him?"

Sabrina switched her position again. "Well—my parents did not want to talk to people about it. They kept telling me to tell everyone I dreamt it. I didn't understand why, but I went along with their wishes. I even wondered if they were right, if maybe it *was* a dream. My mom told me she didn't want the neighbors or anyone to ask a lot of questions. I learned later a reporter did come around, but my parents sent him away."

"How did you feel?"

"At that point I felt pretty good, like maybe I saved his life or something. I felt important."

Meredith smiled. "How do you think your parents felt?"

Sabrina shrugged. "At the time, I thought they felt embarrassed. Later, I learned they were—scared, I guess, is the best way to put it."

"Scared?"

"Yes. They didn't want people to know—especially my mom didn't want people to know—that I had this, this ability— "

There was a rapping on the door, and a masculine voice called out "Meredith?"

"I'm with a patient," Meredith answered.

"Just wanted to drop off those test results you needed."

"Oh, okay. Do you mind if I get these?" she asked, looking at Sabrina.

"No." Sabrina shook her head.

Meredith stood up. "This will only take a moment. Come in," she called.

The door opened, and a man in a white lab coat entered.

He was over six feet, with broad shoulders. He had dark, slightly wavy hair and a handsome face. A hint of a citrusy aftershave entered the room with him.

Sabrina focused on him, and her pulse jumped.

He was handsome, no question, but she had seen plenty of handsome men before.

But this man—she guessed he was a doctor here—also exuded a certain powerful, intense persona that she could actually *feel*. It was jarring.

As their eyes met, the zing that arrowed through her was nearly as sharp and electrifying as the lightning strike she'd experienced as a child.

She tried to quiet her thudding heart.

"Sabrina, this is my brother, Dr. Parker Costigan," Meredith said, indicating him. "You'll be meeting with him sometimes when you're here."

A look of surprise overtook his face for just a second before he smiled at her. Warmth flowed through her at his smile.

But he *had* been surprised. She knew it.

"Parker, this is Sabrina Holt," Meredith said.

"Nice to meet you," he said. Striding forward, he extended his hand.

Sabrina took his warm hand, feeling a little shock of awareness as his fingers touched hers. She could smell his pleasant aftershave more strongly now. His grip was firm, and for a moment, she had the impulse to cling to his hand.

She withdrew hers reluctantly.

"Nice to meet you," she said hastily. She hadn't realized she had risen until she noticed he towered over her five feet two inches. She sat down, folding her hands in her lap. Her right hand tingled where he had gripped it.

He was studying her.

Meredith coughed.

At the sound, Dr. Costigan transferred his gaze to his sister. As they looked at each other, Sabrina could see a resemblance. They both had straight noses, full lips without being overly full, and large eyes, though his were bluish-gray and hers green. Their hair colors were very different—his so dark, hers so bright. And although Meredith was tall—probably about five six or seven—she was not as tall as her brother. But as she smiled at him, the resemblance was clear to Sabrina.

But it was Parker's engaging smile that Sabrina felt herself responding to. She returned it.

"Sorry to interrupt—but you said you wanted to look at these results right away." He handed a folder at his sister. "Let me know what you think after you've had a chance to review these."

He turned to gaze at Sabrina again. "I look forward to working with you." Abruptly, he left the room, shutting the door quietly behind him.

"Sorry about that," Meredith apologized. "I've been anxious to see these test results. Now, where were we? You said your Mom didn't want others to know about your ability…"

"Yes," Sabrina said. "I didn't understand why she

was so anxious to keep things quiet. But each time I had an episode—of astral projection—she urged me not to talk about it." She stilled, remembering the times when she had spoken, and the awful consequences. She bit her lip, not quite ready to speak about that yet. Maybe in the future.

"Were your other projections similar?" Meredith questioned.

"Yes. I projected a couple of times during the next year. I didn't realize exactly what was happening to me. After a couple of times, it seemed to get easier for me to leave my body, and come back. And things started to look clearer than the first few times it happened."

Meredith had been making occasional notes, and now she scribbled on her pad. "And now?"

"Now, the projections are usually vivid."

"I see." Meredith sat back. "I have to admit we're eager to learn more about your ability, here at the center." She smiled. "Let me explain what's going to happen."

Meredith went on to describe how all their subjects were checked to make sure they were healthy, by first the nurse, then the doctor. They were all scheduled to meet with her sister Dr. Pamela Costigan, a psychiatrist; and her brother Parker, who was the neurologist here. "He'll get a baseline reading of your normal brain waves," she said, in her soothing voice. "Then he'll test you again while you're experiencing a projection."

A sudden flare of excitement moved through Sabrina as she thought about meeting with Dr. Parker Costigan again.

Parker left Meredith's office and strode down the hallway, past his twin sister Pamela's office, until he reached his own. Entering, he shut the door firmly behind him, went around his desk, then dropped into his chair.

His heart beat erratically—an unusual sensation.

He pulled open his bottom drawer, the one with his personal papers. Reaching inside, he felt the well-worn folder. He gripped it and pulled it out.

He opened it and removed the sketch Pamela had drawn when they were only sixteen.

It was done with pencil on simple white copy paper. She'd drawn it in the morning, after she'd had the dream, and given it to him. "This woman is going to be someone important to you," Pamela had said at that time. "Maybe, someone you'll care a lot about."

He stared now at the face in the sketch.

It was a shock to see the attractive woman today in Meredith's office.

Because the woman—Sabrina Holt—was the one in the picture Pamela had drawn.

Pamela's precognition dreams were usually spot on. He inhaled sharply, staring at the picture he'd kept and glanced at from time to time over the years. Only six months ago, Pamela had asked him again if he'd ever met the woman she'd drawn that morning long ago.

"No," he'd answered his sister.

But now he had. And his heart had started thudding immediately.

The dark, shoulder-length, wavy hair, the pretty features—all were there. She was more than attractive—she was beautiful. It was a black and white drawing, but Pamela had said the woman in her dream had brown eyes.

As did Sabrina.

The shock of seeing the woman from the picture had reverberated down to his toes.

She was here, in real life. The woman Pamela had dreamed of. The one who was supposed to be important to him.

And on top of that surprise, he'd felt a thrill. An awareness. The kind of feeling he hadn't felt for a long, long time.

As he studied the sketch, that zing moved through him again.

Sabrina Holt. She was here, to take part in their studies. He'd be seeing her, interacting with her.

A woman who, according to Pam, was destined to be someone important to him.

CHAPTER II

Sabrina hesitated at the door to The Lightning Center and looked around. The modern building was discreetly labeled "Medical Offices" but there was a logo of a lightning bolt on the side of the door.

She'd wrestled with the choice of returning, or not, for the last few days. On one hand, she was curious about the research they were doing at The Lightning Center and it was kind of exciting to think she could be a part of it. They might provide her with opportunities to use her ability for something good. There was also the possibility that their studies could help her at some point, perhaps to learn how to have more control.

But on the other hand, what if it made things worse? Or it brought out her feelings of insecurity form the past?

The handsome Dr. Costigan had also been in her thoughts more often than she liked. And the last thing she needed now was a crush on a good-looking guy.

She took a deep breath. Colorful leaves were beginning to show on the trees, typical for mid-September in northwestern New Jersey. On this Friday, her day off this week, their brightness glowed in the autumn sunlight.

Attempting to ignore her ability for over a year hadn't made it go away, a little voice in her head said. She might as well confront it. Slowly, her hand reached toward the doorknob.

A woman with short, snowy white hair appeared on the other side of the glass pane in the door. Opening the door, she smiled and said in a cheery voice, "Don't just stand there, my dear. Please come in."

Sabrina entered, and the woman shut the door behind them.

The older woman wore a white shirt, blue sweater and gray pants with large earrings that looked like sapphires. Her blue eyes twinkled. Her skin was lovely and flawless, and Sabrina guessed she must be in her seventies, but she sensed a vitality in the woman that belied her years.

"I'm Lorna MacIntyre," the woman introduced herself, and extended her hand. Sabrina shook it. Lorna's handshake was firm but her skin soft. "I'm one of the volunteers here."

"Sabrina Holt," Sabrina introduced herself. "I'm a—a client here…" her voice dwindled.

Lorna nodded. "I saw your name on the roster. Emily, you can check off that Sabrina is here," she said to the young woman who sat behind the large wooden reception desk.

Emily gave Sabrina a smile. "Hi. Lorna, she has an appointment with Dr. Pamela Costigan today."

"Dr. Pam is our psychiatrist," Lorna chatted. "Meredith must have told you that, right?" At Sabrina's nod, she continued. "Next, you'll have an appointment with Dr. Parker Costigan, our neurologist."

Dr. Parker Costigan… the man she'd found so

attractive. Sabrina followed Lorna down the hall to the right. Meredith—who had told her she had a doctorate in social work—had mentioned that many of their family members worked here in addition to other staff members.

"Are you a relative of the Costigan's?" Sabrina asked Lorna.

"No, but I wish I was," Lorna answered. "I love them. I've known Katherine and Edward from the neighborhood for many years, and I watched their children grow up—Meredith and Parker and Pamela."

"Were you ever struck by lightning?" Sabrina was curious to know if most of the people working here had been struck.

Lorna regarded her, her expression growing serious. "As a matter of fact, I was. I don't remember, but my mother told me that my carriage was struck when I was an infant and the nanny had me out for a stroll. As far as I know, I've always had this—talent, as I like to call it. But perhaps it did start when I was struck by lightning. Who knows?"

"And what talent—" she began.

"Here we are." Lorna stopped in front of the door labeled "Dr. Pamela Costigan." "I'll tell you about myself some other time." As Sabrina drew closer, she caught a whiff of a subtle but classy perfume surrounding Lorna.

Lorna rapped on the door, and a feminine voice called "come in."

Lorna opened the door and Sabrina entered. She heard the door shut quietly behind her.

The woman who was coming around the desk paused and stared at her for just a moment, a surprised expression on her face. Almost instantly that expression changed to a welcoming one.

"I'm Dr. Pamela Costigan," the woman said. "But please call me Pam." She shook Sabrina's hand. "We're informal here."

Pamela Costigan was a beautiful woman, shorter than her siblings, with dark blond hair with frosted highlights which fit her coloring perfectly. She had hazel eyes and the same fair skin as her sister Meredith. In fact, there was a definite resemblance among all the siblings, Sabrina realized as she took a seat in front of Pam's desk. As Pamela smiled, Sabrina could see the siblings all had similar wide smiles and straight white teeth. Fraternal twins might not resemble each other at all, but Parker and Pamela did look like brother and sister.

"So, I understand you've met my older sister Meredith," Dr. Pamela began, and Sabrina nodded. She caught Pamela's perfume, a fruity scent that she vaguely recognized as a popular one from a specialty bath shop. "And my twin brother Parker."

"Yes."

Pamela grinned. "Parker is older by fifteen minutes." She laughed lightly, a pleasant sound. "So, tell me a little about you, and your family. For instance, what careers are your siblings and parents involved in?"

"My mother is a speech therapist—she worked part time at a school when we were little, and full time now," Sabrina began. "My father was an architect, specializing in office buildings. Your building is very cool," she added.

"Thank you. I read your chart and saw he was

16

deceased," Pamela said, her voice full of sympathy. "Several years ago?"

"He had a heart attack suddenly, a year after I graduated from college," Sabrina said, feeling the familiar dull ache. "I miss him. He'd gotten heavy, and become diabetic, and hadn't watched himself like he should have."

"I understand. And your sister and brother?"

"My sister Lindsay is a lawyer specializing in wills and estates. She just finished law school in May and is working. My brother is in grad school, studying aerospace engineering. I'm a librarian," Sabrina finished.

"What attracted you to library science?" she asked.

Sabrina smiled briefly. "I love to read—and I never minded doing research when I was in school. I got my MLS degree right after college and I work at a small library branch in Sussex County. I'm a reference librarian."

"That's demanding work."

Sabrina shrugged. "Sometimes, but I enjoy it. I really got into doing research after I began to astral project more often."

"How did that interest come about?" Pamela leaned forward.

"I kept trying to read up on psychic abilities— like my astral projecting, ESP, and more," Sabrina stated. "Trying to find information, I realized I like researching."

"That's fascinating," Pam said, and Sabrina realized she was being sincere.

Years of astral-projecting had also given her an instinct for reading people. She didn't think she had true telepathy—reading people's minds—but more of a sense about them and their emotions.

"Don't worry about talking to me," Pamela said suddenly, her face holding a look of empathy that was appealing. A sense of comfort seemed to reach out and wrap itself around Sabrina like an old blanket, and something within her eased. She felt less alone here with Dr. Pam. She believed that Pam *did* understand and feel sympathetic.

Sabrina glanced around the cream and gold office, which was just as soothing as Meredith's. Landscapes hung on these walls too.

"Meredith mentioned you and Parker were struck by lightning." Sabrina veered the subject, curious as to what Pam would say.

Pam nodded. "As a matter of fact, we were. We were playing, kind of tugging on a toy we both wanted, outside on a calm day. Lightning came out of nowhere and hit the toy and we were both shocked." She smiled briefly. "We were only four, but I remember it well. Meredith was seven and she and our mother came running from a few yards away."

"Oh. So, you remember, and understand," Sabrina said. "You're the first person I've met—except for Lorna a few minutes ago—who's ever been hit by lightning," she continued. "I didn't know another soul who… experienced what I did. Do you and your brother have any abilities since that day?" she questioned.

Pam smiled again. "Actually, my brother and I have *always* had the ability to communicate on some level with each other. It comes with being twins," she added, her smile growing. "We're close; and it is not unusual for twins to have the psychic ability to communicate with each other. I've done research on it myself." She leaned back in her chair. "As to whether it grew stronger after we were struck—who's to know if it would have been this strong anyway, or the lightning gave us an enhanced communication? I like to think it's the latter, and so does Parker. But the truth is, even at a young age, we could often sense what the other wanted, or was thinking."

"I've read that twins can do that." Sabrina nodded. The fascinating studies on twins had been part of her own research. "The studies have proved that."

"Yes," Pam agreed. "Although sometimes it's a little embarrassing to have your brother know that you think a guy who's a friend of his is hot."

Sabrina grinned.

"Meredith told me about your first experience with astral projection," Pam said. "What happened after that? When did you experience it again?"

Sabrina hesitated. It had been a long time since she'd spoken to anyone about her experiences, except for the first afternoon when she'd come in to The Lightning Center and had seen Meredith Costigan. If it hadn't been for her friend Leanne's urging, she might not have come here.

"Sabrina?"

"Oh, sorry, I was—thinking." Sabrina sat up straighter. "I'm not sure I should be here. I still have trouble speaking about my projecting."

"Why is that?"

Sabrina sighed. "I was taught to hide it."

"My sister mentioned that. Why do you think your parents didn't like speaking about your ability?"

Sabrina frowned. "When I was younger, I thought it was because they were embarrassed. It's like—well,

I had a friend in college who had epilepsy. Her parents told her to keep it a secret."

Pam gave a vigorous nod of her head. "Perhaps because many years ago, they sometimes put epileptics in mental institutions."

"Yes. I wondered if my mom and dad thought people would be prejudiced against me because I was different."

"We prefer to call it unique, here at the center," Pam stated.

"I wish my parents had viewed it that way," Sabrina couldn't hide the asperity in her voice.

Pam raised her eyebrows but said nothing.

"Sometimes it was hard not to talk about it," Sabrina admitted.

"Did you want to?"

"Yes. Sometimes I wanted to—brag about being able to float, and move around," Sabrina said. "Especially when I was younger. Now, I don't talk about it, or at least, I only talk to a couple of people, like my best friend." She looked away, uncomfortable about admitting how her projections had made her feel different.

Pam looked like she wanted to question her more about this topic. At least that's what Sabrina felt Pam wanted to do.

Instead, the doctor changed the topic. "Why don't you tell me a little about your projections?"

"Well… after the first time, I found if someone or something was missing, I could often find them. I would lay down, and think about the person or thing— and in some cases, an animal—and feel myself flying toward them. It happened a few times in the next two or three years. I found two lost dogs and a lost cat, actually." Sabrina smiled. "I was pretty proud of myself. But—each time, though, my mother made me tell people I had dreamed about it."

She thought about Devon, but she was definitely not ready to discuss the devastating results of telling him the truth.

"Why do you think she asked you to do that?"

"She said that people would accept ESP dreams more easily than the alternative—astral projection," Sabrina admitted. "She really believed that. After I did a lot of reading, I realized that was the term for what I was doing. She—and my father agreed with her—she didn't want people making fun of me."

Pamela gazed at her. "Were people making fun of you?"

"Not at first. They were grateful. But then in high school, I did tell one friend about my—experiences— and she didn't believe me. She said I was lying." Sabrina sighed. "That caused a big rift in our relationship. It was never the same afterwards. She didn't want to spend much time with me after that, and I was hurt. I had other friends, but I didn't tell them after what happened with Joanna."

"To get back to your mother, did she have a hang up about your ability, do you think?"

"I think so. And…"

"And…?" Pam leaned forward again, her look empathetic.

Sabrina sighed, looking down at her hands, which were clutched in her lap. She felt the sharp jabs as her nails dug into her palms. "I did hear my mother talking to my father one night. Apparently, my aunt had projected a few times, and she was never struck by lightning. From

21

what they were saying, people made fun of my aunt, and that's why my mother didn't want me being honest about it. She was afraid they'd mock me, too.

"I believe my mom was worried," she continued. She wanted to tell Pam everything, since she looked so caring. About her struggles to control the projections at night. About what had occurred with Devon too, much as the thought of him made her cringe. But she held back on that subject.

But right now, she'd focus on her family, and how she'd reacted to them.

"My parents' reactions made me mad," she said. "They didn't even want to tell my aunt, who had the same ability! Or my brother and sister. Later—much later—we all discussed it, but for years it was like a deep, dark secret." She grimaced.

"It's understandable that you'd be angry with their lack of support," Pam said. "How did you deal with your anger?"

Sabrina looked away. "Mostly, I avoided it. Avoided every discussion of my ability."

"Avoid—why?"

She kept her focus on one of the landscapes, showing a beach at sunset. "I'm not—comfortable with my feelings about astral projection."

<hr />

Parker was reading over the file on Ray Tarrington when Pam suddenly appeared in his office doorway.

His sister's face was flushed. "Parker!"

"Yes?" He *knew* what had her excited. It was

Friday, and he knew from their early morning staff meeting that Pam was going to see Sabrina Holt this morning, since Sabrina sometimes worked on weekends and had days off during the week.

Pam marched in and shut the door. Plopping down in one of the chairs facing his desk, she speared him with an accusing expression. "Why didn't you tell me?"

He could have innocently asked "tell you what?" but it was no good playing games with his twin sister. On principle he didn't like to lie to his family; but even if he wanted to, he knew he wouldn't get away with it. Not with Pamela. They could read each other too easily—always had.

Before he could say a word, she continued. "The picture. You have it here, don't you?"

In answer he opened his drawer, took out the file he had gazed at only last Friday, and opened it. He handed the black and white sketch to Pam, who had drawn it approximately sixteen years ago.

"Is this what you're referring to?" he asked. But he didn't have to ask. He knew she was.

She took it, studying the sketch intently. Finally, she raised her eyes to his.

"It's her," she said breathlessly. "Sabrina Holt. She's the one I dreamed of all those years ago. This picture looks exactly like her."

"I know," he agreed, sighing. "I recognized her the minute I met her."

Pamela lay the picture carefully back down on his desk. "What are you going to do about it?" she asked eagerly.

"Do?" He found himself shaking his head. "Nothing. Absolutely nothing."

23

"But—you can't, Park. She's the one—she's going to be important in your life!"

"Not if I can help it." He tucked the picture back in the folder, closed it, and placed it back in the drawer before shutting it with a decisive click. "Besides everything else, Sabrina Holt is a patient here. We have to keep things professional."

"But— "

"No." He said it firmly. "Don't even think about that picture and what you thought it meant, Pam."

But even if he hadn't seen the mutinous look on his twin's face, he would have known she didn't agree with him.

Now he would have not only a potential problem with Sabrina, but with his twin sister, too. Because he *knew* she thought the picture represented his true love.

"Have you said anything to Meredith?" he asked. Since she was divorced, his older sister was pretty skeptical about the whole love thing.

"No, but I will. She remembers the picture. Oddly enough, we were talking about it just a few weeks ago—and I don't like to hide things from her. You know that. Just as I don't hide things from you," she said, looking him straight in the eyes.

"Because you can't," he teased, hoping some levity would get them away from the topic of the picture and Pam's precognition dreams.

"You can't either," she retorted. "And, that picture has you more shook up than you're letting on." She gave him what could only be considered a smug smile.

"So you say," he said dryly. "We'll see about that."

"Yes, we'll see." And his sister winked at him.

24

CHAPTER III

Sabrina applied cherry lip balm. Then, picking up her purse, she exited the ladies' room.

She was only planning to do a few errands now—the dry cleaners, the grocery, maybe a nearby shoe store. But her lips were dry after all the talking she'd done with Dr. Pam.

She turned towards the entrance area, and saw Parker Costigan coming down the hall.

Her heart started to beat rapidly.

His footsteps slowed as he drew near her. "Hello, Ms. Holt." He regarded her seriously.

"Hello, Dr. Costigan." Her voice came out somewhat breathless.

"I understand you were meeting with my twin sister today," he said, regarding her.

She played with the strap on her purse. "Yes. She's—very nice. Very sympathetic."

"Yes." There was a note of pride in his voice.

Sabrina knew that her next two meetings would be with Parker's father, the general practitioner here; and then with Parker. And later there were the psychologists who did testing.

That's if she stayed on. She still had mixed feelings. Would it eventually help her?

But her night time projections were interfering with her sleep. If there was a chance that she could get help with controlling her ability, to really harness it for good the way she'd always hoped…

"I like to think we're all understanding here," Parker continued.

"Both of your sisters are," Sabrina stated, breathing in his citrusy aftershave.

"Thank you." For a moment he regarded her, and she found herself staring back.

Why was her heart beating so quickly? She'd met other handsome guys before. Parker Costigan was definitely good looking, but she sensed he was more than an attractive man. There was a certain character, an intensity to his face that made him more than simply handsome. And she wasn't sure why he appealed to her so much. What had caused such a strong attraction towards him?

Footsteps sounded in the carpeted hallway behind her. Turning, she saw an Asian man in a lab coat, wearing glasses, approaching them. He appeared to be in his mid-30s.

"This is Dr. Neal Wu," Parker introduced him. "Neal, Sabrina Holt. Sabrina, you'll be meeting with him and Dr. Alicia Fitzgerald for testing, in the coming weeks."

Dr. Wu greeted her. "Please, call me Neal," he added. "We're pretty informal here."

"Call me Sabrina," she said, smiling.

Neal addressed Parker. "May I speak to you for a minute, Parker?"

"Of course. I was just on my way to the conference room." He waved his hand in the direction

Dr. Wu had come from. He smiled at Sabrina. "I'll see you soon, Sabrina."

"Bye." She watched as they strode off together, their voices pitched low. The only word she could distinguish was "telekinesis."

She was wondering about her own testing when she walked into the lobby and said goodbye to the receptionist.

The following Friday, Sabrina was checked by Edward, the general practitioner at The Lightning Center. He declared her to be perfectly healthy. Then she went on to meet with Parker.

Seeing him again sent another zing of awareness through her system. Her pulse sped up, and she hoped it wouldn't be discernable.

"Hi," he greeted her. He wore an open lab coat over a striped shirt and dark blue jeans.

"Hi." She sat on the examination table.

"I'll be doing some standard testing today," he explained, rolling over a machine. "This is to get a base line reading on your brain waves," he added in a calm voice. "Later, we'll compare it to your readings when you're astral projecting. The machine here is an electroencephalogram. We'll see your EEG waves."

She hoped that her reaction to Parker wouldn't affect her brain waves.

Parker attached various implements to her head, hooking her up to the EEG machine. "We've developed some of our town tests here," he said in a conversational voice.

She made an effort to relax her body.

"Would you like music?" he asked.

"Yes." She watched as he went over to an iPod. Classical music filled the air a moment later.

"Just relax," he told her, sitting down and rolling his chair over to a computer with a screen.

She lay back on the table, and focused on a beautiful photograph on the wall. It depicted the ocean and beach on a tropical aisle. The scene was tranquil.

She was silent, listening to the music and studying the photo. After a few minutes Parker turned to her.

"Very good. Now, I want you to think—just for a couple of minutes—about something that upset you recently."

Immediately, Sabrina flashed back to the discussion she'd had with her mother only a couple of nights ago. She'd told her that she was going to The Lightning Center.

"What are you doing that for?" Her mother's angry tone had come through the phone clearly. "Do you want other people to know about your problem?"

"They don't consider these things a problem," she'd told her.

"But it's weird! They'll think you're weird!"

"No. Everyone who goes there has some kind of ability," she'd defended her choice. But she'd wondered, after getting off the phone, if she was being careless. Did she really want to expose her ability to lots of people, even in a research environment? Did she really want to concentrate on it, perhaps have it brought out more fully?

"That's fine," Parker said. His voice was

soothing. "Okay, I've gotten a good reading on you for when you're agitated. Now, relax, Sabrina." He met her eyes. "And think of something good, something you've enjoyed."

She relaxed her body consciously, thinking about her last vacation. During the summer she and Leanne had visited the Grand Canyon. The beauty and magnificence of nature had taken her breath away.

"Good, very good," he said a few minutes later. He got up. "Okay, we can take off these contraptions." He grinned at her.

"Is that all?" she asked, sitting up.

"Yes, for now. This afternoon we're going to watch you project." His hand removed the first attachment from her head. As his fingers touched her fleetingly, she felt a zap, and shivered.

"Are you cold?"

She shook her head. How could she explain the spark that had zapped her? "No." She left it at that.

Again, he met her eyes. He removed another one of the disks from her head.

"They scheduled a break for you to have lunch," he said, as he took the last one off of her. "You can eat here or go out if you want a change of scene."

"I'll run over to the local Panera," she said, her voice strained. Why did this man affect her so much? "I'll be back in an hour." She rose from the table.

"See you then."

"See you then," she echoed, and left the room.

She spent her lunch wondering just why it was that she was so attracted to Parker.

And... did he feel the same?

When Sabrina returned to the Center, Lorna escorted her upstairs, to a room that looked like someone's living room—only devoid of photographs and items that made it personal. Yes, there were pillows on the blue couch and interesting lamps, a blue ceramic vase that matched some of the blue tones of the room, a white candle on a side table—but it was rather staged looking.

Still, for a room that was kind of a laboratory, it appeared comfortable and homey.

"Dr. Neal will run some simple ESP tests on you next week," Lorna said. "All our clients are tested."

"Meredith mentioned that," Sabrina said.

"Emily asked when you'd like to be scheduled."

"Tuesday evening?" Sabrina asked. She wasn't working that night.

"Okay, I'll tell Emily that. Seven o'clock?"

"That works."

Lorna smiled, and left.

Sabrina was conscious that her heart had begun beating faster than usual. She attributed it to the fact that she was going to have a witness to her astral projection experience—a rare occurrence. Only her college roommate Leanne had witnessed a few of these sessions—and certainly she could count on her fingers the number of times that had happened.

And perhaps her accelerated heart rate could be attributed to the fact that she was going to see Parker again…?

On the heels of that thought, the door swished open, and he entered the room.

He'd taken off his lab coat, revealing the blue and white striped shirt and jeans. His face was set in a serious expression, all business.

"Hi Sabrina," he said.

"Hello."

"Now, the purpose of this session is for us to observe you while you are projecting."

She nodded. "Yes." Her voice came out a little scratchy. "I'll lie down on the couch, then?"

"You get into whatever position is comfortable," he said calmly. "I'll have you hooked up to monitors so we can check your heart beat and your brain waves."

"I told Meredith I like to use a vanilla candle and soft music."

"Yes. We've provided that." He pointed to the candle she'd noticed, then an iPod docked into a station. "We have a variety of music loaded on the iPod. Everything from soft jazz to Rock 'n Roll or classical."

"I use any of those, depending on my mood. Even country-western sometimes." She sat on the couch. Her heart was still beating hard. This was really happening. Would she be able to project as easily as she did at home? She hadn't considered that before, but she did now. "I think I'd like some soft jazz today."

She hadn't had any problems when she'd concentrated on trying to project in the last ten years. And now she was doing it in her dreams—with no conscious attempts—what if she couldn't control it today? She swallowed. She didn't want to disappoint the people here. She wanted to help their research. And find some answers for herself.

"Do you feel ready?" he asked. "I know Meredith mentioned this, but I'm reminding you there is a camera that is over there"—he indicated the small video camera placed unobtrusively across the room—"to record the events here. Neal and Pam will be monitoring that from our computer room next door."

"I'm fine." She cleared her throat. "We can start."

"Okay." He attached some wires to her. Then, dimming the lights, he took a seat on the chair near the couch. "Nurse Maura is also in the computer room, checking the EEG and EKG machines. We find it's best when only one of our staff is with each patient in here." He smiled reassuringly.

Sabrina turned slightly and, moving one of the pillows, slid down on the couch until she was lying looking up at the ceiling.

"Ok, here's the assignment." He handed her a photo. "Pamela says you work better when you have a photo of the person. I want you to find her home."

The photo was of Pamela Costigan. It was her professional photo, the one on The Lightning Center's website. Pamela wore a white lab coat and her long blond hair was pulled back. She was smiling into the camera.

"If you can, please speak while you're projecting," Parker requested.

"I'll try," she agreed.

Sabrina studied the photo for a minute, then let her hands drift to her sides, her right hand still holding the picture. She closed her eyes. "I'm ready." She deliberately relaxed her body. Where her left hand rested against the suede couch, she felt the smooth texture.

She heard him move around, strike a match. Within moments the vanilla scent wafted towards her.

She'd done some experiments with her college roommate, Leanne, the only one of her college friends she'd dare to tell about her ability. They'd discovered that music helped Sabrina to concentrate, and float; and some scents, like vanilla and apple, helped to soothe her.

Within a minute soft jazz music filled the room, swirled lightly around. It was a good sound system, she thought idly. No expense had been spared in this place.

Parker said nothing as she relaxed deeper into the couch. She breathed slowly, rhythmically.

She was ready.

She consciously pushed her inner self up, up. Out of her body. Through the ceiling. Out of the white office building. She was floating. She looked down at its flat, dark roof.

The late afternoon sun slanted over the building, casting some shadows. The trees were bright with color, and here in Mt. Olive it was beautiful, as beautiful as New England in the fall.

She recalled the photo of Pamela, felt the thick paper in her right hand and found herself turning east. She was above Rt. 46, then Interstate 80. Heading east, as if being pulled by an invisible hand. There were cars and trucks below her, more on the opposite side of the road going west.

She seemed to fly as she moved, and could feel wind buffeting her. She heard the traffic as it moved beneath her. It was louder than the music in the room.

She moved away from the Interstate and back on a state road which she quickly recognized as Rt. 46 again, in the Denville area. No—she was turning. She

33

was in Mountain Lakes, a wealthy community with beautiful homes. She was above the Boulevard, the main road through the town.

She continued to fly. She was semi-conscious of the music, the vanilla scent, the electrodes on her forehead—but at the same time they all seemed far away. Far away from where her mind and body were. Her ethereal body.

She remembered that Parker had requested that she speak if she could. "I'm now on the Boulevard," she whispered. "In Mountain Lakes."

She was above some huge houses. Mansions. Many of them were right on the lake, others had a lake view.

She hovered above one home. She dropped closer. The house was lovely. Probably built by Hapgood, the well-known architect who had built many of the homes in this area. She had never been in one, but she did know something about the town. Since her father was an architect, he'd been fascinated by these houses.

She knew this was Pamela's home. Surprised that the young doctor lived in such a large home, she circled it. It was three stories, and she guessed it must hold five or six bedrooms. She caught sight of a sunroom, and a patio, with steps leading to the lake. Potted mums in shades of yellow and crimson were placed at intervals along the steps. The autumn sun reflected on the glassy surface of the lake, making it shimmer.

"I'm above a tan home, three stories—maybe a Hapgood mansion," she said. It's right on the lake, in Mountain Lakes. It's gorgeous."

34

Faintly, as if it was far away, she heard Parker take a deep breath.

"The glare from the sun makes it hard to see in the windows." She continued to hover. A car drove down the road; across from the house, a woman pushed a baby stroller on the sidewalk. "I can go in." She'd done that many times. She directed herself to drop into the house, and did.

She was in a room which must be a formal dining room. Huge, with a large table and ten chairs surrounding it. Where sometimes her vision was misty during an experience—especially if she had traveled a long distance—this time everything was nice and clear. "It's the dining room," she said. "It's got cream colored walls and gold curtains. The chairs are upholstered in red and gold. I can see everything very well. Shall I go into another room?"

"No, that's not necessary." Parker's voice sounded strained.

"Okay…" she murmured. She would return now. She felt herself lifting back through the house, then floating again, going the opposite way. Traffic was growing. More cars and trucks, she could vaguely hear the honking. The sun was blindingly bright as it dipped to the west. It was getting later. "I'm on Route 80 headed west," she said.

She flew along. She was approaching the exit for Budd Lake and Hackettstown. Then she was back on Rt. 46. There, the modern-looking Lightning Center building came into sight. She hovered above it, then dropped down.

She felt herself lower into her body, and settled in. She was acutely conscious of the smell of the

35

vanilla candle, could hear the soft jazz music that before had been a faint, background noise. And Parker's breathing, which was not regular and even, but rapid. As if something had startled him. "I'm back," she announced.

Slowly, she opened her eyes.

The room was dim, with only one small light on a side table, and the candle glowing on another. Parker sat in the shadows on his chair. The probes stuck to her reminded her that she was still being monitored by a couple of machines.

Parker turned his head, regarding her now, not the monitors

"How do you feel?" Parker asked quietly.

She sat up, and had to grip the arm of the sofa as the usual wave of dizziness hit her.

"Fine," she said. "I'm always a little—dizzy, afterwards. And then I'll get tired."

He stood, turned the lights up—but not too bright—and came over to her. He checked her pulse. As he held her hand she couldn't help feeling a shimmer of awareness. His hands were large, the fingers long and strong. Her hand tingled where he touched her.

After a moment, he said, "you're normal." He then proceeded to take off the probes connecting her to the monitors.

Music still played quietly in the background.

"Tell me what you saw," he said. "Again." He was so close she could feel his breath, smell the mint he must have had recently.

She described the large house and its surroundings. She felt rather than saw a little tremor move through him.

"Is that your sister's home?" she asked. "It's so beautiful and elegant."

He sat down on the couch near her. "Not exactly. It *was* her home. It's my parents' house, where we all grew up. They still live there."

She drew in a sharp breath. "Oh. Well, I'm guessing she still considers it her home. That's why I found it."

He studied her. "You're right about that." Abruptly, he got up, moving some of the wires attached to the machines. "She lives in a condo near here, but she always says her real home is the house where we grew up." Parker flashed her a sudden smile, and his serious face became boyish and appealing. "I didn't think of that. But, apparently, something in you connected to that feeling she has."

"My inner self," Sabrina murmured.

He shot her a look.

"That's what I call it," she added.

He brightened the light some more. "Can I get you anything? Water?"

"Yes, thank you."

He disappeared into an adjoining room, and was back moments later with a water bottle. She took a few gulps.

He sat near her again. "How do you feel now?"

"I'm tired. I get a little dizzy after projecting, but that goes away quickly. I'm just left being tired."

"Would you like to lie down?" he asked, regarding her.

"In a few minutes, yes. It's not unusual for me to feel this way," she reassured him, seeing the slight frown on his face.

37

"Then you should rest," he said. "I'll review the heart and EEG records while you do."

"My eyesight was very clear this time, where sometimes things are a little fuzzy." She shrugged. "I have no idea why it was sharper today; except I think it isn't as clear when I have to travel greater distances."

"We'll have to look into that," Parker said. "Do you know how long you were projecting?" he asked.

She met his eyes. "Fifteen minutes? Twenty?"

"Nearly an hour," he told her.

"Oh. I lose track of time when I'm projecting." She yawned, and glanced at her watch. It was three thirty already.

"You're our last appointment of the day," he said, standing. "We try not to schedule appointments too late on Friday so everyone can get home early and start their weekends. But you rest for as long as you want. I'll be here—I have work to do."

"Very considerate of your employees."

"Go ahead and rest," he urged.

"Okay." She slipped back down on the couch and closed her eyes, feeling the familiar weariness. She'd probably doze for a half hour to an hour. She was conscious of his dimming the lights. The couch was comfortable, and she didn't object to the fact that Parker was nearby, although when she'd projected with Leanne, she usually liked to be left alone afterwards. She wondered drowsily why she didn't have a strong desire to be alone…

Hushed voices in the hall woke her. She thought only a few minutes had passed, but when she looked at her watch it read 4:30. She'd dozed off for an hour.

38

She sat up, then waited to see if she felt dizzy again. She didn't. As a matter of fact, she felt clear headed. The nap had been good for her.

"Ok, we've finished up here." She recognized Neal's voice. "Have a good evening, Parker."

"You too," Parker answered.

Sabrina heard footsteps receding down the carpeted hall.

The door creaked open, and she saw Parker peering into the room.

"I'm awake," she said.

He strode in. "When I looked in before, you were deeply asleep. I didn't know how long you would normally sleep after projecting."

"Oh, a half hour to an hour. Usually. I feel well-rested now."

He turned on the lights. When he opened the blinds, she could see outside that the sun was dipping further down.

"How were my medical results?" she asked.

"Everything was perfectly normal. Your heart slowed down as if you were sleeping. Your brain waves were much more active than if you'd been in a resting state, though."

She took the water bottle and drank the cool water, conscious of him standing so close by, his masculine features, the citrus aftershave he favored. "Good to know."

Although the people who worked at The Lightning Center were consistently kind, she knew she was a subject to all of them, someone to study. That's what they did here. Her results were just that—results of testing.

"Are you okay to drive?" he asked.

"I should be. I didn't think of that. Usually, any projecting I do is in my own home."

"Maybe I should drive you home," he suggested, a worried look crossing his face. "Everyone else has left already."

"I'm sorry I made you stay so late—you should have woken me," she said, a flash of guilt moving through her. She hadn't meant for him to stay late at work; she knew how much people wanted to leave on a Friday. Even when she had no plans, she felt the same way herself at the end of a work week.

"It's no problem," he said. "Many of us are often here late, studying some exciting test results."

"I'll get going." She picked up her purse.

"Listen, I skipped lunch and I'm hungry. You probably are too, after that session. Why don't we grab a bite to eat? I'll drive you home afterwards, if you're tired."

She *was* hungry. All she'd eaten for lunch was soup. She wondered how he knew. Maybe other people who projected were hungry afterwards. Not knowing anyone who did what she did, she could only guess. She'd have to ask sometime.

"You're right, I get hungry sometimes after I project," she admitted. "Okay, we can get something to eat." The fact that she would be with Parker was an added bonus. "Thank you."

What the heck was he doing?

He'd driven home a shaky patient once before—but he'd never taken one out to dinner.

Still, he was starved. And he'd known Sabrina was too.

Not that he was about to reveal *how* he knew.

The ride to the local diner—which was a great place to eat—took all of three minutes. He watched as he drove behind Sabrina. She seemed to be driving fine, so he concluded she'd be okay for the fifteen or so minutes she had to drive home after dinner. If she seemed tired, he would do the right thing and either he or one of his sisters could drive her home, and then they could drive her car back for her.

The diner wasn't too crowded yet, since it was early for dinner. They were shown a booth.

"Their food is very good," he said, picking up the menu.

"I know. My family eats here often."

He looked at Sabrina. Although she looked better since her nap—there was color in her face where it had previously looked pale—she still seemed a little bit fragile.

His eyes lingered on her beautiful face. Her thick dark hair invited a man's hands to run through the waves. Her skin looked satiny-soft. He swallowed, all too aware of her presence across form him.

She hadn't opened her menu.

"Do you know what you want?" he asked.

"The hamburger deluxe."

The waitress approached and Sabrina ordered. He ordered a cheeseburger deluxe for himself, and then she brought over their sodas.

His cellphone pinged. "Excuse me," he said. "I'm expecting a text."

"No problem."

41

Taking it out, he saw it was the expected text from Pam. She wanted to know how Sabrina was feeling. She'd left while Sabrina was napping, after watching her incredible projection from the computer room, with Neal. He knew his twin had been surprised that Sabrina had visited their childhood home.

He replied, "Fine. I'm at the diner with her now. She needs to eat."

"Ok. Call me later," Pam texted.

He pocketed his phone.

"Do you live around here?" Sabrina asked, then took a sip of her diet cola.

"Yes, in town, five minutes from here," he said, sipping his own cola. "I wanted to be close to the office, and I like the community of Mt. Olive."

"I grew up here," she said. "We moved here when I was a baby. Now, I'm renting a condo in Stanhope but hope to buy one, or a small house, eventually. You said Pam has a condo in the area?"

"Yes, she has a condo in Hackettstown—just fifteen minutes from here," he said. "It's pretty spacious."

"Does Meredith live nearby?"

"She actually has a house a mile from me in town," he said, "close to the lake."

"She mentioned that she owns a house."

Their burgers were served, and she picked hers up.

He grabbed a fry and bit into the salty, crisp potato. He knew a lot about Sabrina from her files, but there was a lot more he'd like to know. He was going to ask her about where she'd gone to school, when she spoke again.

"Parker's an unusual name. Are you named for a family member?"

"Parker was my grandmother's maiden name, on my mother's side," he said. "But the real reason my mom wanted to name me Parker was, she likes the actor Parker Stevenson. He was, according to her, a very good-looking actor when he was younger. He was one of the stars on a Nancy Drew/Hardy Boys TV series in the 70s," he finished.

"I've seen some of the reruns. Your mom's right—he is cute!"

He laughed. "It always makes me feel awkward when people say that." He chewed some of his hamburger. He'd been really hungry, and the gooey cheese and hearty meat hit the spot.

"It's true." She smiled suddenly. "My mother liked the name Sabrina because it was a character on Charlie's Angels played by Kate Jackson, and she thought the name was pretty. So, in a way we're both named for TV shows," she finished, grinning.

He smiled back. "That's an odd coincidence. And my sister Pamela was partly named for the actress Pamela Sue Martin, who played Nancy Drew on the same show as Parker Stevenson. Plus, my dad really liked the name, and they thought Parker and Pamela sounded nice for twins if they had a boy and a girl."

They chatted about the area and how much it had grown in the last ten years. Parker hadn't known the area well until they opened The Lightning Center three years ago—he was much more familiar with the eastern part of Morris County, where he'd grown up. But he liked it out here, where it was less crowded.

"Would you like dessert?" he asked as they finished their meal.

"No, thanks, I'm full."

The waitress approached, and he held out his hand. "I got this."

"We can split the bill," she offered.

"No, supper was my suggestion."

"Thank you," she said.

"You're welcome." He'd enjoyed the time he spent with her, and hoped she had enjoyed herself, too. "How are you feeling now?" he asked.

"I'm feeling fine." Her wide brown eyes met his.

And that's when the picture popped into his mind.

Him. Holding Sabrina. Their arms were around each other and she was snuggling into his chest. His telepathic ability had read what was in her mind. *Her desire to be held by him.*

The fact that it was also a desire of his, was something he didn't want to think about now.

He coughed, and the image dissipated. Trying to look innocent, he wiped his hands on his napkin.

Along with "seeing" what Sabrina was picturing, he'd felt a yearning. And her yearning had echoed his own.

He would love to hold Sabrina, stroke her silky hair, kiss those pink, lush lips.

"Can I leave the tip?" she asked, interrupting his thoughts.

"No, I've got it." He stood up.

He paid, and she followed him outside.

"You're okay to drive?" He studied her.

She smiled. "I'm fine. I'm going straight home and I'll relax."

The wind had picked up while they were eating, and it felt damp. They'd probably get rain later. He looked up, and saw clouds in the dark sky, hiding the moon.

"You're sure you don't want me to follow you back home?" he asked.

"Certain. I'm fine." She flashed a smile. "Thanks again for dinner."

"Ok, text me when you get there, please," he said. He gave her his cell number and she added it to her contacts.

"See you soon." He waited while she got into her car, started it, and drove away.

He drove home, wondering why he was so attracted to her. Yes, she was beautiful, and he could see that she was a nice person. He'd met plenty of nice, good-looking women. What was so different about Sabrina? It wasn't just that she had an ability, although that was intriguing.

Was it because she seemed trustworthy?

But—he'd thought people were trustworthy before. He'd thought a woman was trustworthy before.

A picture of Dara flashed through his mind.

He grit his teeth. That was one woman he didn't want to think about.

Didn't want to think about her nasty behavior.

***

Sabrina texted Parker when she arrived home, then took a shower, combed her hair, and leaving it to dry naturally, got into old, comfortable pajamas. She dropped on the couch and flipped channels, looking for something relaxing to watch. She settled on a food network show that she watched occasionally.

She was weary—but oddly exhilarated at the same time. And she thought that might be because of Parker Costigan.

The astral projection had gone well—smoothly, nothing that made her upset. Except she had ended up at Pam's and his childhood home, not Pam's current home. She hoped the people at The Lightning Center weren't disappointed that she'd gone to Pam's old home. But then, Pamela thought of that as her home, according to Parker.

Had she somehow read Pam's thoughts? She'd never thought she had any more telepathy than the average person. Now she wondered.

The results of the screening they planned to do soon should prove interesting.

She thought about Parker. She'd felt drawn to him before, but it had intensified when they'd spent time together over dinner.

He'd been thoughtful enough to take her out for dinner, and then offered to follow her home. Clearly, he was a kind, considerate person.

Or a caring doctor simply looking out for his patient.

But besides all that, he was handsome, masculine—and there was something undefinable that drew her to him.

She'd felt an unexpected yearning to be in his arms during their dinner. Which surprised her.

She recalled how she'd been attracted to Devon when they'd first met. The physical attraction had been strong, similar to what she was feeling now for Parker.

But she had been naïve, and Devon had turned on her, cruelly.

Was Parker trustworthy? She wanted to believe he was, but—could she?

And yet her whole self—brain, heart, body—longed to find out what it would be like to nestle in his arms, to be held closely by him, to kiss him.

She sighed. She guessed she wouldn't know.

A commercial came on, and she flipped channels, finally going back to the food program and trying to focus on it before she went to sleep. She was working at the library tomorrow, so she needed a good night's rest.

She made herself get into bed and read for a few minutes—a western historical romance by a popular author that she was halfway finished with. When she saw her bedside clock said 10:08 she put down the book and switched off the light.

She wished, as she often did, that she had a dog and a cat, but she worked weird hours sometimes and it wouldn't be fair to pets to leave them for long periods. Besides, with her recent and troublesome projections at night, she'd been feeling tired.

She fell asleep fairly quickly. And then the realistic dream began...

***

She was floating above her rented condo. It was dark and she knew it must be chilly but she felt fine. Wind bent the trees as she looked down, and there was an almost full moon which appeared intermittently between large clouds.

She was moving, floating, gliding. She was going down the county highway, then arriving on Rt. 46. She was—she was going to The Lightning Center.

No. She passed it.

Now, she was turning on a road she knew from living in town. She floated, going on some twisting and turning side streets. She arrived at a colonial home, which resembled a lot of homes on this street. One of her friends from high school had lived in this neighborhood so she was familiar with it.

She dropped into the house.

No, this wasn't a dream, she realized with startling clarity. She was projecting again. In her sleep.

She was in one of the rooms on the second floor. She could see it clearly. Perhaps it was originally a bedroom, but the multiple bookcases, and large desk with a computer, showed it was being used as someone's office. There was a light on, and a man sat at the desk.

She sucked in her breath. *It was Parker.*

Guilt flashed through her. She shouldn't be projecting to his house. Spying on him. She hadn't intended to do this.

She struggled to move back up, but it was as if she was caught, held in place by something invisible.

Parker was wearing a dark blue T shirt and long plaid boxers. He frowned as he looked at something in a folder he was holding.

As she watched, he looked at the computer screen, then back down at his file.

She floated where she was, temporarily giving up on trying to pull herself up and out of his home. Everything seemed so real, so vivid. Was it her file he was studying, she wondered?

48

She thought about how much she'd wanted to be held by him. Automatically, she reached a hand towards him, wanting to touch his shoulder.

He started, and looked around.

For a moment he looked at the spot where she floated. Then his head turned, and he scanned the room.

But then he turned his head again, and looked directly at her.

She almost gasped, her heart speeding up. Surely he couldn't see her!

Could he?

The fear enveloping her at that thought broke her free from whatever seemed to hold her in place.

She rose rapidly. Through the roof, going backwards. She felt the rush of the wind as she hurried, hurried, back to the safety of her home. She was along the highway, along the county road. She could see her building. She dropped down into her apartment, experiencing a feeling of intense relief.

With her hands she felt the mattress beneath her. Home. She was home. She sagged into the bed.

Sabrina opened her eyes.

Her bedroom was dark, the room-darkening shade protecting her from all light but the smallest glimmers around the edge of the shades. Her eyes moved to the clock. It was 12:15 AM. Parker had been up late, doing work.

Her insides felt knotted. She had projected—right to his home. In her sleep, without meaning to. She'd intruded on his privacy.

She wanted to cry in frustration. She had to get control over these night projections. She had to. It wasn't good for her. She had no control over them, unlike the projections she initiated. Plus, she felt like a voyeur.

She needed help, and her friend Leanne had urged her to get it. She *must* keep seeing the staff at The Lightning Center. She didn't like these night-time, out-of-her-control experiences. They left her uncomfortable. Worse, they were just plain wrong. Unethical.

Nothing quite like this had ever happened before, though.

Because—she could have sworn it—Parker had somehow known she was right there!

Her heart thudded and she gripped her blanket, feeling icy cold.

This was scary. He might not have seen her but— he somehow had known. Somehow, he'd sensed her presence.

She burrowed into the blanket, clutching it close.

That should never have happened!

CHAPTER IV

Parker sat, sipping his hot coffee, as they reviewed the patients that had been seen or tested on Friday. The staff at The Lightning Center always started their mornings at nine o'clock with a meeting to discuss the patients they'd seen the day before. Since it was Monday, they were discussing Friday's patients.

"So, no more questions or comments on Dennis Alward?" Pamela asked, looking around the table in the spacious conference room.

People shook their heads no.

"Alright, then on to our final patient discussion this morning… Sabrina Holt."

It was Pam's turn to lead the morning discussion. It was always attended by Parker, Pam, Meredith, their mom and dad, and Neal and Alicia; plus any other staff members who had questions or input on a particular client. Occasionally one of their volunteers was invited to attend. Since Sabrina was fairly new here, no one else had any other info.

Parker bent his head and took another sip of his hearty beverage. He needed the jolt of caffeine. He'd had trouble sleeping since Friday night. He kept thinking about Sabrina.

"I'm going to be the next one who watches her

astral project," Pamela said. "Can you give us all the results of your observations, Parker?"

He set his mug down on the polished wood table with a clink. He opened her chart now, but he didn't need to refer to it. What had happened during her session was burned into his brain. Along with something else he was eager to discuss with Pam.

"She's quite extraordinary. She's even better than Beryl Vardley, the only other patient we've had here so far, who can astral project," he began. "She was asked to find Pam's home; instead of her condo, she went to our childhood home."

His mother made a sound of surprise.

"She described with complete accuracy the dining room. Her heart rate was typical for resting; but her brain waves were active—not like they would be if she was totally resting. I compared them to her results when I did the base line reading. Afterwards, she was sleepy, which she says usually happens to her.

"We definitely need to do more testing to see how well she does in another circumstance, and if her skills can be made even stronger," he concluded.

"I'll be working with her on that soon," Pamela said.

As he looked at his twin sister, a picture flashed across his mind. Her cat, the gray striped one. She was worried about him.

He tucked it in his mind to question her about him later.

"When will she be tested for ESP skills?" Meredith asked.

Neal spoke up. "Tuesday."

Neal sent Alicia a glance.

Wonder what that's all about, Parker thought, looking from Neal's calm expression to Alicia's. Alicia was wearing her glasses, which made her look intellectual, though she was also quite pretty. She had her hair swept into a clip at the back of her neck right now, making her look all business.

He sensed a certain tension between Neal and Alicia, although he wasn't sure what it stemmed from. Neal had been a parapsychology professor and noted researcher when they stole him away from an Ivy League university nearby. Alicia had just earned her doctorate in parapsychology and was eager to prove herself. Both had done previous research with several different psychic abilities, although not specifically tied to lightning.

"I watched the video of her projection," Neal continued. "She does have a very strong ability. Alicia and I are working on a test specifically for her."

Parker nodded.

"She does have some reluctance to be here," Pamela cautioned them. "Partly from familial prejudices."

"What do you mean?" questioned Alicia.

"Apparently her aunt—her mother's older sister—had some experiences with astral projection as a teenager," Pamela said. "This was in the mid nineteen sixties. Some people believed her—but others made fun of her, ostracized her. Sabrina's mother, Lorraine, didn't want that to happen to her daughter. Neither did Sabrina's late father. So, they put pressure on her to keep it a secret, not to tell a soul. She told few people. Once she did tell someone she wasn't sure of and got ridiculed. Since then, she has confided in only very close friends."

"We've seen that before," Meredith said.

"What made her decide to come here?" Neal asked.

"Good question. Apparently, a friend suggested she come here. But maybe there's something more, something she hasn't shared yet."

"So, we'll do some ESP tests, maybe something more if Neal and Alicia can come up with tests specifically for Sabrina," Parker said. "And we'll have her project several times and see what we can learn. In the meantime, Neal has a video of her projection. I suggest you all watch it. Her ability is uncanny, and fascinating."

"I agree. I'll be with her on her next projection," Pamela said. "This time, I'll ask her to go a further distance than she did with you, Parker."

"Agreed," Parker said.

"Any other questions?" Pamela asked.

There were none, and she concluded the meeting.

As people left the room, he paused by his twin's side.

"What's wrong with your cat?" he asked, his voice pitched low.

"Tobey? How did you know—oh, never mind. I'm usually good at shielding my mind from you, but not always," she said, picking up her folders. "He got sick this morning. This was the second time in two days, and he usually doesn't get sick. I'm going to take him to the vet later."

She'd adopted two cats from a local animal shelter. The shelter had promised to find them a home where they could be together since their elderly owner had been dying, and they had a strong bond. They'd been there five months when Pamela had gone in, having decided she needed a pet to keep her company; and cats were easier when you had a hectic schedule. Besides, two cats could keep each other company, she'd told him.

"Let me know how he is." Parker liked pets too. They'd always had dogs and cats in their family when they were growing up. He'd have gotten a dog for himself if his schedule wasn't so crazy. But he often worked long hours and knew it wouldn't be fair to a pet. Maybe someday…

"Can I speak to you alone?" he whispered, as the others filed out.

"Sure. Come to my office."

He followed Pam to her office. Once there, he shut the door.

"I wanted to tell you about something weird that happened Friday night."

She sat on her chair behind her desk, and waved for him to take a chair opposite.

"The strangest thing happened." He glanced out her office window now, staring at the nearby trees, swaying in the autumn breeze. The day was sunny but cool, and windy. A few gold leaves fell and scattered as he watched.

"I was up late, in my home office, looking over Sabrina's file. It was past midnight, and suddenly I *felt* something. Something—I couldn't put my finger on it. A strange sensation, like I was being watched."

Pam leaned forward.

"I looked around, but no one was there—of course. I was alone in my study. I figured maybe I was simply growing weary. I was about to go back to reading when a picture flashed through my mind."

55

"Of what?"

He hesitated. "I was holding Sabrina close. Hugging her."

Pam's eyebrows shot up.

"I know, I know, you're going to ask if it was my secret desire or something." He frowned. "It wasn't." *Not that he was willing to admit.* "I saw the same image when I took her to the diner, near the end of the meal. It was something *she* was thinking."

"So… she's thinking about you in that way. And, you didn't tell me she thought that before." Her tone was accusing.

Annoyance moved through him. Pam was still thinking of a possible romantic involvement between him and Sabrina. "I didn't think it was important." *He hadn't wanted to think so.* "Anyway, Friday night, as I felt like I was being watched, that image popped into my head. And I couldn't understand how I could be seeing the picture from her mind again? Was I simply recalling the image?"

"Or were you—extraordinarily—reading her mind even though she wasn't nearby?" Pam asked.

"She lives in the next town. Probably less than five miles from me, as the crow flies. But it's rare for me to receive a telepathic image from someone who is that far away. Except for a few close friends," he added. "I don't usually even get them from *you* at such a distance, except in unusual circumstances. Like when our grandpa was sick. But, it was almost as if Sabrina was there in my study, close to me."

"Wow!"

"I even got up and peeked through the blinds out the window. The street was dark and quiet. She wasn't sitting nearby in a car—the street was empty. I could swear she'd been in close proximity, though."

"There's another possibility!" Pam's tone was excited.

"What?"

"She was projecting into your room, and you read her thoughts because her ethereal self was there."

He almost jumped in his seat. He'd been concentrating on the fact that he had somehow reached Sabrina from far away; that his telepathic ability was the talent that was involved here. But what if it was *her* ability that caused them to be close enough for him to read her mind?

"I never thought—" he whispered.

"Isn't it possible?" his sister demanded.

Sabrina's Tuesday evening session, first with Neal Wu, then with Dr. Alicia Fitzgerald, the other researcher/tester, was an interesting one. They tested her with the usual ESP cards. She'd been tested once, in college. Neal and Alicia got the same results as had happened back then: her ESP rating was above average, but not extraordinary.

She was back now on Friday afternoon, and was greeted by both Emily, the receptionist, and Lorna MacIntyre as she entered The Lightning Center.

"Hi," she said, approaching Emily's desk.

"I'll let Dr. Pamela know you're here," Emily said, and lifted her phone.

"How are you, my dear?" Lorna asked cordially.

"Fine. And you?"

"Just dandy!" she said, her smile wide and infectious. She lowered her voice and leaned forward. "I'm going out with some of my girlfriends tonight. I'm a widow, you know, and so are some of my friends—but we believe in going out and having fun. We're meeting at a local restaurant and having dinner and margaritas to celebrate my friend Abigail's birthday!"

"Good for you!" Sabrina said, smiling. She liked the older woman, who certainly seemed lively for her age. Lorna was dressed in a purple sweater and gray pants, with a purple and gray striped scarf, and silver earrings. Next to her Sabrina felt rather plain in her jeans, pink top and sneakers. But they'd told her to dress comfortably, so she had.

Lorna pulled back and looked over Sabrina's left shoulder. She smiled, and nodded.

"Your father is glad you're coming here," she said.

"My father?" Sabrina squeaked. "But—he's gone! He passed away almost six years ago, after I graduated college."

"I know." Lorna's expression turned solemn. "He's with you now, though. And—it looks like your grandfather, his father, is behind him. They're watching over you, Sabrina."

Sabrina felt a tremor move through her. Looking back, she saw nothing.

"I don't see them," she said.

Lorna nodded. "As I mentioned, I too was struck by lightning. I can sometimes see those who have passed."

Sabrina stared at her. "You can?"

"Yes. Some of us working here have abilities.

58

Some—but not all. For instance, Felipe, our grad student who works here part time—but I'm getting carried away, I'll let him tell you when he meets you. We have had a number of patients here who have the same ability I do—seeing those who have passed—and some of them are much more talented than I am." She smiled modestly.

Sabrina turned again. She saw nothing.

"They left," Lorna said helpfully. "I think they felt self-conscious when I spoke. Anyway, they are glad you're coming here."

Glad? Sabrina wondered if she was crazy to believe Lorna's words. And yet... they rang true. And she knew from her own experience that the impossible was often possible. Maybe her father and grandfather thought the people here at The Lightning Center really would help her gain control of her abilities—especially when she was sleeping.

"Did they say anything?" she asked anxiously. "I miss them both." Her father's father had died when she was only fourteen. She would love the opportunity to speak to him, and her dad, in some way. To find out that they were happy—wherever they were.

Dr. Pam opened the door leading to the hallway on the right, and entered the lobby, her dress swishing. She wore a burnt orange dress with stylish brown boots. She smiled as she approached.

"Hi, Sabrina," she said. "C'mon, we'll go upstairs."

"Bye," Sabrina said to Doris. "I hope we can speak again, soon."

"I'd like that." The older woman's eyes twinkled.

Pamela led the way down the hall, and they ascended the staircase that led to the second floor where the "living room" was set up. There were also other rooms up here. Neal and Alicia had tested her in two of them.

As they climbed up the staircase, Pam asked "how are you doing?"

"Okay," Sabrina answered readily. But inside, her mind was still reeling from Lorna's statements.

She'd always believed in ESP and although she considered the existence of ghosts to be possible, she'd never had anyone tell her she had one—or in this case two—around her.

Once in a while, since her father's death, she'd felt a certain comforting presence and had hoped it was him. She glanced back now, but again she saw nothing. Lorna had said they were gone—were they?

Sabrina followed Pam into the same large sitting room where she'd projected the last time. She sat on the couch, as Pamela bustled around, docking Sabrina's iPod in the station, since Sabrina had told them she wanted to bring her own music from home.

"It's The Beatles' *Abbey Road*. My mother listens to it all the time and it's become one of my favorite albums."

"I've listened to it too. It's wonderful. Do you want me to pull down the shades?"

The day was partially cloudy, not too bright. "Just partly," Sabrina said. "As long as it's not super bright I'll do fine."

She settled in the couch in a prone position, and Pam reminded her they would be video-taping as she lit the white candle in the corner.

"Here's the person I want you to find," she said, producing a photograph of a young woman with blond hair, wearing a brown sweater and a serious expression. "She's Tanya Cantrell, one of our staff here. She's a graduate student, studying for her PhD in psychology, and she works here a couple of afternoons a week. You'll have to travel further this time. And if you can, please talk as you project."

"Okay. I've traveled distances before." Sabrina settled in. She breathed slowly and deeply, the vanilla scent soothing.

She closed her eyes and relaxed further into the sofa. A moment later she drew herself together, then pushed herself up and out. She was rising, through the roof, looking down on the building.

"I'm seeing your building from above," she said. "Now… I'm moving—south. Through the free trade zone. I'm on Rt. 206, going south."

She continued to move, watching the light early afternoon traffic underneath. She passed above intersections in Chester, and in the Bernardsville area.

"I'm coming to Rt. 287," she told Pamela. "I'm—yes, I'm going south on 287." She was silent as she felt herself moving smoothly, over the traffic, past a few exits. "I've passed the exit for the Bridgewater Mall." She felt herself smiling. "I like that mall." She fell silent, then found herself turning off at exit 9. "I'm on—it's River Road. One of the ways to get to Rutgers." She floated on top of the road. "I got my graduate degree in Library Science there. I'm by the Bush campus—the science area. Now—I'm going towards the Livingston campus. That's where she is."

Sabrina found herself looking at some buildings she had never been in. She paused, then floated slowly down into one.

Now she was in an office area. "I see her. But—it's a little fuzzy. Not too much, just not perfectly clear." She frowned. She disliked when she couldn't see clearly, but since this hadn't been a short trip, she had expected that. "She's in some kind of office, in a partitioned area. There are a couple of other people at different desks. She's sitting at a computer. She's wearing a black and red Rutgers sweatshirt, and jeans. And glasses. She's staring at the computer monitor."

"Very good," Pamela said softly. "You're doing great, Sabrina."

Sabrina heard the words as if they were from a long distance. "You sound far away," she told Pam.

Pam fell silent.

Sabrina drew closer to Tanya. She could see her studying something on the monitor.

She moved closer, squinting to see. Then gasped. "She's staring at Parker on her computer screen."

Parker watched Sabrina on his monitor as she lay, talking quietly, her eyes closed. He heard his sister praise her in a soothing tone. He was sitting in the computer room with Neal, both of them observing Sabrina and her extraordinary astral projection.

On a monitor to his right, Tanya was staring at the camera from the office at the university which she shared with a bunch of other grad students. He'd connected with her by Skype.

Everything was *exactly* the way Sabrina had described.

He couldn't help the amazement that wound

through him. She could actually see Tanya's computer screen. She could see *him.*

She was the best subject he'd ever seen doing astral projection.

Neal, in a chair on his left, let out a low whistle. "Wow." His expression was one of awe.

Sabrina's ability was strong, very strong. Parker was curious how she would do when near Meredith, who had no abilities.

If their special theory continued to hold true, she wouldn't do quite as well when she projected near Meredith. This one of the theories they were testing at The Lightning Center was that their subjects had improved abilities when they were in close proximity to someone else who also had an ability—any ability. Like him, or Pam.

Sabrina was murmuring again, describing the desk where Tanya worked.

He saw Tanya staring on the monitor. Tanya could see him staring at the monitor with Sabrina, although she couldn't see that monitor herself.

But she must have heard some of Sabrina's description.

"How do you know she isn't reading your mind, visualizing what you are seeing?" Neal whispered to Parker.

"That's a good point. I'm pretty good at blocking my thoughts—even from Pam," Parker said. "And your ability is different, Neal—you can move things. Still, make a note to repeat this test in the future with no monitor."

Neal nodded, tapping on his iPad.

"You can return now," Pamela said. Her face was

in shadows on his main monitor, but he heard the amazement in his sister's voice.

"I'm going up… I'm leaving the campus… back along River Road…" Sabrina spoke slowly.

She appeared to be resting, maybe even sleeping. A few minutes passed. "I'm back on Rt. 287…" her voice was quiet. She was silent again.

Finally, she announced, "I'm back." Her eyelids fluttered, and she opened them.

"How are you feeling?" Pam asked, moving to take her pulse.

"A little dizzy." After Pam finished, Sabrina sat up slowly.

"Impressive," Neal whispered next to Parker.

"Yes." Parker nodded. She *was* amazing. And he was as impressed as his co-worker.

"How did this compare to the time you visited my old home?" Pam asked Sabrina.

"I couldn't see as quite as clearly. But I wouldn't say it was terribly fuzzy; just a little."

Pam handed her a water bottle. Sabrina drank from it.

"How did you feel while you projected?" Pam questioned.

"I felt calm. But when I saw what Tanya was watching on her monitor, I was startled."

"Has that happened to you before?"

"Well…" Sabrina stopped. Parker sensed she was struggling with something.

Pam waited.

"I was—troubled by something that happened last week," Sabrina admitted.

"Please tell me about it." Pam stretched out her hand.

Sabrina sipped more water, and was silent for so long Parker thought she wasn't going to answer. But she must have decided to, because her words began to tumble out.

"For the last six or so months, I've been projecting—in my sleep. I don't have any control," she said, her voice shaky. "It starts as a realistic dream, and then—I realize I've projected."

"Do you project to someplace you want to go?" Pam asked quietly.

"Sometimes. Once I projected to a friend's house— a friend from grad school who lives in Pennsylvania now, and I'd been thinking during the day before how I wanted to get together with her. But—sometimes it's a place I had no conscious thought of visiting."

Parker leaned in close. Had that happened last Friday night?

"Can you give me an example?" Pam's voice was calm, soothing.

Sabrina looked down. "Last weekend, I visited your brother's house," she whispered.

Parker sat straight up. She *had* been in his house!

Neal turned and stared at him.

"Oh." Pam paused. "Go on."

"I saw him working in his—home office. At first, I struggled to leave, but I couldn't. Then—I felt like he *knew* I was there."

"That's very interesting," Pam murmured.

Despite her quiet, even tone, Parker knew his twin was excited. She was thinking that this explained his experience with reading Sabrina's thoughts.

"Why is this happening to me while I sleep?" Sabrina asked. "It never did before!"

"Do you notice a pattern?" Pamela leaned forward. "For example, when you have a stressful day at work, are you more likely to project?"

Sabrina shook her head. "I don't think so."

"It would be beneficial to start keeping a journal about your day and then about your sleep. And—perhaps we should try hypnotizing you just to see if your unconscious mind can give us some answers."

He heard Sabrina take a deep breath. "I guess I could do that." She sounded uncertain.

"Where else do you usually project to when you do it in your sleep?" Pamela asked.

"A couple of times my home—my parents' house. My mom still lives there. Once, the house where my grandparents lived—my grandmother still lives there, too. That's in Union."

"Anyplace else?"

"No, not that I remember."

There was silence for a minute. Then she looked straight at Pam.

"Can you help me? Can you help me control these projections?" There was a desperate note in her voice.

"We can certainly try," Pam said. She moved over to Sabrina, and put a hand on her shoulder. "I'll start researching ways we can help," she added. "And we'll experiment with some."

Sabrina sagged against the couch.

Parker's heart was beating hard. Wow. Sabrina had been in his home—at least, her etheric self—her soul—whatever—had visited him. Pam had been correct.

Why had she come to visit him? He recalled the

66

image of her in his arms, the image she'd had in her mind at the diner.

Had she visited him *because* she wanted to be held by him?

He watched the monitor as Sabrina got up. "I'm going home to rest," she said.

"Do you want a ride home?" Pam asked.

"No, I should be fine to drive. It's a short ride. I'm not as tired as I was last week," she finished.

He reached out with his mind. No, she didn't seem to be too tired. She should be fine to drive.

And he caught a flash of something else.

The big bookstore in the next town. She wanted to go there.

That image wedged inside of his mind.

CHAPTER V

I'm leaving, Park."

Pam stood in the doorway to his office. He'd been so absorbed that he hadn't heard her coming down the hall.

He glanced at the clock. It was almost three thirty.

"Just—tell me, what you thought about the session with Sabrina."

Pamela came in. Dropping to one of the chairs facing his desk, she said "I think she has an extraordinary ability."

He nodded. "Watching it on the video monitor, I totally agree."

"She saw the room Tanya was in and described her, and everything, precisely."

"I know."

"And— "she waved her hand— "there's no chance she read your mind as you were watching. Neal says she doesn't have any more than slightly above average abilities in that area. You're good at shielding your thoughts and Neal—well, his ability is telekinesis. No, she was *there*. In that room with Tanya. But more importantly"—she leaned forward— "is this problem she's having. Projecting at night, and not being able to control it."

68

"Projecting into my house," he said dryly.

Excitement glowed in his sister's eyes. "I know! That is something! In her sleep she visited your home—" She paused, then gave him a sharp look. "Parker, I really think this means she *is* going to be very important in your life."

He didn't want his sister jumping to that conclusion. "Uh—no. I think the reason she projected there was—well—" he hesitated.

"What?"

"Maybe she's—fantasizing about me, or something."

Pam regarded him. "Maybe she has reason to."

"No." He said it firmly. But he knew, deep inside, that he had equal fantasies about her. About running his fingers through her thick, glossy mane of hair. About stroking that satiny-looking skin.

He looked out his window. He had to stop daydreaming about her. The cloudy day had grown grayer. He saw wind whip the trees and a few leaves falling.

When she was silent, he looked at his twin.

She was grinning.

"Don't get any ideas—" he began.

"None that you haven't gotten yourself, already," she said, looking as satisfied as one of her cats.

Seeing her expression, he changed the topic. "How's your cat?" He'd forgotten to ask her again after Pam had first reported the cat had a dental problem.

"Since they extracted that tooth Tuesday, he seems much better. He's on antibiotics for a while." She smiled. "But he'll be okay. Now, don't change the topic."

69

"I am changing it." he declared. "I'm glad your cat's better. Are you and Merry going to mom and dad's for dinner Sunday?"

"Yes. I'd carpool but I may be stopping at the mall first." She stood up. "See you there. And" —she grinned—"I *know* Sabrina will be important to you."

He refused to answer that remark. "Don't forget, Monday morning we have the appointment with the two professors from Rutgers." They were meteorology professors, doing some research for The Lightning Center. "And in the afternoon, we're skyping with the two researchers in New Mexico." They were meteorological researchers too.

"It's on my calendar. I really think we're going to have to hire a full-time scientist to do the research we want."

She'd been pushing for that for a few months, and he was starting to agree with her. Meredith had been in favor all along. They had to convince their parents, though, that it was a good idea. Fortunately, they did have extra money in their budget.

"Bye, Park, see you soon." And she whisked out of the door, her skirt swishing.

He looked after his sister as she strode down the hall. He heard her call goodbye to Emily, and Emily answered. People were packing up to leave. Meredith had said goodbye a while ago; his parents, who worked part time, only worked occasional Fridays. The center was only open every other Saturday, and tomorrow wasn't one of them. So things were quieting down.

He wanted to watch the video of Sabrina's projection one more time before he left, and settled back to do so. He was barely aware when Emily and Neal and Madison, one of their part time grad students, called their goodbyes.

He immersed himself in studying Sabrina's video. Her heartrate had been normal, he saw from the EKG they'd had monitoring her. After he was finished watching the video, he studied her EEG info on the computer.

It showed an unusual amount of activity for someone who was lying still and whose heartbeat was slow. Her brain had been very busy with the projection.

The video plus the test results proved Sabrina's projection had been extraordinary. He'd never seen another projection like it in the three years The Lightning Center had been open.

When he looked up it was nearly five o'clock and the center was silent and empty feeling.

Time to leave. He sent his collected info and notes to the private drive all the researchers shared, shut down the computer, and turned off the light in his office.

Most of the lights were already off. One low light was always left on in the reception area, and he checked it. He checked upstairs and down to make sure no one else was there. But even Alicia, who often stayed late—trying to prove herself, was his theory— had left for the day. Leaving from the back door, he set the alarm and walked to his car.

The wind had turned gusty, bringing the late September temperature down. He placed his briefcase containing a few files he wanted to study in his trunk, then got into his car.

71

For some odd reason, he didn't feel like going home. It was the start of the weekend, time to relax. He had no plans for the evening.

He remembered the flash he'd gotten from Sabrina. What if he went to the bookstore? Would he run into her there?

Without another thought, he turned his car in the direction of the big bookstore ten minutes from their building.

He needed to get something new to read anyway, he told himself. He'd relax with a book this evening. Not one of the texts he often pored over, but something different and exciting.

Once there, he browsed through the mystery section, picking a new book by a popular author. Then he turned, almost instinctively, towards the occult and new age area.

As he rounded the corner, he almost ran straight into Sabrina.

She had a book in her hands, and was reading the back-cover copy, looking absorbed.

"Hi," he said.

She looked up. "Oh—hello!" she answered.

She looked cute in her light pink top, her jeans which showed her curvy but slim figure, and the white and pink sneakers she was wearing. She wore little jewelry—small gold oval earrings and a simple gold necklace. On closer inspection, he saw that the necklace held a small medallion of a crab. Cancer, her zodiac sign. He didn't think he'd seen her wearing it before.

"Find anything good to read?" he asked.

"Between the library and this store, I read plenty on psychic abilities," she said. "But there's often something new out, so I like to look." She grimaced slightly. "Maybe something will help me learn to control my ability. I guess you heard me while you were monitoring my session."

"Yes. I know you're having a problem with night projections," he said.

"I need help." Her expression was beseeching, and something in him wanted to answer her plea.

"I'm hoping we at TLC will do that," he said solemnly.

"TLC—oh, right." She smiled. "The Lightning Center. Yes, I hope you will, too." She changed the topic. "What did you find to read?"

"A new mystery by Dick Donahue. I like his books. And I figured I'd take a look here and see if there's anything interesting. Aren't you tired, after projecting?" He pitched his voice low.

"I went home and took a short nap. I owe you a dinner, you know," she said suddenly. "Do you want to come over and I'll cook? It won't be anything fancy, but I'm a good cook."

He wished, suddenly, that he could. He stared at her for a second, fighting the temptation. A temptation like the scent of a savory meal, beckoning him.

Or the tempting presence of a beautiful woman.

"I'm not sure it's a good idea," he said. "The doctor-patient relationship and all."

"Of course." He thought he heard a soft sigh. She looked disappointed.

"But—why don't we go to that seafood place that's practically across the parking lot?"

"I'd love to." Her sunny smile seemed to light up the whole area.

"Do you need more time?" he asked. He didn't. He was anxious to get to the restaurant with her.

"No, I'm fine." She held on to the book she'd been looking at, plus another one. He followed her to the cashier's area. As they stood in line, he noticed the second book was a romance with a western-themed cover.

"What's that?" he asked idly.

"A book by an author I haven't tried before," she told him. "I like romance novels, especially those that take place in the old West."

"Cowboys and Indians?" he asked, raising his eyebrows.

She said in a spirited voice, "cowboys and marshals and bounty hunters. And strong women. Women had to be strong both physically and mentally in those days. Life wasn't easy, but it could be exciting."

"I'm sure it could be," he said. "I was just teasing."

"Oh." She flushed a pretty pink.

"Have you ever been out west?" he asked as the line moved up.

She shook her head. "No, but I'd love to go someday."

"New Mexico and Arizona are beautiful," he said. "As a matter of fact, we're working with two meteorologists at a university in New Mexico. They're doing some research on lightning for us."

"That sounds interesting," she said. "You'll have to tell me more about it."

He did, over dinner. As they ate their salads and the rolls the restaurant was known for, he described how he and his father had decided not just to contact researchers in New Jersey, but in New Mexico and

Florida as well—areas known for particularly strong thunder and lightning storms.

"Both sets of meteorologists are doing studies on the kinds of lightning that most often strikes people, and the numbers of people who survive," he said. "You know that at TLC, we study those who've been struck by lightning and have developed psychic abilities. We don't know yet if different kinds of lightning are more likely to cause abilities than others. Of course, not everyone struck by lightning develops an extra ability. We're doing long term studies. My dad is hoping that someday we may have branches of The Lightning Center in other areas, too," he finished.

"How did you come to start The Lightning Center?" she asked, sipping her soda.

He picked up a forkful of salad. "When I was in high school, I was talking to Pamela one day about the day we were struck. Both of us wanted to be doctors, like our dad is, and I suddenly had the idea to start a place where doctors—and parapsychologists—could study those who had been struck by lightning and developed abilities. Like our neighbor, Lorna, who was struck when she was a baby," he added. "I approached my dad and he thought it was a great idea. He'd gotten very interested in the subject after Pam and I were struck by lightning, and thought there was a real need for research." Yeah, he thought, after he and Pam had started exhibiting their own unusual abilities, their mom and dad had become *really* interested.

"It must have been tough to start," she remarked, picking up a freshly-baked roll.

"My mother's father was a well-known lawyer, and my father's father a pediatrician, and they both had money." he said. "We got a grant to do research from a large scientific group, and another grant from an investment group looking for cutting edge projects. My grandparents invested. And of course, my parents invested too. We did get some other private investors who were excited about our mission. We're doing a lot of ground-breaking research. Like trying to figure out if lightning strikes cause stronger abilities in people, than abilities people were born with."

She regarded him. "It does sound exciting… except…"

"Except?" he prompted.

"Except when it's happening to you, it's less exciting, more… disturbing, at least at first."

He knew that to be true for a fact—but didn't say so. He'd found his own ability to be more exciting than disturbing, but Pam had had conflicting emotions about her abilities. "Yes, a lot of people feel that way," he said. "Some embrace being—different—while others dislike it. Still others simply want to get used to it." As he and Pamela eventually had.

He didn't want to go into his own ability. After the catastrophe with Dara, he only talked to his family, and coworkers about it. He switched the topic and asked her why she'd become a librarian.

"I always loved to read," she said. "From the time I was young and got into my mother's Nancy Drew books. But I read all kinds of things. Then, in high school, I started researching psychic phenomena—I wanted to learn more about abilities like mine. I discovered I liked doing research." She paused as the waiter brought their main courses.

He kept thinking about her projection into his

house last week. He decided to bring up the topic, although he suspected she'd be uncomfortable. She had, after all, asked for help, so the topic was not off-limits.

"About your projecting into my home last Friday," he said, trying to sound casual so she wouldn't feel ill at ease. "You had no conscious thought of doing that?"

She paused with a forkful of fish halfway to her mouth. "I—I'm so sorry," she said hastily. "I never meant to—go there. To sneak in."

"I realize you didn't have control," he said, making his voice as soothing as he could. As he regarded her, seeing her down-turned mouth, he knew she felt not just embarrassed, but guilty. And he didn't want her feeling that way.

She put the fork down, and he noticed she was flushing.

He reached over and covered her hand with his.

Instantly, tingles shot up his arm.

She stared at him, and he knew her thoughts.

She felt this spark, too.

He withdrew his hand. She picked up her fork again. Her hand trembled. Yeah, she'd had a reaction, just like him.

She switched the topic abruptly, asking him about some of the other employees at the center.He decided to go along with it.

"Carol is our office manager," he said. "She's very efficient. You've met Neal and Alicia; they're our PhD psychic researchers. We also have three grad students who help them, working part time—Tanya, Felipe, and Madison."

"Tanya—the young woman I saw today?"

"Yes. Then there's Maura Linden, the other nurse; Harold, our part-time bookkeeper—he's a retired CPA; and you've met Lorna, our head volunteer. We have two other volunteers—Ben and Melissa."

He asked Sabrina about her family. He knew her father had died; and she had a sister who was a lawyer and a brother in grad school. She told him a little about their personalities—her sister was outgoing but meticulous with details; her brother was very focused on work but easy going in life.

"And my mother is dating someone on a regular basis now," she said, sipping her coffee.

"Is it awkward?" he asked.

"It was, at first. But I really like John. He treats her well. His wife died of cancer a few years ago. He has two sons."

They finished their dinner and he insisted on paying the bill. As he signed the receipt, he was tempted to ask her to come back to his place and watch a movie. But he reminded himself that wasn't a good idea. It was too personal. It was enough he'd gone to dinner with her.

"Now I have a new book to start reading tonight," he said as they left the restaurant. He had to stop himself from reaching out and grabbing her hand.

"Me too. I think I'm going to enjoy both books. Thanks again for dinner," she added, smiling up at him.

"Goodnight." He fought the urge to lean over and give her a quick kiss. Even a small one would be unprofessional. They parted, and he watched her get into her small white Nissan. As she drove away, she waved, and he got into his car, sighing.

If she hadn't been a patient—if he had simply met her at a party or something like that—he'd be asking her out.

He'd be kissing her and hoping for more.

He suspected that thought had been at the back of his brain since he'd first met her. She was beautiful, though not in a flashy way. He'd love to touch her, hold her, bring her to heights of pleasure. His body tightened. He'd felt a compelling urge to hold her before, but it seemed to be stronger every time he saw her.

But it was more than that, he suspected. He *liked* Sabrina. She was kind, and although she was intelligent, she didn't show it off. She wasn't conceited about her talent. She was modest.

He started his car. Time to go home, relax, and try to get Sabrina Holt off his mind.

Once home, Sabrina showered and threw in a load of laundry, then curled up with the romance novel she'd bought.

She had to work part of the day tomorrow, but was planning to go to the movies with her friend Amanda, from grad school, in the evening. So, she was looking forward to Saturday.

Snuggling down on her favorite chair, her mind wandered back to Parker. He was not just handsome, but warm. He seemed to be a thoughtful person too. He hadn't been angry about her unintended projection into his home, the way she imagined some people would be. He had been interesting to talk to and dinner had sped by. She'd hardly noticed the food.

She understood his reluctance to see her on anything more than a casual basis. He worked at The Lightning Center, and she was a client there.

But she *wanted* to spend time with him. If they had met under different circumstances, she'd be hoping to date him, wanting to get to know him much better.

She'd be dreaming of being in his arms…

She already was dreaming of that, she thought ruefully. Just two nights ago she'd dreamed he was holding her, murmuring loving phrases in her ear. Fortunately, she hadn't projected.

She sighed, trying to concentrate on the book in her hands.

She read several pages, then realized she was picturing the sheriff hero looking exactly like Parker.

She put aside the book, deciding to go on her computer for a while.

But even then, her mind kept returning to Parker Costigan.

***

Saturday afternoon Parker sat in the second-floor media/computer room of The Lightning Center, once again studying the videos of both sessions with Sabrina Holt.

He could have watched them at home.

He could have *not* watched them, too. He'd practically committed the videos to memory.

But he'd felt compelled to watch them again. Why, he wasn't sure. He didn't want to dig too deeply into that question.

She had such an incredible ability to project. He was almost mesmerized.

The video ended. He shut the computer down. Turning off the lights, he went downstairs to his office to give her file one more look.

The building was quiet, almost—spooky. The gray day brought little light to the rooms. As he entered his office, he heard a noise. The back door?

"Hello?" he called out, returning to the hall.

"Hello. Parker?" Alicia rounded the corner into the main hall. "I came in to review some files," she said hastily. "I want to reread them."

"Sure—whose files?" he asked lightly.

"Ray Tarrington—I wanted to review the results of the tests he did with Neal. And Sabrina Holt. I saw the tape from yesterday last night, and I'd like to look at it again."

She could access it from the shared drive. But he'd observed before that Alicia liked to come in and work here. Perhaps she was trying to impress them with her diligence. Or impress Neal, her supervisor.

"I just watched it again," he told her, when his cellphone rang. A glance showed him it was his friend Kyle. "I want to take this call."

"No problem. I'll lock up if I leave after you," she told him, and went upstairs.

He sat down behind his desk and took the call. "Hey, Kyle." Kyle was one of his best friends from high school and a police lieutenant in a town nearby.

"Hi, Parker. Do you have a minute to talk?"

"Sure."

"I'm in the neighborhood. Are you at home?"

"No, at work, but I was getting ready to leave and visit Mark." Mark was another friend from high school.

Kyle's voice sounded strained. "I can be at your office in five minutes. Okay?"

"Okay. See you then." He wondered what the problem was.

He didn't have to wait long. He heard the front door buzzer a few minutes later, and went to let his friend in.

Kyle wore a serious expression. "I'm hoping you—or someone here—might be able to help us."

Parker shut the door behind him. "Come into my office and tell me what's on your mind."

"Actually, it's friend of mine. He's having a problem, and so far we—the others on the force—haven't been able to help him.

"This is what's going on." Kyle dropped into a chair. Parker sat beside him instead of taking the chair behind his desk.

"Dan—a member of our force—went through a nasty divorce. He has a five-year-old daughter. He has custody because his ex-wife is an alcoholic, but she has visiting rights. She had permission to take her out for dinner Thursday night. They never came back."

"Kidnapped by a non-custodial parent," Parker said, nodding. "I guess that happens often."

"Too often. We've been following up clues, checking every lead. The mother's landlord doesn't know where the she is, her own parents claim they don't know—and we got a search warrant. She's not in their house. We've checked a few other relatives—there aren't too many—but so far, no clues." He was frowning, his voice deep with concern. "I know you have a lot of patients here with—with unusual abilities—like ESP. Do you think one of them could help us?" He leaned forward, his voice becoming hopeful.

Sabrina. She might be able to help.

Aloud Parker said, "we have a couple of people who might—and there's one woman I'm thinking of, who has exhibited some strong abilities. But I need to ask if she'd be willing to do so."

It wasn't the first time the police had turned to The Lightning Center for help on cases. Once, it was for help in telling if someone might still be alive, of if dead, where they might find a body. Another time it was going to the scene of a crime and asking someone with ESP if they could describe something about the perpetrator. When their clients filled out their paperwork at the Center, one of the questions they asked was if the person would be willing to use their skills to help someone else. They'd started doing this after their first year in business, because of these requests.

"Let me check something," he told his friend, and starting up his computer, accessed Sabrina's file. "If this woman I'm thinking of is willing to help, I still have to get her to sign a 'hold harmless' form, etc."

"Yes, yes." Kyle's tone barely hid his impatience.

Parker opened her file and found Sabrina's forms. She had agreed to help. *Great*. Finding someone who was alive—that was something Sabrina excelled at.

"Okay, let me call and see if she's available. And—do you have a photo of the girl and her mother?"

"I have one of the girl. I can get one of her mother." Kyle was already pulling his cellphone out.

Parker picked up his desk phone. "Can you give me some privacy?"

"Of course. Dan would be so grateful if she tried." Kyle walked out of the office and down the hall.

Parker took a deep breath, and called Sabrina.

Sabrina was getting ready to leave the library at two o'clock when her cellphone rang.

"Hello?" The phone number came up as The Lightning Center.

"Sabrina? It's Parker."

At his voice, her insides warmed. He'd been on her mind so much—and now, he was calling.

"Hi Parker," she said, hoping she didn't sound as excited as she felt.

"Sabrina, I wonder if I can ask a big favor."

"What?" she asked cautiously.

"A friend of mine is a detective. One of his friends has a daughter, whom he has custody of. She was taken by her non-custodial mother. They're both missing." He took a breath. "I know you wrote on your form that you would be willing to help if needed," he finished.

"You want me to help find her," she said. But—what if she didn't succeed? Her stomach knotted as she recalled the one time she hadn't been able to help.

"Yes. We have a picture of her and are getting one of her mother."

Thinking about the child, frightened and with an unstable parent, there was no question she would try. "I'll help. But—I can't guarantee I'll find her."

"All we want is for you to try. Thank you." Relief was evident in his voice. "I'm at The Lightning Center with Kyle now."

"I'm finishing work at the library. I can leave in a few minutes," she said after glancing at her watch. "So... I'll be there in about twenty minutes."

"Perfect. And Sabrina—thank you."

"You're welcome." She clicked off.

Would she succeed in finding the child? Or would she fail?

CHAPTER VI

Parker darted out of his office and found Kyle, relaying the message that Sabrina had agreed to help and would be here within a half hour. Kyle said the station was sending him a photo of Dan's ex-wife and he should have it soon.

Parker sprinted up the stairs to find Alicia. He knew that it could be important to tape this session, and having Alicia there would be helpful.

"Of course I'll help! I'll start setting up the equipment immediately," she declared, her smile wide.

Not knowing how long this could last, he called his friend Mark, and told him about the emergency situation.

He could have called either Pam or Meredith and asked if they wanted to observe, but instinct told him that Sabrina would want less people, not more.

Twenty minutes later Sabrina arrived, and he took her up to the "living room" where she'd projected before. The candle was still nearby, and he plugged in the iPod they kept there, tuning it to the soft jazz music she liked. Alicia and Kyle were both in the computer room. Alicia had everything set up to record while they observed.

Now Sabrina sat stiffly on the couch, and Parker

knew she was feeling uncomfortable. He lit the candle from yesterday, and the scent of vanilla began to waft through the room. Smooth jazz wound around the room.

"Please relax," he said, striving to make his voice as calm as he could.

An image flashed in his mind: Sabrina, with a young woman. She was thinking of something that had happened in the past. Something—not pleasant.

He tucked the picture away for future consideration. He hooked her up to the EEG and EKG machines, then took a seat on the chair near her. She lay down on the sofa.

She was wearing business casual clothes today. Black pants, flat black shoes. A white top with a bright blue sweater. She looked professional but not stuffy.

But her brow was furrowed, her mouth turned downward.

"Relax," he said again, smiling. He disliked seeing the tense expression on her face.

"I'll try."

He handed her both photos—he'd printed the one Kyle had received—and she studied them for a minute. Then she laid the one of the mother aside, and gripped the one of the little girl. She closed her eyes.

"Please tell us what you see," he requested.

She breathed slowly, almost in sync with the soft music.

He watched her. Sabrina was worried about failing. He could sense it. With something big at stake, he recognized it put a lot of pressure on her. He glanced at the EKG machine. Her heartbeat was steady. Physically, she was reacting fine.

Several minutes went by.

"I'm on Rt. 46," she said, "now I'm turning to go up Rt. 206. I'm on the Brooklyn Stanhope Road now." Then she fell silent.

She lay quietly for several minutes. He was wondering if she'd fallen asleep when she said, "I'm now on Lakeside Boulevard. I don't know this area." She was silent for a long time, then she said, a note of excitement in her voice, "I'm on the River Styx Road. I'm in the town of Hopatcong." She paused. "I'm taking some side streets. Some of them aren't marked with street signs," she added.

"You're doing great," he praised her, his voice low.

Once again she fell silent. Parker guessed that Kyle was observing carefully, waiting for some clue as to exactly where the little girl and her mother were. And Alicia was probably taking notes as she stared at the monitor.

He had his iPad on his lap. So far he hadn't noted anything different from her last projections. As he sat, he breathed in her fruity cologne. The same one she'd worn previously.

According to what Sabrina had already relayed, she was in the Boro of Hopatcong —actually not too far away from their location. But the town had narrow, winding streets that crisscrossed at odd angles. It was easy to get confused there.

"I see the house!" she said excitedly. Her fingers tightened on the photo. "It's a little bungalow, painted tan. It has a very tiny yard." She stopped, then said "I'm going in," and was silent again.

He observed that her heart rate had increased, and

made a note of it. He found himself holding his breath. Would she find the child?

"There she is!" she said, her voice triumphant. "She's in a bedroom, playing with some dolls. The room is painted purple. Her mother—" she paused. "She's not in this room… wait… her mother is in the kitchen, having something to drink with another woman. An older woman."

"Can you tell us the name of the street, and the number on the house?" Parker pressed. They were close, so close—and they needed this vital information.

"I'll look." Two long minutes went by. "There's no number on the house." She sounded frustrated. "Or on the mailbox." She fisted the hand not holding the photo.

"How about the street?" If they could get the street name, he was sure they could check for a house matching her description. He jotted a note about her fist.

"It's…" Sabrina frowned. Again, a couple of minutes went by. "I see a sign—finally. I think it's on Northwestern Ave. But the street winds around and is crossed by other streets so it's hard to tell."

"Great," he said encouragingly, keeping his voice low. "If there's no number, the police can drive up and down the street and look for the house."

"There's a couple of houses that look similar. But—this one is tan, and one of the shutters on the window to the left of the front door is missing." She pointed a finger. "I'm going back inside. The little girl is playing, and she seems safe." A moment passed, and he saw Sabrina frown. "I can see the mother is lying down on a couch now, and the other woman is doing something on her phone and smoking a cigarette. I think I need to come back… so you can send in the police…" her voice dwindled. She sounded weaker than she had before. "Do you need me to stay?"

"No." He knew the projection would fatigue her, and wanted to get her back safely. He guessed that finding the house, in what must have been an unfamiliar and possibly confusing area, was tiring her out more than usual. "Come on back," he told her. His gut clenched, an unusual sensation. He had a strong urge to reach out and caress her hand, to reassure her. But he remained still.

He'd given Alicia and Kyle instructions to stay where they were until she was "back" in her body. He had no idea what might happen if she was interrupted, and didn't want to take a chance on her well-being.

He knew Kyle would be anxious to call in the information, but he didn't want him disturbing Sabrina in any way. Even though he was in the next room she might hear him and possibly feel confused.

She was silent again. Then she announced, "I'm back on the Brooklyn-Stanhope Road. I know where I am." He caught the note of relief in her voice.

"Back on Rt. 183…" she said after a couple of minutes. "I'm… coming back here." He observed a shudder move through her body, then a small smile. "I'm back." She opened her eyes.

He felt relief too, and instinctively moved to the couch where she was sitting up slowly.

"Are you alright?" He reached for her hand, to take her pulse.

"I—I guess so." She pushed back a lock of her dark, wavy hair. She looked tired. "I—I don't like the vibes I got there."

Her pulse was more rapid than usual. A glance at

90

the EKG monitor showed her heart rate was faster than normal, too.

"You did well, Sabrina," he said soothingly. "What vibes?" He felt the tension beginning to ease out of her.

"The girl's mother. She's—not a nice person. I could *feel* something negative around her. Negative vibes. It made me uncomfortable."

"But you found the girl anyway. Despite your feelings of discomfort." His gaze swept over her. She was admirable, pushing past her discomfort to help them. He wanted to give her a big hug, but refrained.

He let go of her arm, and made a note about her physical reaction, and her negative feelings.

"Here." He handed her a water bottle, then unhooked her from the machines. Being close to her, touching her, his own heartbeat accelerated. "Do you mind if I speak to Kyle for a minute?"

"Go ahead." She waved at the other room.

He walked rapidly into the adjoining room, where Alicia was tapping out notes on a computer and Kyle was grabbing his cellphone.

"Go ahead and call in the info," Parker said.

Kyle gave him a nod, then tapped hard on his phone. "Hopatcong Boro," he said to whoever picked up. "Northwestern Ave." He looked at Parker. "Thanks, buddy. I owe you one."

"You owe her." Parker inclined his head towards the room where Sabrina sat.

"I know." Kyle smiled, then refocused on his call. "No," Kyle said, "I don't have a number, but we do have a description—" he repeated what she had said about the tan bungalow with the missing shutter.

Returning to Sabrina, Parker shut the door behind him so she wouldn't be disturbed by Kyle's excited conversation. "Want something else to drink—coffee or tea? Or a cookie or something? We have snacks in the 'break room'."

Later, he'd compare her EKG and EEG results to the video, but he suspected the change in her heart rate and probably brain waves had been more acute when she'd felt the negative vibrations.

"I'm fine." She sipped her water. He noticed her hands shook slightly.

"You're certain you're okay?" he asked.

"Just… very tired." She placed the water on the coffee table. "That was difficult, with those negative vibrations I felt. Do you think they'll be able to find her?" She regarded him anxiously.

"I think it's likely. You gave us a good description and we have the street name." He admired the fact that she was so concerned for a child she didn't know. She really was a compassionate person.

"But there was no house number."

"They'll find it," he affirmed. He sat down beside her on the couch, and reaching out, took her hand. It was cold. "Do you want a blanket or something?" Without thinking, he caressed her hand with his thumb. He skin was so soft.

"No, I'm alright. I think I'll lie down though." She met his eyes. "I saw everything very clearly. The last three sessions, the ones I've had here—I am seeing things more clearly than I have before."

He suspected that was because she'd been with him, and Pam. In which case the future session with Meredith might not be so clear, if their theory was

92

correct. But he wasn't going to comment on that right now.

"I'll make a note of that for the files," he said.

She looked away. "I was afraid…"

"Afraid…?" he asked.

"That I—that it wouldn't work." She met his eyes then, and he saw uncertainty in her expression. It tugged at his heart. She doubted her ability. He could see it.

"You did a fantastic job."

"Not always," she whispered, looking away again. "I'm going to lie down."

"Of course." He stood up. "Want me to wake you in an hour or so?"

"Yes. Please."

He went into the other room. It looked like Kyle had already left by the main door from the room to the hall. Alicia was still tapping away on her keyboard.

"That was amazing, simply amazing." She looked up at him. "I'll make a copy of the session as soon as I finish my notes. Kyle said he was heading out to get a search warrant."

"I'm going to make my own notes." He sat down at the long counter which contained four computers, and added to the notes on his iPad.

When he finished, he looked up. Alicia was standing up.

"I'm going to my office," she said.

"Okay." He stood as Alicia left the room, and went to check on Sabrina. She appeared to be deeply asleep. He was reluctant to wake her, and decided to let her continue to nap.

For a moment he watched her. She looked innocent, curled on her side, her head resting on a blue pillow, her long black lashes fanning her face. Emotion curled up in him. He wasn't sure exactly what it was. He admired her, certainly. She had such compassion for others, including a little girl she'd never met.

But he suspected the tugging he felt towards Sabrina was something more than admiration or respect. He cared about her.

He tried to push aside that thought. After his disastrous relationship with Dara, he didn't want to care about another woman. He figured it would be many more years until he did.

But Sabrina had gotten under his skin.

Unwilling to consider that observation further, he returned to the computer room. He emailed his notes to the shared drive. After that he looked for, and found, Alicia in her small office.

"I've made one copy of the video already," she said, "and I'll upload it to the drive. Should I email the others and tell them it's there?"

"Yes, good idea," he said.

"Sabrina has an extraordinary ability, doesn't she?"

"Yes," he agreed. "What did Kyle say about the information?"

"He was very excited—he thought they might be able to locate the little girl."

"Thanks again for helping out," Parker added. "I know this was on your own time."

"No problem!" She beamed at him. "It was exciting. I just want to check over my notes and make sure I didn't forget anything. I'll stop in tomorrow to do what I planned to do today."

He stepped into the hall and walked further down into a smaller sitting room. Before he watched the video of Sabrina's session, he called his friend Mark, and told him he couldn't meet him this evening. "We had a problem at work," he said. "I'm not sure how long I'll be here. I'm sorry." He intended to make sure Sabrina was okay and that she got home safely.

Mark took it in stride, and they agreed to meet another evening.

Parker got down to business, returning to the computer room and watching the video again, marveling at Sabrina's projection. He added a few notes on his iPad, which he could put in the file later.

"I'm leaving." Alicia's words startled him and he jumped.

"Sorry, I didn't mean to scare you," she said.

"I forgot you were in the building," he admitted.

"Need anything?" she asked.

"No, I'm fine. You can lock the door and I'll relock it and set the alarms when we leave."

"Is she okay?" she tilted her head toward the next room, where Sabrina was still sleeping peacefully.

"Just sleeping," he said.

"Okay, see you soon." Alicia exited the room. He heard her walking down the hall and then the stairs. The click of the back door shutting two minutes later seemed very loud in the silent building.

He got up. He'd been monitoring Sabrina on the computer, but now he went into the living room and quietly approached her.

She was breathing slowly, deeply. Fast asleep.

He returned to the desk in the next room and studied her EKG and EEG results.

When he was done, he glanced at the clock. It was 6:02.

Sabrina must really have needed the rest.

He remembered that Beryl, a subject they'd had here over a year ago, had been tired after projecting, but not as tired as Sabrina. Sabrina had been much better at projecting—more accurate in her descriptions, going places based on where someone was, not just simply going to a nearby mall or park as Beryl had. So perhaps accuracy was more exhausting to the person traveling.

He added that thought to his notes, amending the notes on the shared drive, then turned off his iPad and placed it in its carrier. He began turning off the computers and lights in the room. He could simply sit in the room with Sabrina and wait for her to wake up.

"Hello?" her sleepy voice reached him at that moment.

He hurried into the adjoining room.

"Hi," he said.

She was sitting up, her hair tousled, but her cheeks had more color now. She looked adorable. He felt compelled to reach out and touch her, but resisted.

"How are you feeling?" he asked, his eyes moving over her, looking for any signs of distress. Automatically he moved his fingers to take her pulse.

He couldn't help noticing again that her skin was silky smooth and soft.

Her pulse was back to normal. Reluctantly he released her hand.

"I'm okay." She did sound a little breathless.

"I'll take your blood pressure," he began.

She shook her head. "No, I'm fine." Her cheeks were pink, and a small smile played around her mouth.

God, he wanted to touch her again. He had to restrain himself. It was one thing to take her pulse, quite another to let his fingers linger.

He cleared his throat. "How about something to eat?"

"I— "she shook her head, as if she was dazed. "I want to go home and take a shower."

"I don't know if you should be driving," he said. She still looked fragile.

"I'm fine," she insisted.

"I'll follow you back to your place, and pick up a pizza," he offered.

She stared at him, as if considering. "Did they find the little girl?" she asked.

"I expect Kyle will call me when they do," he said. "You gave them enough information, according to what he said to Alicia. I'll call him when we reach your place if I don't hear from him before that."

"Alright," she acquiesced. "We can order the pizza from my condo. There's a place right nearby that delivers."

She went to the ladies' room, and he turned off the remaining lights in this room and the computer room. While he was alone for a few minutes, he also checked his email on his cellphone, then the office email.

The return address for one leaped out at him: E Lassiter.

Hmph. He could guess what *that* was about. He wasn't about to spoil a decent day reading an email from Evan Lassiter. It could wait.

Sabrina returned, and she gave him her address in case they got separated on the road. "I rent the condo," she said.

He set the alarm, locked the back door, and they left together. He was soon following her car with his. She appeared to be driving fine, which was a relief.

As he drove, he felt a niggling emotion at the back of his brain. Guilt. He felt like he should tell Sabrina about his own ability.

But his awful experience with Dara had taught him to keep it strictly to himself.

He made the turns, watching closely as Sabrina drove. He knew where her condo development was, and it was easy to reach. They pulled into a parking lot for one of the many buildings and she led the way to her apartment.

He was curious about her place. He had actually looked at condos here when he was looking at houses, but had decided he preferred a house.

It turned out she lived in one of the smaller models. They walked into her combined living-dining room and she said simply "make yourself at home. I'll call for a pizza. Is plain okay?"

"Perfect." He glanced around as she picked up a landline phone in the large, bright kitchen. There was a small deck off the kitchen.

Sabrina had decorated her apartment with attractive, modern furniture. A comfortable-looking brown couch and dark wood coffee table and side table offset the light beige carpeting. The coffee table held a coaster, a copy of "Cosmopolitan" magazine and an orange fabric pumpkin. The walls of her apartment were white—probably the landlord wanted them that way—but contained a lot of photographs and a couple of paintings.

There were several bookcases, all filled to the

brim, a TV and Cd player plus an iPod, and a desk with a laptop computer. He noticed many books by the author Heather Graham, a writer who his mother, Meredith and Pam all read.

"The pizza should be here in a half hour," she said. She paused. "I really should be making dinner for you," she added.

He shook his head. "No, you helped me—us—out. And you're probably still tired. You shouldn't cook."

"Well… I need to take a shower," she said. "Did you hear from Kyle?"

"I'll try to reach him now," he told her.

She went into the bedroom, came out, and then went into the bathroom. In moments he heard the shower going.

He tried hard, very hard, not to picture her slim, curvy body as she must be stripping off her clothes—

He swallowed, feeling his body twitch. This was *so* not appropriate.

He picked up his cellphone, determined to call Kyle and get his mind off the beautiful woman in the shower nearby. And he should probably text his sisters. Alicia had emailed them about the afternoon's events, but he wanted to let them know he was watching over Sabrina for a while. Making sure she was okay.

Who was he kidding? He was concerned about her. He cared about his patients, but his feelings were ratcheted up when it came to Sabrina.

Sabrina showered, liberally using the vanilla shower gel and lotion which she found so soothing. She refused to get into the pajamas she normally would have worn, or even into yoga pants and a T-shirt. Parker was here and she didn't want to look like a mess. She'd felt a little cold earlier, so she chose old, faded jeans which were comfortable and a dark red sweater made from a fabric that wasn't too heavy.

She'd already texted Amanda that she'd had a friend with an emergency and couldn't see her. Amanda replied that she thought she was coming down with a cold so it was probably better if they didn't get together tonight.

As Sabrina was getting dressed and toweling her hair, she heard Parker on the phone. She assumed he was talking to Kyle, until she heard him say his sister's name.

"Yeah, Pam, I got the email too," he said. "No, I didn't read it—I don't want to interrupt a nice Saturday by reading one of his complaints. It can wait 'til Monday."

There was a pause, and she guessed Pam was talking. Then he said "And I have stuff to tell you. We'll talk tomorrow." Another pause, and he said, "Yeah. See you soon."

She finished toweling her hair, leaving it damp to dry in waves around her shoulders. She wasn't going to put on make-up again—she was with her doctor, and he'd made it clear this was a professional relationship, not personal. He was merely concerned about her welfare like any good doctor would be. So all she put on was some lip gloss.

She was a little anxious. Had she been able to

help? That was so important. Had they found the girl? Was she still alright?

Her vision had been especially sharp. Although most of the streets she'd floated above had been unfamiliar, she'd had no trouble zeroing in on the correct house. She'd been drawn to it as if by invisible threads. She'd only been frustrated because she couldn't find a number. But with her description, hopefully they'd find the right one.

She left the bathroom.

Parker was sitting on the couch, looking at his cellphone.

He sprang up. "How are you?" She saw anxiety on his face.

"I'm alright. Really. Did they find her?"

"I'm waiting for a call back from Kyle. He called when you were in the shower and told me they thought they would find her soon. Apparently, the girl's grandmother lives in Hopatcong—on a different street. They checked the grandmother's home yesterday and she wasn't there. But she probably has friends in town. They were driving down the street, looking to find a house that matched your description. I believe they got another warrant. He said he was confident they'd find the girl soon, and he'd call."

Her body sagged visibly. "Oh that's good!" She went to reach for her purse on her desk.

"The pizza should be here any minute—"

"I'm paying. You were a big help today. It's the least I can do." He reached into his pocket, and removed his wallet just as the doorbell buzzed. Striding forward, he opened the door before she could reach it. "How much do I owe you?" he asked the delivery boy. She saw him hand over several bills. "Keep the change."

"Thanks!" The boy's smile was huge. Parker must have given a generous tip. He shut the door and brought the pizza box into the kitchen.

The smell made her mouth water. Cheese and tomato sauce, spices and garlic. She was suddenly ravenous.

While she got paper plates and napkins, he opened the box. "Smells good."

"I have diet cola, ginger ale and water," she said. "I don't have beer. What would you like?"

"Ginger ale."

She took out a can for him and a diet cola for herself. They sat at the table and started eating.

For a minute or two they were both silent. Then Parker asked, "How did you feel about today's session? I mean, you weren't prepared for anything like this before hand. It wasn't like when you had an appointment with us to be tested, and were expecting to project. Was it more difficult?"

She swallowed a bite of the tasty pizza, then took a sip of soda. "I was nervous," she admitted, although she didn't go into why. She wasn't ready to discuss that yet. "I—there's a lot of pressure when people are expecting you to perform, to locate someone. Especially when it's important, not just a test." She took another sip as he gave her an encouraging nod. "But—fortunately—once I was projecting, things were extra clear and I found the house without any problems. I did feel bad, and frustrated, that I couldn't find a house number."

"I can understand that. But, Sabrina, you did great!"

"I hope so." She met his eyes, and with a start she saw admiration there.

That was a welcome sight to her. She added "thanks" again, then switched the topic to the books they'd bought yesterday and were now reading.

As they were finishing their meal, he got a call on his cell. "Kyle?" he asked eagerly, and she tensed. Had they found her?

He smiled at her, giving her a thumbs up. "That's great. She's okay...? Yes, I'll tell Sabrina. Thanks for letting us know." He ended the call, and beamed at her.

"They found her, safe and sound, with her mother and her grandmother's friend at the exact house you described. They'd driven around, found it, and identified her mother's car in the driveway. The girl is reunited with her father and the mother's under arrest. The mother was drunk when they found her, by the way."

The tension inside Sabrina eased as he spoke. "I'm so glad they found her!" She took a deep breath. "Now I can *really* relax."

"I never doubted you would succeed," he said suddenly.

"I did." She met his eyes.

"I didn't," he shot back.

Warmth flowed through her at his words. His confidence in her ability made her happy. No one except her friend Leanne had ever showed so much enthusiasm for her ability to project.

"Thanks." As they cleaned up and put away the leftover slices, she asked, "do you want to watch a movie?"

103

She could see him visibly hesitate. Then, he said, "yes, that would be nice."

She felt a shot of gladness at his words.

They debated about a few movies available on Netflix plus a couple she had on DVD. They chose the classic, first "Ghostbusters" movie.

"I haven't seen it for years," Parker admitted as they sat on the couch.

They sat apart—not too far, but certainly not close. It was as if he was keeping a careful distance, Sabrina thought. "Want some popcorn?"

"Maybe later." He leaned back.

The movie was funny, but about halfway through Sabrina found her eyelids growing heavy. She never fell asleep during the movies, but today she was fighting to stay awake.

She heard music and opened her eyes to see the credits of the movie rolling.

Her head was leaning against Parker's shoulder. She must have scooted closer to him without realizing it. His even breathing told her he, too, had fallen asleep.

She rested against him, feeling unbelievably comfortable and content, and took a minute to simply enjoy the sensation of being propped against Parker.

She wished... she wasn't sure what she wished. That, maybe, this could go somewhere... that he wasn't merely her doctor...

He stirred. A minute later he opened his eyes.

"Hi," she said softly.

"Hi... sorry, I must have fallen asleep."

"I did too. I guess we were both tired."

"Yes." He pulled back, and she sat up, feeling her cheeks flush.

He shook his head, as if trying to wake up and pull himself together. "What time is it?"

She focused on the digital clock on her TV. "10:22. Do you want some coffee or something?"

"No. I better go." Was that reluctance she heard in his voice? She had an impulse to wrap her arms around him and hold him there, and had to fight herself. She knew he wouldn't want that.

But he was gazing at her, and she could have sworn his look was one of longing.

And then he reached out, and with his finger tilted her chin up slightly.

She caught her breath.

His lips brushed hers softly, sweetly. And then returned, lingering.

Hunger sprang to life inside her. Her arms slipped around his neck and she clung, returning the kiss.

She felt warm, she felt hot—all over. She sank into the kiss, relishing it—when he pulled back, freeing her lips.

He stared at her.

Then, slowly, he dropped his hands, and pushed himself further away on the couch.

"I—" he swallowed. "I shouldn't have done that, Sabrina. I'm your—doctor. I'm sorry."

"It's alright." Her voice was scratchy. She wanted to shout "I liked it!" but stopped herself. He was her doctor, and it was evident he was feeling guilty about the kiss.

But oh, it had been such an exciting kiss! Her heartbeat was rapid and she knew her temperature had shot up.

He was still staring at her. "I better go." He stood up.

105

She stood up too.

As if he couldn't help himself, he suddenly placed his hand against her cheek. His touch was warm and seemed to brand her skin where it settled against her.

She'd never, ever had such a strong reaction to a simple kiss, a simple touch.

This man did something to her.

He stepped back. "Take care of yourself. I'll call and check on you tomorrow."

"Okay." She followed him as he walked to the door.

He turned, and his blue-gray eyes met hers. "Goodnight. And—thank you, Sabrina. What you did today—it was extraordinary."

"I'm glad I could help," she whispered.

He left, and she watched him walk down the outside stairs. Then she shut the door.

From her kitchen she watched him get into his car and drive away.

Her confused feelings about her night-time projections were nothing compared to her confused feelings about Parker.

She was attracted to him. She liked him.

Yet he seemed strangely hesitant, and that made her hesitant, too.

After he left, she got into comfortable pajamas, poured herself a glass of wine, and opened her book. She was afraid that after napping, she wouldn't be able to sleep right away, even though she was tired.

But instead of reading, she relived the kiss they'd shared. Relived it more than once.

She sighed. Their relationship was not going

anywhere. She shouldn't kid herself. He was her doctor. And… could she trust him? He seemed trustworthy, but—memories of Devon echoed in her head.

She tried to focus on the book instead of the memories.

But once again the hero appeared in her mind to look like Parker.

"Are you ready?" Meredith asked when she finished with the monitoring equipment.

"Yes." Sabrina lay back on the couch.

It was Wednesday, early in the evening. She'd had a quick dinner after work and come here for her session with The Lightning Center's social worker. She knew both Pam and Parker were in the computer room to watch this next astral projection.

"You did a wonderful job finding that little girl," Meredith said as she lit the white candle. "I was so impressed when I watched the video."

"I'm happy she was found safe," Sabrina said.

The little girl was now living with her father and her father's mother again. Parker had texted her a couple of days ago to let her know.

"Do you feel comfortable?" Meredith asked now, lowering the light.

"Yes." Sabrina recalled how Lorna had told her that her father and grandfather wanted her to be here. Was it true? she wondered for the umpteenth time.

She had dreamt about Parker last night. Nothing specific she could remember. Just—dreams of being with him, and she thought they'd been dancing. She knew she hadn't projected though. That would have been clear, and she would have seen a specific room. These were simply ordinary dreams.

She relaxed into the comfy couch, holding the photo Meredith and given her—a photo of a friend of hers, she'd said. A friend named Kim who lived further away than where she'd projected previously.

The brunette woman was attractive, and smiling in the photo. Sabrina gripped it now, closing her eyes as soothing classical music filled the room.

She soon found herself floating easily up in the building, through the roof, looking down at Rt. 46. Night traffic was busy at the nearby shopping centers; but she was going the opposite way, headed east, flying over Rt. 80.

"Please tell us what you're seeing," Meredith suggested.

"I'm headed east on Rt. 80." Sabrina continued to move, silently. After a while she was on a highway she recognized. "I'm on Rt. 3," she announced. "I feel the wind, but it's not making me cold." She looked down at the area below. "I can see the Meadowlands, all lit up. But it's not totally clear." There was a little fuzziness around the edges of her vision. She'd had that happen often, but her last few projections had been so clear that this surprised her now. She continued east, then realized she was getting close to the Lincoln Tunnel. "I think I'm going to New York City."

"You're doing fine," Meredith said.

She was over the river now. "Yes, I'm over the Hudson… I'm in New York City." She could see the grid of streets, car and traffic lights, buildings and skyscrapers brightly lit up. The Port Authority. And—there was the Empire State Building. "It's beautiful," she breathed. "The city at night, with all the lights... but it's a little blurry around the edges. I'm not seeing as clearly as I did with my last few projections." She frowned.

But the lights of the city shone through the haze. Quite suddenly, she wished she could share the sight with Parker. Despite not being crystal clear, the city sparkled, unlike anything she'd ever witnessed during an astral projection.

Then she was moving, although more slowly. "I'm turning... north," she said. "And..." she stopped, sucking in her breath. "Wow." Was that someone else, projecting too? Yes... the woman who was flying through the air was smiling at her. She had long blonde hair, which glowed in the city lights, and appeared to be about Sabrina's age. She nodded, and Sabrina smiled as they passed each other. They were going opposite ways. Sabrina reached out towards the other woman. She felt air move around her arm.

"That's the first time that ever happened!"

"What?" Meredith's question was low. Sabrina realized somewhere in her mind that Meredith didn't want to disturb her.

"I just passed another woman who was projecting too!" Quickly, she described the woman, then continued to move. "That's never happened to me before." She looked down at her surroundings. "I'm on Broadway... passing some theatres, restaurants... now a lot of stores. Starbucks, Old Navy," she continued, naming a few. "I think—yes, I'm here."

She was dropping down. "I'm in an apartment.

This woman—Kim—she's talking on her cellphone. She's on a couch, facing a TV. The TV's on—looks like an advertisement for laundry detergent. It's a decent-sized living room."

"What else do you see?"

"The door to the bedroom is open but the light's not on. There's a tiny kitchen—*really* tiny. There's no stove!" She couldn't help the surprise in her voice.

"That's correct, Sabrina. You're doing great."

"Can I leave now?" The apartment was small. "I'm feeling a little claustrophobic in here."

"Yes. When you do, can you see the number on the building?"

She moved upwards, through several apartments. One smelled so strongly of garlic she could almost taste it. Then she was back on the roof. "I actually smell garlic," she said. "Sometimes I can smell things when I project."

Now she floated downwards outside of the building, looking for the number. "I can't see... oh, there it is." She read it to Meredith. "It's right by the corner of 83rd Street," she added.

"You're doing great," Meredith praised. "Okay, come on back now."

The return trip seemed shorter. She didn't see the other woman who had been projecting again. She was flying, moving steadily and surely. Again, she felt a touch of the wind on her face. She moved over the highways, past the Meadowlands... soon she was on Rt. 80, which had little traffic at this hour. Before she knew it, she was arriving back at the building, and dropping down. She felt herself settle in, and announced "I'm back."

"You did wonderfully, Sabrina." Meredith sounded sincere.

Sabrina opened her eyes, and sat up slowly. The room was dimly lit by the one small lamp, and the single candle burning on a side table. She could smell the pleasing vanilla scent from the candle. She felt the familiar wave of dizziness, and stayed still until it passed.

Meredith sat nearby, leaning forward, smiling.

Sabrina reached for the bottled water someone had placed on the table before she started her projection. She drank for a moment and then set it down with a click.

"Can you tell me a little bit about the other person whom you said was projecting?" Meredith's tone was eager.

Sabrina described her journey again, in more detail; the apartment and building, the beauty of the city lit up at night. She eliminated the fact that she would have liked to share the vision with Parker.

She finished by describing the woman she had seen, who had recognized another soul traveling the same way; and how they had acknowledged each other.

"This is very intriguing," Meredith murmured.

"It's the first time that's happened to me," Sabrina repeated. She yawned. "Is there anything else? I'm tired."

"Do you want to rest here?" Meredith asked.

"I'd rather go home and get into my own bed," Sabrina said. She stood up. "It's getting late, and I worked all day."

"Just one more question—you said you didn't see

quite as clearly as you had the last couple of times you projected?" Meredith questioned.

"That's right. Usually it's a little blurry around the edges; but the last three times I was here, my vision has been very sharp. Why do you ask?"

"We are hoping, by studying your normal projections, that we'll find a clue to help you control the ones you've been doing at night," Meredith said. "There may be something happening during the night that is different and causing them. Pam, Parker, Neal and Alicia and I have all been doing some research. We don't have a conclusion yet, but we will let you know as soon as we can figure out something. And we're all working on ideas that may help you."

"Oh, okay."

"I want to make sure you get home okay," Meredith added. "Pamela volunteered to follow you home."

Pamela? Not Parker? But of course, he had followed her home last time—and come in. Maybe he was going to be busy later this evening. With a woman? she wondered, and then squashed the thought. Parker was a free agent. He probably had many women interested in him—some of whom he'd be interested in, too.

"Whenever you're ready I'll get Pam," Meredith was saying.

"Now is good," Sabrina said.

"You sure you'll be fine?" Meredith repeated. She pushed her long red hair back.

"Yes. I'll shower and go right to sleep," she told her. "Well, maybe I'll have a snack first." She smiled.

"Pam can stay with you—"

"No, really, it's not necessary," Sabrina said firmly. "In fact, she doesn't have to follow me home."

"I insist." Pam entered the room. "I know how tired you get after these sessions. Just let me check your EKG and EEG readings, and your pulse."

Afterwards, they left. She only caught a glimpse of Parker at his computer in the next room. He met her eyes and smiled, then returned to work.

Sabrina felt a comforting feeling as she saw Pam's headlights in her rearview mirror. Still, it wasn't as warm as the feeling she had gotten when Parker followed her home.

"What do you think?" Meredith asked, coming up behind Parker.

He had made a copy of the session, and wanted to watch it again, later. Now he was comparing her EKG and EEG results from this evening to her previous projections. They were very similar, except for the fluctuations when she'd declared she'd had "bad vibes" when she found the missing girl.

"I noted," he said to his oldest sister, "that she said she didn't see quite as clearly this time. I'm glad you asked."

"Which seems to prove your theory that she 'sees' better when she's with Pam or you. We should test her with another person who has an ability," Meredith suggested. "Another control—just to be sure."

He glanced at his sister. She had her pad of paper in her hands, ready to add more of her own observations on Sabrina's session. Meredith preferred paper and pen to using a tablet. When he pointed out that it took extra time because she then had to type her notes into the computer, she just shrugged and told him she thought better that way.

"Sure, we can do another test. That was exciting when she 'saw' another person projecting," he said. He'd made his own notes. The fact that she had "seen" someone else projecting, which was something he'd never even heard of before, was astonishing. And that she'd seemed to take a long time to get to her destination—even though it was further than before, it had taken her considerably longer. Was that because she was with Meredith and not him or Pam? They'd discuss it at their next meeting, he was certain.

And—there was one other fact. One that he didn't want to share with the others.

She'd been projecting, and she'd announced she was in New York City, and it was beautiful. Then, flashing through his mind, he'd seen the image she was thinking about.

She was thinking about projecting—with him. Flying through the night sky in New York City hand-in-hand with *him*.

He'd been so startled he'd almost fallen off his seat.

He was pretty sure Pam had noticed something strange in his behavior, and would be questioning him about it tomorrow.

The image had been very clear. Sabrina was thinking about—wishing perhaps—that he was on this spectral journey with her.

He swallowed as he remembered the picture now.

Too bad he couldn't draw well like Pamela. But he wasn't sure he wanted to capture the image on paper anyway.

He wasn't sure he wanted to share it with anyone else.

Meredith sat down and watched the projection again with him, and Neal. When they all finished, they turned off lights, and locked the building.

Parker felt tired when he reached his home after ten o'clock. He had to work late again tomorrow, so he knew he shouldn't stay up too late. He should be doing a load of laundry; he probably should relax or at least check emails. But he had a strong desire to watch the video of Sabrina again.

He had to force himself not to. There were other patients he was going to see tomorrow and notes to go over at some point. And he knew he needed a few minutes to unwind.

He took a shower, then sat and surfed the TV channels until settling on an old sci-fi movie he hadn't seen in years.

He must have fallen asleep, because the next thing he knew, he saw Dara's face. "Cheater!" she yelled, pointing a finger at him. "He cheated!"

He gasped and woke.

He was in his family room, on the couch. He'd fallen asleep. There was an unfamiliar movie on now, and the digital clock read 2:19.

He hadn't had a nightmare about Dara in a long time. He hadn't even consciously thought about her for days, maybe a week or two. So why was he having nightmares about the woman he'd once been involved with, now?

115

Dragging himself upstairs, he brushed his teeth and got into bed. As he drifted off, he turned his mind to Sabrina, not Dara. He wondered if he would have any more nocturnal visits from her…

Parker took his seat at the large oval conference table and sipped his strong coffee as Pamela seated herself to his right.

Automatically, he psychically probed his twin's mind. No picture. But then Pam had learned a long time ago to shield her thoughts from him—and much of the time, she was successful. He psychically pulled back. He shouldn't be trying to read her mind unless there was a really good reason, anyway.

He wondered idly if she had had any dreams recently that foretold future events. He'd have to ask her.

Meredith dashed in with a bunch of folders. He could often read her thoughts. He reached out with his mind, and saw she was thinking about Sabrina.

Who would be an important topic of conversation today.

It was Friday morning, and after two long days, he was looking forward to a shorter one today. He'd worked twelve-hour days both Wednesday and Thursday.

They scheduled meetings almost every morning, but yesterday had been so hectic the meeting had been cut short. They planned to complete going over the Wednesday and Thursday patients today.

His father was calling the meeting to order. Both of

his sisters and parents were there, along with Neal and Alicia and Maura Linden, the other part time nurse; and Larry Weissman, the other part time general doctor. Also joining them, as he sometimes did when his schedule permitted, was one of their interns, Felipe.

"On our agenda is our new patient, Roger Blaine; the yearly check-up with Anne Norton; Neal's latest research into telekinesis; Sabrina Holt; and the emails we've received from Evan Lassiter," his father announced.

That was going to be an interesting discussion.

They talked about Roger first. He'd come in because he'd started to experience telekinesis after being struck by lightning four years ago. Neal had done a lot of research on the subject since he had this ability himself. He was going to be testing Roger next week. Parker and his dad, Edward, had done the usual screenings and determined that Roger had no medical or neurological issues. Pam had done an evaluation too. After a session with Meredith, Roger would begin further testing. They mapped out his next few visits, then moved on to their other patients and topics. Neal also gave a brief report on his research.

Finally, they reached the subject of Sabrina.

"You've all seen the videos of her sessions with Parker, Pam and Meredith," Parker's dad began. "The one when she was searching for the little girl was especially fascinating since Sabrina was unprepared for it ahead of time."

"She did an extraordinary job," Neal commented. Murmurs of agreement sounded from around the table.

"But Sabrina struggled more when it was me she was with, then when she was with Parker and Pam,"

Meredith pointed out. "It appears she could draw on their power in those sessions to enhance her own; but since I don't have an ability, she had to rely on herself alone."

"Meredith—" their mother protested.

"You know it's true," Meredith stated, regarding her.

"Not completely," Kathrine said.

"Yes, I have slightly above average ESP abilities, but nothing like Parker and Pam. Even though I'm working to improve."

It was the first time Parker had heard his older sister admit to the entire group that she was working on improving her ESP. He sent her an encouraging smile.

Meredith took a breath and glanced around at the others seated at the oval table. "This supports the hypothesis of our first study: that patients with a paranormal ability will have that ability, whatever it is, enhanced when they're in close proximity to someone else who also has an ability, no matter what kind of ability it is."

Heads nodded.

This was the most important study of the ones The Lightning Center was doing now, and Parker was excited that tests with Sabrina seemed to be confirming their theory.

"I observed her carefully," Meredith continued. "You may notice in the video she frowns, and almost squints with her eyes closed, as if she is having problems seeing. It also took her a considerably longer time to travel. Now, I know it was further; but proportionally, she took almost twice as long to arrive at her destination as she did when she went to Rutgers to find Tanya; and she was with Pam that time. I checked the timing and mileage on both."

Parker studied Meredith. As usual, his older sister downplayed the fact that she hadn't been hit by lightning, but he could remember when they were kids and she'd been a little jealous of the fact that he and Pam were getting attention because of that fact. Still, as she'd grown she'd become a wonderful, giving and caring person—one of the nicest people that he knew—and no longer seemed fazed by the fact that he and Pam had abilities she didn't share.

"That was a good idea," his father was saying. "Any other observations?" He looked from one to another around the table.

"I was surprised that she saw someone else while she was projecting," Alicia said. "I've never even heard of that occurring."

"I agree," Neal said. "I looked through some of our research; no one else has reported that particular phenomenon."

Parker sipped his coffee, silently agreeing. He watched as Neal gave Alicia a look he couldn't read.

"Yes, this may be a significant find," Pamela said, seeming ignorant of the tension between Neal and Alicia.

"What's next in her testing?" asked Maura.

Ed glanced at the papers. "I'm not sure. What do you all think?"

"I'd like to run some additional ESP tests to see how she does with those," Alicia said.

Ed nodded. "Everyone else agree?" When he got affirmative answers, he went on.

"Hopefully, within the next year, we'll have enough data to publish a study regarding our theory and the testing results," he concluded.

"We should do another session with Sabrina soon, projecting even farther away; perhaps with Parker or Pam this time," Neal suggested. "And one with another person who has an ability. I can do that."

Everyone was in agreement.

Parker felt himself tense up, and reached for his coffee mug. Since Sabrina had found the missing girl, he'd started to feel guilty about keeping his secret ability from her. He knew, instinctively, she'd want to know about the effect it had.

"I'd love to try again next week," Pam was saying.

"Okay," Ed said, making a note.

Meredith got up and helped herself to more coffee, and their mom followed. She whispered something to her older daughter that Parker couldn't hear; Meredith nodded.

He wondered if they were speaking about Sabrina. But why whisper?

Maybe they were speaking about him. He reached out with his mind.

And felt a wall rebuff him.

Hmph. Looked like Meredith had been taking some lessons from Pamela!

His mother, on the other hand... she *was* thinking about him. But he wasn't sure in what way. All he could get was a hazy picture of himself—then it disappeared.

As usual, sometimes the image came in stronger than other times... and this time it was not clear. But apparently his mother and oldest sister had some concerns about him.

He didn't want to let them know he knew that.

He leaned back in his seat. "You know," he said, "as usual I find it difficult to keep the information to myself that Pam and I have abilities and these enhance—"

"We have to remain professional," his father said firmly, setting down his own coffee mug. "We can't influence our subjects by suggesting that we can make their abilities stronger. The power of suggestion could change our results."

Parker sighed. His father firmly believed that they had to keep the information to themselves—the information about the fact that their abilities had an effect on other's powers—at least until they'd done more testing with that individual. But it was easy for his father to say that, since he had no more than an average ESP ability. He wasn't the one put in an awkward position.

And having lived through the experience with Dara turning on him—which his family all knew about—Parker had conflicting emotions. To tell—and risk results he might later regret—or not to tell? His feelings remained mixed.

"Okay, so we'll set up Sabrina's schedule," his father was concluding. "Any other questions? Comments?"

"Remember, we have to try to find out why she's projecting in her sleep," Pam reminded them."And help her control it. This is a priority."

"True," Alicia said, nodding. "Meredith and I are going to speak this week to some researchers at Duke University to see if they have suggestions."

"I'm having Sabrina keep a journal, to see if there's any pattern to her night time projections," Pam finished.

"Okay. More comments?" his father asked. When there were none, he continued. "Moving to our final topic…" he gave a big sigh. "Evan Lassiter."

"You've all seen the email he sent to our general address," Pamela said smoothly, "once again outlining his objection to our methods."

"And threatening to make those objections public," Meredith said with a grimace.

"And complain to the medical board," Katherine stated.

"I've written a reply to him," their father said. Standing, he passed around papers. "Take a moment to read this, then give me your input. I'd like to respond with all our names, but to keep it short."

He gave them a few minutes to read. Parker made his own mental notes, but he saw Pamela and Meredith scribbling. Alicia was reading, frowning. Neal, his expression guarded, read without making notes, but Parker knew that he was probably making them mentally. Neal was extremely intelligent.

"So… what do you all have to say?" Edward asked.

"This is a crock!" Pam exclaimed. "We've been very careful in all our testing. We screen people carefully and eliminate those with psychological problems or neurological problems that could influence any test results— "

"We know that, Pam," their mother said soothingly.

"Well *he* doesn't seem to!"

122

Meredith leaned over and put a hand on her sister's arm. "He probably does—he's just making trouble."

They all knew why Pam was so upset. Years ago, she'd had a serious relationship with Dr. Evan Lassiter. And things had ended badly.

"Really, what can he do?" Alicia asked. "I mean, is he capable of giving us a reputation or is he just bluffing? And will the medical board really listen if he goes to them? We're a research facility. We don't do medical procedures."

"He's capable of making things uncomfortable for us," their mom said, making a face. "Very uncomfortable."

"Now, Katherine—" Edward began.

Their mother glared at their father. "Ed, you know perfectly well he can stir up more trouble if he chooses. Let's not sugar coat this."

"Let's not panic either," his father retorted. Then his expression softened as he looked at his wife. "We've all met him. I believe we can reason with him if we sit down together. He is a professional."

Pam remained silent, staring at her coffee mug. But Parker felt the trepidation rolling off her.

"You're being optimistic," his mother insisted.

"We can at least try," put in Meredith.

Parker sipped his hearty coffee. His oldest sister was a born peace-maker. As he met her look he gave a brief, hopeful smile.

Pamela sighed. "Mer—why don't you try to meet with him?"

"I'll go with her," Parker volunteered.

Edward glanced around the room. "I don't want

to bring too many people in if we do meet him in person. I think I'll go myself. If it requires subsequent meetings, then we'll discuss who should speak to him."

He watched as everyone nodded—everyone except Meredith. She looked dismayed.

Edward turned to her. "You, my dear, are a wonderful negotiator. The best, actually. I'd like to save your skills for a second meeting or if I sense trouble on the first go-round."

His oldest sister looked mollified. "Alright," she agreed.

But as his father concluded the meeting, Parker wondered if it would be as easy as Edward thought it would be. After all, he'd met Evan Lassiter years ago when Pam was involved with him, when The Lightning Center was still a dream.

And the guy was a highly opinionated man. Plus, as a successful psychiatrist now, people looked up to him. Listened to him. That could make things decidedly uncomfortable for The Lightning Center.

CHAPTER VII

So tell me about this dreamy-sounding doctor," Leanne said, settling into the corner of Sabrina's sofa.

Sabrina sighed, licking the cake from her fork. It was Friday evening, and Leanne, who lived about an hour and a half away, had come up to Sabrina's home. They were enjoying the cake Sabrina had baked her since her birthday had been earlier in the week.

"There's not much to tell. He's handsome, caring—but I'm a patient, and he's a doctor, and we need to keep our relationship strictly professional. So... forget about anything between us." Sabrina sagged back on the couch. The sweet chocolate taste lingered on her tongue.

"Why?" Leanne pursued the topic with her usual enthusiasm. "If you're really attracted to each other—"

"I'm attracted to him," Sabrina admitted. "And he seems to be attracted to me. But he's made his thoughts on the subject clear. It's hands off."

"Hmm. You're beautiful, and sweet and personable and charming—"

Sabrina held up her hand. "You're my friend, and you're prejudiced."

"It's the truth." Leanne sounded adamant. "And

125

you'll just have to wear him down!" she finished with a laugh, tossing her blond hair.

Sabrina had to grin at that. Her friend was making everything sound so easy. As if all she had to do was wear Parker down so he wouldn't care about their doctor-patient relationship.

If only it was that easy.

"Don't forget," she said, "I'm not quite sure I'm ready for another relationship. Devon-"

"You can't let that jerk keep you away from a potential relationship," Leanne declared. "He was a jerk. Don't let him keep ruining your life years after he messed with you."

***

She was here.

He knew it, in every part of his being. He *knew* Sabrina was in the room with him. A sizzling awareness moved up his spine.

He glanced at the small clock on his desk automatically. 12:08 AM on Friday night—Saturday morning, he corrected himself.

He *felt* her presence. Physically. He sniffed the air. There was the slightest scent in the air, something fruity, like melons. Slight, but there. Her cologne.

Rain pinged against the window suddenly. He looked around, but saw nothing.

He hadn't intended to stay up so late. He'd only wanted a few minutes to look at the file of a new patient.

Now he felt the slightest movement of air. A draft from the window as wind blew the damp air outside? Or—someone nearby?

"Sabrina?" he whispered.

The very air seemed to still.

Was she watching him, projecting even now?

Anger darted through him. Why was she watching him?

And then he remembered that when she projected in her sleep, she was unable to control her power. That she had asked the staff at The Lightning Center for help in managing her gift.

Perhaps she was sleeping and had drifted in on a dream. At this hour it was quite probable she'd already gone to bed.

He swallowed, feeling a twinge of guilt. He shouldn't judge her harshly. She was trying to control her ability.

They *had* to figure out what was causing her to project in her sleep, and teach her to stop doing it. He'd make it a priority. First thing Monday, he'd speak to his coworkers about it.

That decided, he looked around again. "Go back to sleep, Sabrina," he said, gently. "Back to your bed in your own room."

The room was silent.

And yet, he felt a presence. Someone watching him. It was spooky, in a way—but also comforting, because it was not an unknown. He knew who this must be.

His eyes saw nothing, but he sensed she was still present. He looked at the corner of the room where her energy seemed to be coming from.

He closed his eyes, and this time reached out with his innermost mind.

The picture flashed again—the picture he'd seen

before. Him with his arms around Sabrina, holding her close and tenderly.

She was thinking of them. Of being held by him, embraced by him.

She wanted this.

So did he.

He tried to deny the thought, but he couldn't. He shouldn't be having such thoughts, craving to pull her into his arms, to kiss her, soothe her—and do much more. But he couldn't help it. He wanted her, wanted her badly. And not just physically.

He wanted to hold her, make love to her—but also to keep her safe, to guard her, to keep the demons away that caused her to project and have little control over her night wanderings.

At that thought, he felt some relief. At least Sabrina had showed up here. Uninvited, maybe, but his home was a safe place for her.

He was a safe person for her.

He reached out his hands, his eyes still closed. "It's alright," he whispered. "You're safe here, Sabrina. Nothing can harm you."

At his words, he felt the air tense, electrified.

Had she heard him?

And then—he could swear he heard a small popping noise. Then—nothing.

He opened his eyes. He reached out again with his mind, but there was no image or presence with him at the moment. He knew she had left, that she had gone back to her own home, her own bed.

He felt relief… and a strange feeling of being alone.

He glanced at the clock. 12:17. More time had passed than he'd realized.

Time for him, too, to get some rest.

He closed Martin's folder, turned off the light, and got ready to go to sleep.

He didn't feel Sabrina's presence again as he got into bed. But once there, with his eyes shut, he could see clearly the vision from before: him holding Sabrina, her head resting on his shoulder, her dark hair tickling his neck, his lips brushing her forehead...

Sabrina dropped down, into bed, and sat up abruptly.

She felt dizzy, her mouth dry.

She had projected into Parker's home—*again*.

She'd seen his frown, felt annoyance roll off of him. He'd known she was there. *He'd spoken to her.*

That had never happened to her before. She felt another wave of dizziness, and gripped her comforter until it passed.

Once she felt steadier, she cautiously got out of bed. She padded through her living room, past Leanne who was sleeping on the couch so they could spend part of Saturday together. Once in the kitchen, she took a cup and pulled the pitcher of cold water from her fridge. She took several gulps of the cooling liquid, letting it slide down her throat. Placing the pitcher back and the cup in the sink, she tiptoed back to her bedroom and got into bed, shivering slightly. The air was warm in her home but she still felt cold.

How had Parker known she was in his home, watching him? How could he possibly know? Had he somehow heard her? *Sensed her*?

And she'd felt such a longing for him, such an intense wanting, that she'd reached out her hand to touch him. But before she did, she'd seen him frown, and pulled her hand back.

She didn't know how on earth he had sensed she was there. She scrunched down now, pulling her comforter up to her chin. If he knew she had been projecting into his home, he must be feeling anger and annoyance.

She could only hope that he'd think he had heard a mouse, or the wind.

But she was afraid he *knew*.

By late morning Sabrina and Leanne were at the Rockaway Mall, doing some serious shopping. Leanne had declared that she wanted to get a second pair of Australian boots with birthday money she'd received. She and Sabrina had bought identical chocolate brown boots in the basic design several years ago, and she wanted another pair in a different color, perhaps in a different design. Impulsively Sabrina decided to get herself a pair too, and they both ended up with short boots with a button, Leanne's in dark blue, Sabrina's in dark red.

They wandered in and out of several stores. Leanne bought herself a navy blue sweater that would look nice with the boots, and Sabrina chose a red and gold scarf that would be perfect for the holidays with a sweater she already had.

They went to the food court to have lunch, and chose Chinese food. As they started to eat, Sabrina spotted Meredith Costigan with a tray, looking for a table.

The mall was crowded and most of the tables were taken. "That's the social worker form The Lightning Center," Sabrina told her friend. "Do you mind if I ask her to join us?"

"Not at all. I'm curious to meet her, after all you've told me about the whole family. Hell, I'd like to meet them all, especially Parker."

Sabrina sent her friend a warning look before waving and calling "Meredith!'

Meredith spotted her, and came towards them. She was wearing a forest green long-sleeved T shirt and jeans, and carrying a denim jacket and a Macy's bag.

"Please join us," Sabrina invited, and introduced Leanne as Meredith slid her tray next to Sabrina's and sat down.

"Thank you," she said to them both. "It must be the fall sales—it's really crowded here today."

"What did you get?" Leanne asked, spearing a piece of her General Tsao's chicken.

"A birthday gift for my mom—a green sweater," Meredith said. "Her birthday's next week."

They chatted a little about shopping and their purchases. As Sabrina ate her tasty chicken with broccoli, she decided this might be a good opportunity to ask for help. "Meredith," she began, "would it be possible to speak to you later about my night projections? They've been happening more frequently and—I'm concerned."

As Meredith glanced at Leanne, Sabrina added, "Leanne is my best friend ever since college. She knows what's been happening."

"Of course. Want to meet me at the center later?" Meredith asked, a sympathetic look on her face.

"Leanne has to leave the area by three," Sabrina said, "to go back to her apartment in Plainsboro, since she has plans for tonight." Leanne had a boyfriend who was taking her out to a show for her birthday. "Would it be okay to meet after that? We could meet for a cup of coffee."

"We'll have more privacy at The Center. I'll make a pot of coffee when you get there," Meredith volunteered. "Want to meet at three thirty?"

"That would be fine," Sabrina agreed.

They talked for a little while longer about their favorite stores, while they ate their food.

"I better finish my shopping." Meredith stood, and smiled at both of them. "I want to get new boots too. Nice to meet you, Leanne."

They said goodbyes and after she left, Leanne leaned forward. "She's very nice and down-to-earth. I like her."

"I do too," Sabrina said. "In fact, I like everyone there. Meredith is particularly approachable."

Leanne nodded, and sipped her diet iced tea. "How about we finish our shopping?"

They shopped for another hour. Sabrina had given Leanne a purple and blue scarf for her birthday, and Leanne found a purple sweater that would go with it perfectly.

As they walked back to Sabrina's car, the wind whipped their hair across their faces. The day had grown cooler, and it looked like rain was approaching. They were soon back at Sabrina's condo and by three, Leanne had hugged her and left, promising to call during the week.

Sabrina felt a little bereft after her friend took off.

It was Saturday, with the day still young, and she had no plans for the rest of the day except for her meeting with Meredith.

Normally she didn't mind spending some Saturday nights alone with a good book or a movie, especially if she had worked during the day. But she felt unusually restless and wished she had made plans for the evening since she'd known Leanne would be leaving in the mid-afternoon.

Wind rattled the window, and she decided to wear her new boots since the temperature had dropped. They went well with the gold-colored vest she was wearing over her black long-sleeved T-shirt.

She left a few minutes later to meet Meredith, stopping to buy a couple of muffins at a nearby coffee shop.

There were no cars in the parking lot when Sabrina arrived there.

As she approached with her goodies Meredith unlocked the front door. "Come on in," she greeted her, then locked the door behind Sabrina. "We're closed every other Saturday."

"I didn't see any cars," Sabrina said, "and thought I might have beat you here."

"We have a parking lot in the back. The staff usually parks there."

"I'm sorry to ask you to come in on your day off," Sabrina apologized. "Are you sure you don't mind?"

"It's no problem." Meredith smiled. "Except for shopping I had no plans. I like your boots. Red looks good on you." She extended her right foot. She was wearing the same brand of boots Sabrina and Leanne

133

had purchased, in a similar style, in gray. "See, I was inspired by you two to get almost the same boots."

"Nice! Here's some muffins." Sabrina handed the bag to Meredith.

"I just started the coffee," Meredith said, taking the bag. "Thanks! Why don't we go to the break room?"

Sabrina hadn't been in this room. It was pleasant, with a rectangular table surrounded by eight chairs. A small couch and a couple of chairs, plus a refrigerator, stove and microwave were in the room. The employees probably ate and hung out in this room between appointments. The furniture was newer but comfortable and the room had a cozy air.

"Alicia's upstairs, doing some work," Meredith said as she stirred low fat milk into her coffee. "Want some?" She passed it to Sabrina. "She often comes in on Saturdays to do some stuff on her own. Just wanted you to know in case you hear someone walking around."

"Okay." Sabrina added the milk and sweetener to her coffee, then took one of the muffins. "I would have brought her a muffin if I knew she was here."

"That's okay." Meredith sat beside her, then turned her chair to look at Sabrina. "So… what's on your mind?"

"I'm still projecting at night," Sabrina admitted. "I can't help myself, and it seems to be happening more often." She frowned. "I'm visiting places I shouldn't, and I did it again last night."

"Places like…?" Meredith prodded.

"Your brother's house."

At that Meredith looked startled. She placed her coffee cup down. "Parker's house? Again?"

134

"Yes. You know about the first time. Now I've been there twice. And—" she hesitated.

"Go on," Meredith said, her voice calm. She placed a hand on Sabrina's arm.

"I feel like a voyeur—like I shouldn't be there, spying on him," she confessed.

"Do you think you have any control over the places you go in your sleep?" Meredith asked.

That made her pause. Sabrina thought about her answer. Did she?

"I feel like I *must* go places in my sleep," she admitted. "Like I'm compelled. And—I don't want to be."

"I can understand that," Meredith said sympathetically, shifting slightly in her seat and removing her hand. She grasped her coffee cup, and raised it to her lips to take a sip. "But since you have no control, you shouldn't feel guilty when you visit Parker—although I imagine it feels awkward afterwards."

Sabrina picked up her own coffee and drank before setting it down. "Very awkward. Not only that, but—the strangest thing happened last night. I could swear that Parker was aware that I was in his home office with him. He looked at the place where I was hovering."

"Well, we can ask him if he was aware," Meredith said slowly. "But—how do you think he would know? Has anyone ever sensed you being there—whether you're asleep or awake, when you're projecting?"

"Not that I know of. Except for the time when I saw that other woman projecting."

"So we don't know for sure if he was conscious

of you being there," Meredith went on crisply. "It's possible he was staring into space, pondering something—he often does—when you were projecting into his house."

Sabrina sipped her coffee, inhaling the rich, comforting aroma of the fresh brew.

"I will find out," Meredith continued, "on the chance he somehow was aware of—something, even if it wasn't you specifically."

Sabrina shifted in her chair. "Can't we—can't we just try to find a way to make this stop?" she asked anxiously.

Meredith nodded. "We—Pam and Parker and I—have discussed that. We're doing research. Tell me, have you had any recent changes in your diet, exercise, anything in the last six months?"

"You asked that before, and I said no," Sabrina pointed out.

"Did anything that caused you stress or upset you happen?"

"Nothing—" Sabrina stopped, as a thought occurred to her.

Meredith was observing her carefully. "You've thought of something?"

"Maybe… it's kind of far-fetched though." Sabrina pondered the idea.

"Tell me anyway," Meredith urged, her voice soft. "It may be important."

"Well… last April I was in a restaurant near here with a couple of friends eating dinner after work," she said. "I went to the ladies' room and when I came out, I saw Devon. My old boyfriend. We had a—painful break-up."

"What happened when you saw him?"

"He told me—he'd been drinking quite a bit, I suspect—he bragged that he'd gotten engaged. Then added it was to a wonderful girl, a beautiful girl who was normal." She flushed, remembering his exact words, which had stayed with her. "He said, quote, 'she's normal in every way. Not like some freaks I know, not like some kind of circus act'. And he laughed."

Meredith's creamy skin grew splotchy, and when she spoke her voice held suppressed anger. "What a jerk! That was a cruel thing to say, just plain nasty. Lots of people have unusual abilities!"

"I know." Sabrina flashed back to that day, seeing the scene vividly. "I very calmly congratulated him even though I was seething inside. I didn't respond to his insults, just went back to my friends. We were finishing up dinner and I left soon afterwards. I held my head high when I passed his table and ignored him and his friends, but I heard them laughing, and I'm afraid he was making fun of me." She swallowed. "I felt like I was back in high school."

"You're better off without a man like that," Meredith said, covering Sabrina's hand where it lay on the table. "But I can see that the experience disturbed you."

"I pushed it to the back of my mind and when I think of him, it's usually about the time we broke up. Do you think—could just *seeing* him have caused my night projections?"

Meredith considered this for a minute. "It's very possible. Seeing him that night upset you. Why don't you see if you can think of anything else that happened around that time? In the meantime, I'll discuss this with Pam and Parker and we'll try to come up with a plan to desensitize you on this incident—to get him, basically, out of your system."

Sabrina wondered about sharing this information about her ex-boyfriend with Parker. But she couldn't tell Meredith that without admitting she had feelings for Meredith's brother. Feelings which seemed more intense than a simple crush.

"Devon's out of my system," Sabrina said with some asperity. Of course, he hadn't been when he'd first broken up with her. She's been devastated.

"Perhaps there are some lingering… bad feelings," Meredith said carefully, as if she was tiptoeing around Sabrina. "In any case, let's see if dealing with this helps you control your night time projections." She smiled sympathetically.

"Also, Pam suggested to me yesterday that we give you something you can keep nearby, when you're sleeping, like an object to anchor you. We can train you to hold onto it if you feel yourself projecting. That might help center you."

"I'll try it," Sabrina said eagerly. "Thank you." She wished she felt as confident as Meredith. Even if the problem was caused by some kind of unresolved or bad feelings regarding Devon—would the doctors be able to stop her nocturnal wanderings? Would the anchoring object help?

* * *

"Park, do you have a minute?" His sister Meredith's voice on the phone sounded more anxious than her usual calm tone.

"For you? Always." He strove to sound light-hearted. Meredith was more private than Pamela, and didn't always share her problems; but he always tried to help when she did.

He glanced at the nice shirt and tie he'd taken out, preparing to get ready for his date tonight. Kyle had introduced him to Nadine at a party a few months ago, and they went out occasionally. Nadine was a lawyer and a tall, leggy blonde.

But even though he'd made this date about ten days ago—her schedule was pretty busy—he'd found he wasn't looking forward to it with his usual enthusiasm. In fact, he was wishing he'd called Kyle or Mark or another friend and was having a few beers or going to the movies with one of them. Or even hanging out for a quiet evening at home, with the book he was reading and a video game.

"It's about Sabrina."

Holding his cellphone, he dropped into the comfortable chair in his bedroom. "Anything wrong?"

"Well... she's been... projecting at night. A lot."

"I know," he said, wondering where this was leading. Could it be Meredith knew about...

"And—you're not going to like this—but last night, she's ended up in your house. Again."

He'd been correct. "She *was* here last night," he said, sighing. "I—got a picture in my head that I'm certain came from her thoughts." He wasn't about to describe the image to Meredith, or anyone else. "I knew she must be close. You know it happened before."

"She's not happy about it, and I'm sure you're not, either," his oldest sister said. "I think she feels like a peeping Tom or something."

139

"She can't help it," he defended her, automatically. And she couldn't. "It's just— "he ran his hand through his hair— "kind of weird. Awkward."

"I know. Park, we've got to help her."

His sister sighed, and he got a pretty good image from her—the one of the picture Pam had drawn. Obviously, Meredith had some kind of idea that he and Sabrina were meant to be together.

An idea that he fought.

And yet, he was drawn to her. He wanted to be with Sabrina. To put his arms around her. More than that. He liked her.

He wished it was Sabrina he was going out with tonight.

Sabrina found she was still restless when she arrived at her complex. The gray day had grown darker, the wind was whistling and the temperature had dropped while she'd been with Meredith. She knew that sunset was coming earlier and earlier now that it was October, and between the darkening sky and the clouds the day had turned dreary.

She greeted a neighbor as the woman walked by with her little Maltese dog, then climbed the stairs to her second-floor apartment. Letting herself in, she locked the door behind her, turned on a few lights, and dropped onto her couch.

Had she done the right thing in confiding in Meredith about her new projection to Parker's house?

She knew it would eventually get back to the

whole team at TLC. Parker would find out. And she still had the feeling he'd somehow known about her presence.

She sighed. She felt embarrassed, and uncomfortable. What if the whole team at The Lightning Center thought it was because she had feelings for Parker? Even though she recognized she did, she didn't want everyone to know.

She needed to get control of her astral projections at night if she was ever going to lead a normal life. And if this kept happening, she wanted to be honest with him. She didn't want to eavesdrop.

Oh my God, she thought suddenly. What if he's with a woman when I project?

She felt her face flushing. She had never, ever dropped in on anyone during an "intimate" moment—but there was always a first time. It was better, she thought, if she warned him about her projections before anything like that could happen.

Meredith had seemed confident that the team at The Lightning Center could help her. Sabrina leaned back on the couch and closed her eyes. Could they? Maybe it really was Devon and her unexpected encounter with him that caused her disturbing nocturnal wanderings.

She wished now she had said something nasty to Devon. Like "you're not man enough to handle a woman with extraordinary abilities!" or something like that. She sighed. Why did she always think of these great retorts *after* the fact? In this case, months afterwards?

When he finished the call with Meredith, Parker stared at his phone for a moment. Then, without another thought, punched in Nadine's number.

"Hi, Park," she drawled.

He grimaced. Only his closest friends and his family called him by that name. He'd never suggested she do it, and he felt resentment—illogical though it might be—that she was using it.

"Hi Nadine," he said. "We've had an emergency at work. I'm really sorry, but I can't make it tonight." And waited for the fall-out.

There was a long pause, and he could almost feel the frost-filled silence.

"Are you giving me the brush-off?" Her voice was no longer warm and come-hither. It was strident, angry.

"No," he said simply. "I'm a doctor, and we have emergencies. There's a patient I have to see."

"On a Saturday night?" she demanded.

"Yes." He refused to get involved in a war of words. Short and simple, that was the best way to answer her.

"Hmph. Somehow I doubt that."

Annoyance shot through his system. Did she think she was so wonderful that no one would dare to change plans with her? "It's part of my job as a doctor."

"Either you're just too devoted a doctor—or you're making plans with someone else," she snarled. "Well, it will be a long time before you make plans again with me, buddy."

"It's a risk I'll have to take," he said, purposefully keeping his voice even, not wanting to escalate the argument. But inside, he was thinking, *it will be a long time until I want to make plans with someone as shallow as you.* "My patients come first— "

"But you're no emergency doctor. Your patients don't have life-or-death emergencies. So long, Parker." She hung up before he could.

He stared at the phone. Surprisingly, he felt a surge of relief.

He hadn't wanted to see Nadine. And now, he didn't have to.

But he *did* want to see Sabrina. And now he could. Even though he knew he had to keep a doctor-patient relationship at the forefront of his mind.

He was calling her number before he could change his mind.

She answered on the first ring.

"Sabrina?" He couldn't help the eager note in his voice.

"Parker?"

"Yeah. Listen, I just spoke to my sister and she told me what's going on." It came out in a rush. "Can I come over? We can discuss the situation."

"Now?" She sounded astonished.

"If it's not a good time, I understand," he said, feeling a pang deep inside. Did she have a date tonight?

"No, it's ok. I was about to make—uhm, chili." She said it in a rush. "Why don't you have dinner here? I owe you."

"Thank you, I'd like that." He was surprised by the pleasure which dashed through him. "I'll bring something for dessert. Suppose I get there about—" he glanced at the clock. It was five minutes after 6:00. "Between 6:30 and 6:45?"

143

"That's fine," she said, sounding slightly breathless.

"Ok, see you then," he said.

"See you then."

He stared at the phone for a moment after she hung up. Was he insane?

But he didn't want to see Nadine. And he *did* want to see Sabrina.

And from what Meredith had said, it could be a good idea.

His phone rang suddenly, startling him, and he almost dropped it. "Pam" showed on the display.

"Hey, Pam," he started, "did Meredith call you—"

"We have to find a way to help her, right away," his twin said, her voice taking on an urgent note. "If she's visiting you at night—that could get *real* awkward, real fast."

"For her as well as me," he said. "You might as well know, I'm going over there now to discuss the situation with her."

There was a moment of silence. "I see," Pam said, without any inflection, and Parker rolled his eyes although she couldn't see him. Maybe she saw more than he did.

He had broken his date with Nadine, hadn't he? And he was glad he'd learned that she was a self-centered bitch. He didn't want to waste any more time with her.

Pam continued as if he hadn't told her something surprising. "We could try giving her something to help her sleep…" she said slowly, and he recognized the reluctance in her voice. "But we've discussed this, and I know you feel the same as I do, that it's a last resort."

He gripped the phone tighter, the plastic digging into his palm. "Agreed."

"Meredith and I discussed giving her something to hold on to, kind of an anchor," Pam continued. "We'll talk more on Monday. Unless you have any brilliant ideas after seeing her today—and if you do, please let me know tomorrow. I'm heading out for dinner and a movie with my friend Tracey."

"Okay, talk to you soon."

Once he'd hung up, Parker looked at his clothes, decided to stay in his comfortable red flannel shirt and jeans, and ran a comb through his hair. He'd stop at the grocery and pick up something for dessert, then head over to Sabrina's.

He hesitated as he got into his car. Odd, he thought. He hadn't looked forward to a ritzy dinner with Nadine, who was a glamorous woman. But he was *so* looking forward to spending time with Sabrina, having a home-cooked meal, and talking to her.

Sabrina sprang in to action. She rapidly made cornbread from a mix, then started browning the meat for the chili, and soon it was simmering on the stove. On a chilly autumn night this would be perfect. She washed up and reapplied her make-up. She felt re-energized, and knew it was because Parker was coming here.

The cornbread was ready and the chili smelled good when her doorbell rang.

She smoothed her hands over her jeans and went to answer the door.

Parker stood there, looking handsome in jeans, a red flannel shirt and gray sweatshirt. She tried not to reveal how rapidly her heart beat as he thrust a grocery store bag at her. "I bought a chocolate cake."

"Chocolate—perfect," she said. "C'mon in." She'd sent the rest of last night's cake home with Leanne.

She set the cake on her kitchen table and then took the heavy sweatshirt he'd shrugged off and hung it in her coat closet.

He was sniffing the air. "It smells delicious." For a moment he looked like a typical guy, interested in home-made food. Then, his face grew more serious as he regarded her. "How are you, Sabrina?"

"I'm okay," she replied. "This has to simmer for another ten or fifteen minutes. Why don't you sit down?"

They sat on her couch, and she turned to face him.

He began speaking immediately. "Meredith said you remembered a reason why you may be having these projections at night—why they could possibly have started."

Briefly, she told him the same story she'd told Meredith, about running into Devon. She guessed Parker's older sister had shared the tale with him, but that he wanted to hear it firsthand. He didn't take notes, just listened.

When she came to the part about Devon calling her a circus freak, his mouth visibly tightened.

"What a jerk," he said in a disparaging voice. "You're no more a freak than any other human being is. We all have different abilities, some more than

146

others, some undiscovered or hidden until something happens—like being struck by lightning."

"Thanks." She cleared her throat, feeling the familiar tightness when she spoke about Devon. Yet, she no longer felt teary-eyed, and the hollow feeling in her had lessened—quite a bit, she realized. Maybe Meredith was right, she thought. Maybe talking about the whole thing would be therapeutic.

"It might help if you talked about your break-up with this guy," Parker went on. "If not to me, then maybe to Pamela or Meredith."

She silently weighed whether she should tell Parker or not. She glanced at her watch. "Dinner is ready now. Let's eat. We can talk some more after dinner."

They ate, and Sabrina tried to keep the conversation lighter during dinner. They discussed recent movies they'd seen or were looking forward to seeing, and the local national and college football teams. Parker was more into football than she was but Sabrina followed the New York and New Jersey teams enough to be able to have a conversation about them.

"This is delicious," he said for about the third time as he finished his second helping of chili. "You're a good cook."

"Thanks." She smiled. She rarely got the chance to cook for anyone else. "It's nice to be appreciated."

He scowled. "Don't tell me your old boyfriend didn't appreciate your cooking."

"Actually, he did," she said. "He admitted I was a good cook. But I'm afraid he didn't appreciate anything else."

"He sounds like a first-class jerk," he said firmly.

She smiled at his words.

147

They agreed to have dessert a little later, and Parker helped her rinse off the dishes and load the dishwasher. She offered him coffee or hot cocoa, and he chose the latter. She made instant cocoa and they took their warm drinks back to the living room.

"Do you feel comfortable enough to talk about your old boyfriend now?" he asked, sipping the drink.

She blew on hers, then took a sip. The liquid was sweet and chocolatey. "I guess so," she said slowly. She squared her shoulders. Maybe it was time she faced this personal demon.

"Tell me about him." He placed his mug on a coaster on her wooden coffee table, then relaxed against the couch. She caught a whiff of his familiar masculine aftershave.

She placed her mug down, then leaned back in the corner of her couch.

It was dark outside, but lights from neighboring buildings shone through her living room window. She studied Parker. She had a crazy desire to run her fingers through his thick, dark hair and had to suppress it. Instead, she brushed the smooth couch with her hand.

"I met Devon at a party the beginning of my senior year in college," she said. "We fell for each other—hard. We started seeing each other constantly." She pictured Devon's good looking face, his short brown hair, his easy smile. "He was—more concerned with himself than anyone else, although I didn't realize that at first. I was just head over heels." She sighed.

"At the end of January, a girl in one of my classes was very upset because her teenage sister was missing. They thought she had run away. She asked if anyone could help her. I approached her after class and volunteered to try to help." Even now, the memory was like a slap in the head. Her one big failure.

"Yes…" he said.

She realized she had fallen silent, gazing at her TV, which was off, but seeing another time and place. Seeing that girl's worried face.

"I went back to her apartment and tried. I really tried. I projected, but kept spinning around the town they grew up in. I just couldn't seem to focus on the girl. I couldn't get a handle on where she was!" Her voice rose with remembered frustration. Her fingers dug into her palms before she felt the pain and realized what she was doing.

Parker leaned forward and covered her hand. It felt like a comforter settling over her on a cold winter night. She unclenched her hands. He squeezed hers, and warmth flowed from his hand, into hers, then up her arm, and into her head, her shoulders, and her heart.

She swallowed. "After a while I gave up. I felt awful. Both the other girl—Erin—and I were in tears. I told her the truth, that this had never happened to me before, and she said she believed me, and thanked me for trying." She met Parker's eyes, and his expression was warm and sympathetic.

"No one succeeds one hundred percent of the time, at anything," he told her gently. "No one is perfect."

"I know, but my track record had been good until then." She sighed. "I was so disappointed. I called Devon and asked to come over to his place so I could tell him what happened." Her hand tightened in Parker's as she recalled what happened next.

"What did he say?"

"I went over there and told him the whole story. I

149

was crying, looking for a little sympathy." She swallowed the lump in her throat. "He—he *laughed.* He actually laughed at me!"

"What an asshole!" Parker exploded. His hand tightened on hers. "Sorry. I couldn't help myself. The guy's a total jerk."

"Yes, well... I was shocked. And he said—he said I was crazy. I was like a circus act, a freak!" Even though her voice rose with indignation, she could feel the tears clogging her throat as she remembered the pain she'd felt. Still felt.

"And even when he saw how upset I was, he mocked me," she continued. "Finally, I told him we were through, and ran out of there and back to my apartment. My roommate—Leanne, she's one of my best friends—said he was a bastard to act that way, and I had to accept that he was, but his words hurt. A lot. I really—cared about him." Her voice broke. She fought back the tears gathering in her eyes. She hated to cry in front of other people.

Parker moved then, and gathered her into his arms. "It's okay, Sabrina. He's the one that acted badly, but you're entitled to be hurt by his actions."

His compassion seemed to loosen the dam inside her, and the tears began falling. She leaned into him, erupting into sobs. He stroked her hair. "I—I tried to keep busy, and eventually—got over him." She struggled to get control over her crying. "Our paths didn't cross much on campus, and—and then I went on to grad school. I heard he was living in—Jersey City. A few months ago is when I ran into him at the chain restaurant." She took a ragged breath, fighting to control her tears.

Parker continued to hold her, and she relished the warmth that emanated from him. Warmth and caring. Somewhere in the back of her brain she realized it wasn't merely physical. She could feel emotional support coming from him.

Was this her slightly-higher-than-average ESP at work? Or was she imagining his feelings?

"You know the rest," she said. "When I saw him at the restaurant, he told me he was engaged, and she was normal in every way. 'Not like some freaks I know, not like some kind of circus act'." She quoted the words that still echoed in her brain when she thought of Devon. "And he laughed. I simply told him good luck and left him, then left the restaurant as soon as I could. But— "

"But?" Parker prodded when she fell silent again.

She turned to him, and saw his face held not one ounce of mockery like Devon's face had. Instead his expression revealed compassion. "But I kept thinking of that song by Britney Spears, the one about a circus, being in the center of a ring— "

"I know it. It's not a bad song," he said. "And that's when the night projections began?"

She got up, feeling cold as she left the protection of his arms, and went into the bathroom where she grabbed a tissue. She blew her nose loudly before sitting back down on the couch. "Not right away. That's why I don't know if this is really the reason those nightly projections are happening."

"It is possible, since it was an upsetting incident. We'll find out, Sabrina." His voice was firm. "We can try several things to de-sensitize you to thoughts of him. Pam's good at helping in that way. Do you think of him often?"

"No, not really." At least, she didn't think she consciously did. Especially since she'd met Parker.

"To keep you from projecting at night, we can also try hypnosis, suggestions—and as a last resort, drugs," he said slowly.

She shook her head. "I don't like taking medicines unless I really have to. I'd rather not take any."

He regarded her. "Look, Sabrina, the guy was a total ass. You deserve so much better. And I understand that you don't want to depend on medicines; we try to only prescribe meds if it's really necessary." He reached out and touched her cheek, trailing a finger down softly. "There's nothing at all wrong with you. He couldn't handle you and your gift, and so he turned it around, trying to make it out to be something weird; trying to blame you for his lack of understanding." His voice was hard as a rock. "He's a complete jerk."

She swallowed. Parker was certainly supportive, and right now he was speaking as a friend more than a doctor. She knew it instinctively.

And the thought flashed across her mind: *I wish he could be my boyfriend. He's a lot better than Devon any day!*

But he was her doctor, and their relationship was professional. It had to be. He was just being supportive.

"Parker…" it came out as a whisper, as if the word simply appeared on its own. "A lot of people think this way, I'm afraid." *Except you.*

"Not all people do," he protested. "You're better off without an idiot like that!"

She'd heard it before, of course. From her friends—Leanne, other friends, and her sister. They all thought Devon was a jerk and she was better off without someone like that in her life.

And she knew intellectually they were right. She'd known it then—and she knew it now. But knowing it emotionally was another thing.

"You're right, of course." She nodded. "But running into Devon and hearing him say those awful things—it hurt like hell at the time."

"That's natural." He bent forward, and cupped her chin. "Sabrina—believe me, he's not worth worrying about. Any guy who puts you down isn't worth your time. There are many men out there who would appreciate your talents, like you for who you are— " he stopped.

Like you? She wondered.

But she didn't say it. She held her breath, looking at him.

And she sensed he *wanted* to say it. But something—his professional job, his desire to keep that job separate from his personal life—was preventing him.

But she was glad, because she was pretty sure it was what he was thinking.

"I wish things could be different," he whispered, his eyes locking with hers. "But I'm your doctor, so..." He dropped his hand.

"I know." She found herself leaning closer. She touched him lightly on the shoulder. "If things were different..." her voice drifted off.

For a long moment, they regarded each other. The moment stretched, and spun out. Her breath caught, and then, he bent forward, and brushed his lips against hers.

Without thinking, she wrapped her hands around his neck, and pulled him closer.

His lips hardened against hers, the kiss going from tender to demanding in an instant.

She felt electrified, heat licking her nerves from her head down to her toes. Her heart accelerated, and she felt the bursts of energy and desire throughout every cell.

He pressed her closer.

She could smell his lively aftershave, feel his springy hair by his neck. She could hear the quick breaths and feel the rapid beat of his heart against her body as he held her tightly in his arms.

She couldn't think; she could only feel these things, feel the acute awareness of being held by Parker, kissed by him.

But even as she relished every little sensation, he loosened his grip, and pulling back, gazed into her eyes.

"I'm sorry."

"Don't be," she said simply.

"I shouldn't be kissing you—you're my patient, for God's sake—"

"I think we *both* wanted that," she said, chagrinned that he was trying to be so professional at this moment.

He barked a laugh. "Yeah, I sure did." He stared at her. "But—we—I'm sorry, Sabrina, this really is my fault." And then he gave a lopsided grin. "I can't seem to resist you. Every time we're together I want to hold you…"

Her heart leaped. He wanted her. She'd guessed it, but now she *knew*.

154

And she knew she wanted him too.

"I feel the same," she confessed.

He shook his head. "What are we going to do?"

She dared to suggest it. "Maybe after my—uhm, treatments are over—"

"Maybe." He sighed. "But we don't know how long that will be. And in the meantime—we have to refrain from—anything like this." He started to move further back on the couch. "Unless—" he stopped.

"Unless?" she asked.

"Unless you want to give up trying to stop the nightly projections—or give up projecting. But—" he was already shaking his head. "I can't ask you to do that. It wouldn't be right. You need to get a good night's sleep—so we need to help you stop your night-time wanderings. And if you're helping others with your astral projections, I can't ask you to give it up."

She swallowed as he spoke, a hollow feeling in her stomach. Give up projecting? There was a time she would have said yes. Now, she wasn't so sure. She'd seen firsthand how she had helped a little girl and the people who cared for her.

"I—don't think I want to do that—at least not immediately," she stated. "But, Parker—it's something that could happen in the future.'

He stared at her. "I can't ask that of you. It's part of who you are." He shook his head.

"Maybe—" she cleared her throat, and willed her heart to slow down. "Maybe this is a good time to go eat that chocolate cake.'

"That's a good idea." He stood, and extended his hand. She placed hers in his, and he pulled her up too.

Even that touch electrified her whole body.

She stepped back, putting the distance he said he wanted between them, as reluctant as she was to do it. She knew he was right, but she also knew she wanted to move right back into his arms. That she craved him, and she would be dreaming of being held by him in the future.

"Let's have that cake." Somehow, she managed to keep her voice light as she led the way to the kitchen.

Driving home, Parker couldn't stop thinking about Sabrina.

He'd wanted her. In every way. In his arms. In his bed, or hers. Touching her silky skin. Running his hands over her curves. Tasting her mouth.

But besides that, he wanted to hold her, care for her, show her that not every guy was like that stupid fuck of an ex-boyfriend who had put her down and called her a freak. He wanted to cherish her.

And beat the other guy to a pulp.

It was an unusual feeling. Sure, he'd wanted other women before. He'd had his share of girlfriends, lovers, some just for fun. Women like Nadine.

But his feelings for Sabrina—there was desire, but something else. He felt protective towards her. A level of caring he hadn't felt for a long time. Maybe not ever before.

It was something he had never felt about Dara.

They'd had their cake, and then he'd left. He'd given her a mere peck on the cheek when he did. Trying to keep things professional.

Ha, a little voice inside him chortled. *If you were a real professional you wouldn't even be there. Or at least you wouldn't have stayed after you spoke to her initially.*

Regardless, he'd kept a professional distance after that kiss.

But that kiss…!

God, he'd felt as if every nerve ending had ignited. Pure fire had zoomed through his entire body, his entire being. He'd wanted to keep kissing her. To touch her everywhere, to make sweet, hot love to her.

The rain that had struck his windshield on and off as he drove began to come down in earnest, and he adjusted the wipers to a quicker pace. He turned on to Rt. 46, going west towards his home, and puddles reflected the lights from cars going the opposite way.

He turned on the radio to a station that played a mix of current and older hits. Oddly, the music of Britney Spear's "Circus" flowed through the car.

What a coincidence. But the song reminded him of Sabrina's old boyfriend and his calling her a freak—although the song had to do with getting attention, not being a freak.

Sabrina was worthy of plenty of attention.

He turned onto the side road which would lead towards his home, driving slowly through the wet darkness.

All the time, he was wondering how he was going to be able to keep his hands off Sabrina, keep things strictly professional, next time he saw her. It was going to be hard. Dammed hard.

He wondered if, now that she'd spoken about her old boyfriend, it would prove to be cathartic. Perhaps

157

she had gotten Devon out of her system, and would be less likely to project at night.

Or would she once again visit him in the dark of night?

He considered that. And—for the first time—he wasn't averse to the idea.

Huh. That was a change, for him.

He wondered why his viewpoint had changed. Before, he'd thought Sabrina's night-time visits were an invasion of privacy. But now he wasn't sure. Maybe she was coming to him unconsciously for help?

And he *did* want to help her. Maybe… more than a professional doctor would want to. Maybe he wanted to help her personally. Because he cared.

Monday started with the usual meeting. They went through the info on the patients, including Sabrina.

Meredith caught the others up with the fact that Sabrina's night time projections were more frequent; as well as a brief summary of Sabrina's relationship with her old boyfriend and her run in with him before the nightly projections started.

His mom gasped loudly when Meredith quoted Devon's cruel words. The others around the table grimaced.

"What a jerk." Neal said.

"Idiot," Pam declared.

"Bastard." This from Alycia.

They discussed her projections at night, and Pam and Meredith agreed to work with Sabrina on an "anchor" she could clutch at night to help keep her from projecting.

Fortunately, his sisters didn't bring up the topic of Parker visiting her, although they knew. He had asked them to keep that fact from the rest of the staff. He was uncomfortable, afraid he'd appear unprofessional.

Which, he thought, he likely was. When he told her about his own ability—if he did, which was still a question—then that might be the time to bring up the fact he wanted a relationship with her that wasn't strictly clinical. It was just too soon, right now.

"Now, about Evan Lassiter." His father frowned.

Parker noticed Pam sat up straight at the guy's name.

"I called him, and he's refusing to meet with me," his father said.

"I think I should handle this," Meredith volunteered.

"I think we should wait a few weeks then you or Meredith should try again," Neal said.

"Maybe I should try," Parker's mom said.

Pam said nothing, looking at her iPad, which lay on the shining wooden surface of the conference table.

"Maybe I should just go with dad and show up at his office without any notice," Parker suggested. He was getting more irritated by Evan Lassiter. Who did he think he was anyway?

"Then we might waste a trip for nothing," his father pointed out. "Besides, that's not professional."

They discussed it for several minutes before concluding that Meredith should try contacting him next.

When the meeting ended, Parker scooted out quickly.

He saw the look Pamela gave him, and he knew, without attempting to read her mind, that she was wondering about him and Sabrina. He'd talked to her on Sunday, giving her the bottom line on his meeting with Sabrina at her apartment. He hadn't gone into his feelings for Sabrina; but he knew his twin well enough to know she could read between the lines.

His day was busy, and Mondays he typically worked late. It was 8:30 before his last session ended. He'd been doing a follow-up visit with Cecelia, a patient who had come in after being struck by lightning, and developed the ability to see auras.

He finished his notes, then packed up for the night. He heard Pam, who had stayed late also, saying goodnight to Neal, who was heading out after a long day too. He told them both to have a good evening and left by the back door.

He spent the rest of the night watching TV and doing laundry. Nothing unusual.

But his mind kept going back to Sabrina. When he got into bed, he tried to think about something else. Football.

But as he drifted off, her face came back into his head.

Hours later, he was awakened by a feeling of someone nearby.

He sat up in bed, looking around.

It was dark, and the clock read 2:17.

He opened his mind, and an image flashed; he and Sabrina, sitting on her couch, kissing. Exactly what had happened on Saturday.

So, she *was* here. She was projecting again.

"Sabrina?" he asked, his voice low.

160

The air around him seemed to move.

"It's okay, Sabrina," he said. He wished he could actually see her, reassure her she was not some kind of freak. Put his arms around her and hug her.

Again, he felt movement. Then, that peculiar popping noise he'd heard before.

"Sabrina?"

She was gone. He felt it. Reaching out with his mind again, he drew a blank.

He sighed out loud, then pulled the comforter over him and lay down, wishing she was lying here beside him.

Tuesday, Parker planned on working from 8:30 to 5:00. Around four o'clock, he was in his office, making notes on Martin, the man who could predict earthquakes. It was the first time they'd seen that ability at TLC, and they were all excited about it.

His cell phone buzzed, and he saw it was Kyle.

They'd spoken several times during the last week. Kyle had passed on info about how well the little girl was doing and had thanked him, TLC, and especially Sabrina for all her help.

He greeted his friend.

"Parker, we could use another favor." He sounded anxious.

Parker tensed. "Don't tell me there's more trouble?"

"Not with the same family. No, this is another matter."

"What's going on?" he asked, leaning back in his chair.

"A woman has somehow gotten out of a nursing home near here," Kyle began. "We don't know how, but she slipped out last night, and with nightfall coming again, and the weather getting colder, the staff and her family are very worried about her.

"We've had the police and community searching; dogs, volunteers, you name it," Kyle added. "I was wondering… do you think your patient Sabrina could help again?

"I don't know," he said honestly. "I can ask. I presume you have a picture?"

"Yes, I have one already."

"Ok, I'll call her and see what we can do. She's probably working at the moment."

"Whatever she can do is much appreciated. If we have to wait until she gets out of work then we'll wait. Let me know and I'll bring a copy of the photo over or email it to you."

"Okay." He got off the phone, then dialed Sabrina.

She didn't pick up. He left her a brief message about another emergency with a missing person. Hopefully, she'd call back soon.

She called back ten minutes later. "I'm sorry, I was helping someone with research," she said. "I see I missed your call." She sounded a little rushed.

He explained the situation, ending with, "would you be willing to help?"

"Of course," she said. "But I can't leave work until five o'clock. My day has been pretty busy, so I honestly don't know how effective I'll be."

"Kyle said whatever you can do would be helpful. She's an older woman, and they're worried about her being out in the cold."

162

"I'll get there as soon as I can."

"I can pick up a sandwich for you or something," he offered.

"Okay," she said. "I'll see you later."

After their call ended, he leaped up and went to see if anyone else could stay for her session as he clicked on Kyle's number.

Sabrina felt tired before she even got to The Lightning Center. She's dealt with a cantankerous older woman who wanted to look up information early in the day; then some demanding students in the afternoon, who were unappreciative of her efforts and eventual success in finding the historical facts they needed. She really wanted to go home, eat, and put her feet up with a good book.

But she couldn't ignore the need to find the older woman.

On top of that, she'd had an uneasy feeling in her stomach from the time Parker made his request. She was a little afraid about seeing Parker again. She wanted to be close to him. But she'd projected into his home on Monday night, and somehow, someway, he'd known she was there. She could barely believe it. But he'd spoken to her. He'd told her it was "okay."

How had he known? She'd wrestled with that this morning before she left for work, and it was at the front of her mind now. How could he have known? That had never happened to her before when projecting, at night or any other time. It had only happened with Parker.

Plus, she knew it would be hard to maintain a professional-only relationship when she was alone with him.

But she knew her help was needed.

CHAPTER VIII

When Sabrina arrived, Parker was waiting for her, along with Pam and Alicia, who were seated in the computer room next to the living room area.

"Whenever you want to start," he told her, "it's fine with us. Why don't you have something to eat first? Alicia picked up a few sandwiches at the sub place."

She declined, explaining she'd rather eat later. She was slightly hungry and knew she'd be very hungry later; but she wanted to get this done. The woman's life could be at stake.

"Here's a photo of the missing woman, Clarisse," he said, handing it to her. The picture showed a gray-haired woman with large glasses, in a yellow dress, smiling.

He drew the blinds to block out the late afternoon light, lit a candle, and put on classical music.

Sabrina took a sip of water before laying down and consciously trying to relax her body. She held the photo of Clarisse.

The scent of vanilla and the music were calming as she rose up through the ceiling and roof to look down on the building.

As usual, she felt those invisible threads tugging

her and she turned east, passing traffic headed west on interstate 80. Rush hour traffic, horns honking and cars moving slowly. She floated along and reached Route 10, continuing east.

Recalling they liked her to talk while she projected, she said, "I'm near Randolph and Denville. I'm not quite sure where the dividing line is… I may be right in between." She paused, then went on, "there's traffic and it's getting dark. I see stores."

She hovered over a big building. "I think… I'm over the nursing home."

She floated. She seemed to be staying in one spot.

And then she began to circle the building. She clutched the photo of Clarisse in her right hand.

"I'm looking for her," she said aloud.

She stretched her left hand out, appealing to Clarisse to let her know where she was. She willed herself to go in Clarisse's direction.

Nothing happened at first. Then, she felt unaccountably confused. Like she couldn't tell where she was. She was closer to the ground now, the waning sun casting shadows. The air seemed to press on her. She felt almost dizzy.

She cried out.

"Do you see her?" Parker's voice was calm.

"It's getting dark," she whispered. "And I'm closer to the ground than I should be. It's—I don't know what direction to go in. I'm spinning around."

"Take a deep breath." His voice seemed far away. "Try to focus. You're safe."

She did try to focus. But she couldn't seem to go in one specific direction. She kept going around in a circle.

"I can't seem to go in one direction—I keep going round and round. I—I can't find her!"

She heard the sharpness in her own voice. And suddenly she had a flash to another time and place.

"It's—it's the same as when I tried to find Erin's sister," she said, her voice raspy. "I'm—confused." She felt her heartbeat accelerate.

"It's ok." Pamela's voice had joined Parker's. "Can you rest for a moment, Sabrina? Take a deep breath?"

She tried simply floating. But the air seemed to whirl around her.

"I'm trying," she whispered. "But—I can't find her."

"That's ok." Pam's voice was tranquil. "Try to hold still, and just relax."

At Pam's prompting, Sabrina made an effort to relax her body. Pam instructed her in a soothing tone to relax her head, her neck, her shoulder muscles. She could feel herself calming down.

"I'm more relaxed now," Sabrina stated. "I can see the building—the nursing home. There are police cars here and an ambulance." She continued to hover, studying the activity below. But she was still not pulled in a specific direction.

"I'm staying in the same place—not being pulled towards anything, like I usually am," she said. "I'm not sure what to do." She could feel her facial muscles beginning to tense again, and consciously tried to relax them. "I'll try to circle the area." She began to move.

She was aware, though, of a creeping sense of discouragement. She wasn't being pulled toward Clarisse. What if she couldn't find her?

She shivered. This was too much like when she

couldn't find Erin's sister. She could feel her own confusion, her loss of focus, her inability to search effectively.

What if Clarisse was dead?

She felt a lump wedge in her throat.

"Is Clarisse on some kind of drugs?" she whispered.

"It's very possible she takes medications," Parker said. His voice sounded far away. "But those drugs would be to help her be less confused, not more. However, if she hasn't had any of her medicines for 24 hours..."

The conclusion was obvious.

"She could be confused, maybe feeling ill." Suddenly Sabrina felt close to tears. "I'm circling the building... and I'm going to go search a wider area. I still can't feel her!"

She thought she heard Pamela murmur something but couldn't hear exactly what was said.

"I'm going to try looking in the woods to the north."

Sabrina directed herself to drift over the wooded area. She went over the circumference of the woods, then tried zig-zagging across it. Defeat began to build up in her. "I'm covering the wooded area in a zig-zag pattern," she stated. "I'm not getting any readings from Clarisse. *Nothing*."

She continued to look, first to the north, then to the east. She found nothing there. She moved south, telling them at intervals what she was doing.

She was starting to feel cold. By the time she moved west, she was shivering.

She could feel someone laying a blanket on her, but that didn't help much.

Finally, she said, "I've been all over the areas to the north, south, east and west. I can't find any sign of her!" Her voice cracked.

She was also conscious her shivering had increased, despite the blanket on top of her.

"She's shivering." Pamela's voice was far away but still distinct. "And her blood pressure is dropping. I don't like this."

"We've got to get her back here. Now," Parker emphasized, and she was surprised to hear the urgency in his voice.

"Agreed," Pam said.

Sabrina kept looking as she circled the building, and then Pamela's voice, clear and close to her, said, "Sabrina. Sabrina… we think you should come back now."

Part of her was relieved. She was cold, and fatigue was seeping through her. But she hadn't found Clarisse, and she was worried.

They'd all be disappointed, too. She knew it, having experienced that before.

"Just one more time around." She continued the search.

"Sabrina, I'm afraid we're going to have to insist you come back," Parker said emphatically. "We're worried about you."

"Yes, please," Pam pleaded.

"I can't find her!" Sabrina exclaimed. But she knew they were right. She was going to be exhausted soon, and she was afraid extra time wouldn't help the search. She better head back before—she didn't know what would happen if she stayed in this state for too long.

She had failed.

That knowledge hung heavily on her as she forced

herself to head west, following Rt. 10 and the traffic there. It was dark now, and the traffic was lighter than she expected. Somewhere in her she recognized that more time had passed than she'd thought.

She had been searching a long time.

She was soon traveling on Rt. 46, and found The Lightning Center building.

She dropped through the roof, the ceiling, and back into her own body. "I'm back," she said. It came out as a groan.

She sat up abruptly, and blinked her eyes open. Dizziness assaulted her, and she gripped the sofa arm. The suede fabric felt firm yet soft against her palm.

The room was dim. She stared at Pamela and Parker's anxious faces.

"How do you feel?" Pam asked. She began taking Sabrina's pulse.

Parker extended his hand, holding the water bottle. She grasped it and drank.

"You're shivering," he said. "I'll get you another blanket."

"No—no, it's alright." She still felt cold, but not as cold as before. There was a tightness in her middle. "I couldn't find her," she choked out. "I couldn't find Clarisse."

"We know. The important thing is, you tried," Parker said, his voice even, his blue-gray eyes regarding her with kindness. "No one can succeed one hundred percent of the time."

"It's all right," Pamela soothed. She stepped back, dropping Sabrina's wrist. "You should eat something, Sabrina."

Sabrina sat up straighter. And suddenly she felt

tears rolling down her cheeks. "I'm so sorry," she said, struggling to stop her tears. "I—I wanted to find her. But this was like the time with Erin's sister. I looked and looked but I couldn't feel her, couldn't see her—nothing was clear! All I could feel was a—a confusion. A feeling of unreality."

Parker and Pam glanced at each other, and Pamela got up, got a tissue, and handed it to Sabrina.

Sabrina wiped her eyes and blew her nose as her tears slowed.

Parker knelt beside her on the couch. "It's okay, Sabrina. We know you tried your best." He put a reassuring hand on her shoulder. Warmth flowed from his touch into her body.

"It's not ok." She shook her head. "People expect me to do this, and they'll be angry and upset that I couldn't."

"Only Kyle knows, outside of this office; and he wouldn't be angry," Parker told her. "He'll know you tried your hardest. And no one would be mad."

"Maybe I should try to go back—"

"No." Parker's mouth was set in a firm line. "We pulled you back, Sabrina, because your physical body was showing signs of stress."

"We're not going to put you at risk," Pam stated. "Your blood pressure dropped."

Pamela crouched down too, and covered Sabrina's hand with her soft one. "Please don't be upset," she said. "We're more upset because we see you're distressed," she continued. Her sympathetic gaze made Sabrina feel a little better. "Look, why don't you have a sandwich now, and one of us will drive you home? You probably need to rest. And we can ask you questions tomorrow."

171

She *was* exhausted. She blew her nose again, and said, "I can drive home. I'll just use the ladies' room first." She got up slowly, her feet oddly shaky.

Parker and Pam stood up too, and she knew they were studying her as she walked somewhat gingerly to the door and out of the room.

Once she'd used the ladies' room and splashed cold water on her face, she felt a little better, though still shaken and drained. Returning, she found Parker and Pam talking in low voices to Alicia.

Pam turned to her. "I'm going to drive you home in your car," she said. "Parker will follow so he can give me a ride back here to get my car. We'll make sure you're all settled before we leave."

"That's not necessary—"

"It is," Parker interrupted. "You need to lay down and rest. Since your blood pressure dropped low, you could be at risk of fainting."

"Alright," she agreed reluctantly. She sighed with resignation. She was okay to drive, she was sure; but she didn't have the energy to argue with them.

"I never told you," she said to them all, "what happened to Erin's sister, Maureen."

"What?" Parker queried.

"They found her the next day, at a friend's house. She'd taken LSD, and had been higher than a kite. I concluded that I couldn't find her because she was so high; and she'd lost her perspective and sense of self," Sabrina finished.

Parker and Pam exchanged glances. "That's fascinating," Pam said.

Sabrina pulled on her jacket, grateful she'd worn a heavier one today, since she still felt colder than normal. Someone had blown out the candle and shut off the music. "I'm ready to leave."

"I'm ready too." Pam held her purse, a bag and a coat.

"I'll follow you in a few minutes," Parker said.

As they went down the stairs and out the door, Sabrina told Pamela "you really don't have to drive me." The chill air struck her and she shivered again.

"It was either me or Parker," Pam responded lightly, holding out her hand for the keys as they reached the car. "We insist. I brought a couple of sandwiches for you." She held up the bag.

Sabrina got into the passenger seat as Pam took the driver's seat. She seemed to know where everything was and explained that she had a Nissan, too.

Sabrina closed her eyes briefly as Pam drove, chatting about the weather and the predictions for a cool weekend. She opened her eyes when Pam asked for directions to her exact building.

"I find your theory that you can't connect with people who may be drugged or medicated very probable," Pam said, as she turned onto Sabrina's street. "We should explore that further."

"I felt like I failed, both times."

Pam shot her a look. "But it wasn't you! Their brains may have been scrambled. Maureen's because of drugs. Maybe Clarisse's because of the lack of her usual medications, or dementia, or something. Not finding her was not your fault."

Sabrina shook her head. "We don't know that."

"You have an extraordinary ability," Pamela insisted. "No one bats one thousand."

Sabrina directed Pam to her assigned parking

173

space. They got out and Pam clicked the automatic locks, then handed the keys to Sabrina. Sabrina led the way to her apartment. "You live in a condo too, right?" she asked as she trudged up the stairs. She couldn't wait to get comfortable and be alone. She didn't feel like company. Unlocking her door, she led the way in.

"Yes, in Hackettstown. I looked at these and liked them; but there was one particular floor plan in a development in Hackettstown I just fell in love with, and that's where I ended up moving, although this would have been a little closer." Pam shed her coat as Sabrina turned on the lights.

"You don't have to stay long," Sabrina told her abruptly. Then, seeing Pam's surprised expression, she added, "I didn't mean that the way it sounded. I just meant I'm okay."

"I want to be sure," Pam said. "I'll only stay a few minutes. Parker will be here soon to pick me up. Where should I put the food?"

"In the fridge. I'm fine," Sabrina repeated. "Of course, you can stay here til he arrives. Sorry, I don't mean to be ungrateful. I'm just tired."

"Of course—who wouldn't be?" Pam smiled.

"I hope you don't mind if I take a shower right now," Sabrina said. "I—I feel sweaty and uncomfortable."

"No problem."

She left Pam seated on the couch, and went into her bedroom. She grabbed her oldest, most comfortable blue and white plaid flannel pajamas, and got into the shower.

As the warm water pelted her, Sabrina hoped it would wash away the frustration she felt. And the despair.

Why hadn't she been able to find Clarisse? Had medicines—or the lack of her regular prescriptions—messed up the missing woman's mind to the point she was totally confused? Was that why she couldn't connect with Clarisse? If that was true, maybe it really wasn't anything to do with her.

She felt a little better when she got out. After combing her hair, she left it to dry naturally in waves.

Sabrina returned to the living room. Pam was staring at her iPhone, probably checking emails or texts, Sabrina guessed.

"How do you feel?" Pam's hazel eyes met hers. Sabrina read real concern there.

"Exhausted," she admitted.

"Parker should be here any minute— "

The doorbell rang.

Sabrina went to get her old red robe and when she returned to the living room, Parker was standing in what she called her "study" area, by her desk and bookcases. He held a bag in his hand and was looking at a couple of photos on her bookcase.

He turned at her approach. "I brought you some soup from the restaurant near our office."

She didn't feel much like eating. But soup would probably be more nourishing than the sandwiches. "Thank you," she said solemnly, taking the bag.

"Would you like one or both of us to stay a little longer?" Pam asked.

"No, but thank you for offering." Sabrina just wanted to be left alone.

"Check in with us in the morning, ok?" Parker asked. He regarded her anxiously.

"Alright. I'm working late on Wednesday and I

175

won't go in until one, so I'm sleeping in," she told him.

"Whenever it's convenient." He hesitated. "And, Sabrina, please don't feel bad. You found the little girl a couple of weeks ago. You can't find everybody who's lost."

She sighed. "I know that in my head, but—I feel like I *should* be able to."

Pamela stood up, and now she came over and gave Sabrina a comforting hug. "Call us if you need anything, okay?" She pulled back, regarding Sabrina carefully.

"I'm okay. I just want to sleep. Thanks for the soup. I promise I'll eat it right away and go to bed."

They left, and she ate the soup. It was chicken and rice, soothing and delicious, and warmed her inside. Afterwards she channel-surfed on the TV for fifteen minutes, but she could barely keep her eyes open. She plugged in her cell phone to recharge, brushed her teeth, and crawled into bed.

For a few minutes she lay in the dark. She pictured both Erin's sister Maureen and Clarisse in their respective photos, and the images blurred together in her mind. Hopelessness welled up inside of her, and Sabrina felt tears slip out. She buried her head in her pillow and cried, and then, exhausted, she fell asleep.

* * *

The top headline on the New Jersey TV station was "Nursing Home Resident Found Dead."

Sabrina felt her stomach lurch as dismay raced through her. It had to be Clarisse.

176

She raised the volume on the TV and then picked up her first morning cup of coffee.

"Early this morning, a nursing home resident, missing since Monday night, was found dead in the woods nearby," the anchorwoman was saying.

Sabrina scrunched into the corner of the couch, clutching her mug, absorbing its warmth. She listened as the woman spoke. Clarisse was found early this morning by a policeman and his dog, about a mile away from the nursing home. Authorities suspected that she had become confused without her medication and was the victim of hypothermia or had suffered a heart attack.

Sabrina bit her lip, fighting the tears. She hadn't been able to help.

In her head, she knew it wasn't her fault. She had tried, tried hard. Clarisse's own confusion may have made it difficult to pinpoint her location. Or perhaps she had even been dead by the time Sabrina set out to find her.

But in her heart, she felt guilt. Intense guilt.

She reached for the Kleenex box she'd left on the coffee table last night, and wiped her eyes. She'd failed again. Maybe it wasn't her fault, but she'd failed.

Maybe she wasn't very good at astral projection. Maybe she should just give up.

The thought stayed with her all day, like a dull headache that wouldn't go away.

Parker put down the phone in frustration. "I can't get hold of her," he said to Meredith.

177

His older sister sucked in her breath. "Do you think she's avoiding you?"

"I don't know. She was upset when Pam and I left her last night," he told her.

Meredith had been filled in on the events of last night after he and Pamela had left Sabrina's home and returned to TLC. Like them, she had expressed worry that Sabrina's failure to find Clarisse would lead to her feeling discouraged and helpless, maybe depressed.

This morning they'd all agreed to call later so that she could sleep. But it was now a quarter to twelve. She had to go to work at one; she must be awake by now. He'd called at eleven thirty, eleven forty, and again now.

"Maybe Pam or I should try getting hold of her," Meredith said.

"Why one of you?" he demanded.

"Because sometimes a woman feels more comfortable talking to another woman."

And because you two may have feelings for each other. He could read his sister's thoughts.

His siters knew Sabrina had projected to his house. They'd seen Pam's drawing. They obviously thought there was something going on between him and Sabrina.

There was.

"Ok, Mer, why don't you give it a try?"

She glanced at her watch. "I'll wait 15 minutes, then call. If I don't get her, I'll have Pam try later. She's still with Dana Schmitt."

"Okay," he agreed.

He left the break room and returned to his office. He'd have lunch later. His next patient wasn't due until 2 o'clock.

He wanted to watch the session with Sabrina again. He couldn't help worrying about her. She'd looked so upset yesterday, so fragile.

It was the first time Sabrina hadn't succeeded in finding someone since she'd started coming to TLC. Which was enough for them to investigate further.

And the news had come in this morning that Clarisse had been found, dead.

Parker knew it was very possible that the woman had died before Sabrina had even gone searching for her. An autopsy would tell them the approximate time of death. Or perhaps Clarisse was totally confused without her meds, cold and alone in the dark.

Also, there was the factor of chance. When you tried to find someone, there was a probability that sometimes, you wouldn't succeed. No one was successful one hundred percent of the time—even the most gifted of psychics, who had been doing this kind of thing for years. He knew this logically, but maybe he would have to repeat it to Sabrina. He had seen the image of Clarisse in her mind last night. And he had felt Sabrina's despair.

It bothered him. A lot. He didn't want to see her feeling this badly. He felt a hollowness in his stomach when he thought about her despondency over the whole incident.

Maybe, he thought, she *shouldn't* be projecting and trying to find these people. Not only did it take a lot out of her physically, but seeing the anguish on her face last night, he knew it was taking an emotional toll too. She was too nice a person not to be emotionally invested in the outcome.

That thought stayed with him as he went about

179

his business. Despite the fact that he was going over tests from some fascinating clients today, including earthquake-predicting Martin, Sabrina was never far from his thoughts.

And the findings about Martin were intriguing. He'd predicted, with dead-on accuracy, the earthquake two weeks ago in northern California.

Yet still, thoughts of Sabrina poked Parker's mind, worrying him.

Meredith came into his office at 12:30 to say that she had finally reached Sabrina, and Sabrina said she expected to be busy at work, and was okay.

"Do you believe her?" he asked.

"She didn't sound too good," Meredith confided. "She heard the news about Clarisse's death."

He sighed. His sister's words were not surprising.

By six o'clock, when he took a break for dinner, Parker decided he had to see Sabrina. To make sure she was okay.

She was working tonight, she'd said. He was scheduled until seven thirty but often stayed later. And he knew the libraries in the area all closed at nine.

She probably wouldn't want to speak to him while at work. So he decided to go to her condo and wait for her. He doubted she would refuse to speak to him if he simply showed up.

With that decision, he felt a little better, and got back to studying Martin's test results.

He knew it would take Sabrina at least ten minutes to get home from the library—and that's if she left promptly at nine. Still, he arrived at 9:02, parked by her condo in the guest lot, and waited.

He didn't see her car arrive until 9:18.

She got out of the car, pulled out a tote, and locked her door. Then she trudged towards her condo.

He scrambled out of his own car. "Sabrina?" he called, slamming the door shut and clicking his key fob to lock it.

She stopped, looking towards him. "Parker?"

He sprinted forward. "Sorry, I didn't mean to startle you. I came to see how you're doing." As he drew near, he saw how tired her face looked. "Can I come in?" He reached for her tote. "Here, let me get that."

She relinquished the bag without protest, and led the way silently to her place.

Once inside, she turned on lights, and he got a better look at her as he dropped her tote on a chair.

She was pale, and her mouth was set in a straight line instead of its usual upturned curve. There were shadows under her eyes and her large, beautiful brown eyes held sadness.

He sucked in his breath, and without another word pulled her into his arms.

She rested her head on his shoulder, and as he held her, he was startled by the feeling of *rightness* he experienced with her in his arms. Like she belonged there. He could smell her fruity shampoo—or was that her cologne? He brushed his lips against her soft hair.

"I failed," she said, her voice low and choked up. Her arms slid around his waist.

"You did not," he replied indignantly. Pulling back, he stared into her face. He couldn't stand it.

Couldn't stand seeing her like this, hurt and anguished. He bent his forehead until it was touching hers.

"You did not fail," he repeated. "You tried your best. I called Kyle this afternoon. He said Clarisse died of a heart attack. They're estimating it was between three and five o'clock. So, it's likely she was already dead when you went out searching for her." His heart thumped hard as he held her.

"But we don't know that," she said.

"No, we don't." He pulled back a little, to regard her steadily. "She was also missing her meds, confused... there's a lot of things that could have happened even before the heart attack. Maybe a bear scared her. They're in the area. I don't want you blaming yourself!"

"I can't—help it," she said, her voice breaking. "I—it was the same with Maureen, the fright, the confusion—and being unable to help her."

"Come here." He led her to the couch, and shrugged out of his jacket. She did the same.

Sitting beside her, he took her cold hands in his and chafed them, trying to warm her up. "Sabrina." He sighed. "I've been thinking... maybe projecting isn't such a good idea. Maybe you shouldn't be doing that for our studies—or at least you should take a break from them." He looked into her eyes. "It takes a lot out of you even when you succeed, but I can see it takes even more of a toll on you when you don't."

She sighed too, echoing his. "Actually, Parker... I've been considering the same thing. I was a little reluctant to come into the Lightning Center. And now... I don't know, but I keep thinking maybe I shouldn't continue doing this, projecting. Even though I want to use my ability to help others."

182

He knew it went against the needs of TLC and their important research studies, but he urged her on. He was more concerned with her well-being. "Then stop. At least for a while. Maybe we've been expecting too much of you. We've moved too fast, done too much in a short period. I'm not saying you have to stop permanently. Just take a break from our testing, at least for a few weeks."

"I was thinking of stopping altogether. But perhaps you're right, and a break—a few weeks, a month, maybe longer—is precisely what I need." She sighed again. "Although I can't seem to take a break from my night-time projections." She grimaced. "But I'll definitely consider it." She stood up. "I was going to make myself some herbal tea. Want some?"

He agreed, and followed her into the kitchen. "If you leave, even temporarily, Meredith and Pam will still work on helping you with those uncontrolled projections." He was certain his sisters would do that.

"I'd appreciate it."

He'd felt disappointment when she'd agreed that taking a break might be a good idea. But it had been rapidly followed with a feeling of hope.

He examined those feelings as she boiled water and took out two mugs and a box of decaffeinated tea.

He knew why he was feeling glad. It was because if she was no longer participating in studies, was no longer a patient, he could feel free to have a relationship with her.

It had occurred to him also that she might eventually be someone they could hire for TLC. It was becoming clear to them all that they would need another psychic tester in the near future, since Neal and Alicia were stretched to the max; and their three grad students, while good, could only work part time. He had even discussed with his parents at one point the need to get someone to do research and free up Neal and Alicia to concentrate more on testing.

Who better to do research than a reference librarian?

He filed that thought for a later date.

Once they were seated back on the couch, each with a mug of mint tea, he studied her as she sipped her drink.

She met his look. She'd been mostly silent while making the tea, but now she spoke again. "I am going to take a break from projecting at the Lightning Center. For now."

And as he studied her, he felt the usual pull, the yearning, to get close to her. To take her in his arms.

To make love to her.

For the first time, it was a real possibility. Without the confines of a professional relationship, he was free to date her, have a relationship with her. Explore this attraction further.

For a second, Dara's face flashed across his mind.

No. He was not going to think of the last woman he'd had a serious relationship with. The woman who'd burned him.

He set his mug down on the book-shaped coaster she'd provided. Without preamble, he spoke.

"I'd like to take you out."

She looked at him, her mouth opening in surprise, then quickly shut it. "Take me out?"

"As in, a date." He found himself grinning. "Before, we had a doctor-patient relationship. But if you're going to stop projecting—at least for a while— well, I'd like to date you."

A smile broke out on her lovely face. He hadn't seen that on her for two days.

"I'd like that," she said simply.

"How about Friday night?" Friday he got out of work early, and he knew she sometimes did.

"I'm working, but I'll be out at four. I have Saturday off if that's better."

"I only have to be at work for a short time on Saturday," he said, wondering if she'd agree to go out two nights in a row. He'd take it one day at a time, he decided. "How about dinner on Friday? I could pick you up at six if that works."

"That would be great!" The enthusiasm in her voice was surprising—and welcome.

"It's a date." He smiled as relief and a feeling of gladness streamed through him. Picking up his mug, he drank some of the sweet tea.

She smiled back. "Where are we going?"

He named an Italian restaurant nearby, which he liked a lot. "The food is excellent and it's got a comfortable and cozy atmosphere," he finished.

"I've been there, though not for a while," she said, nodding. "That sounds perfect." He would make sure she had wonderful time, and forgot all her troubles, he determined.

Aloud he said, "Great."

He noticed that color had returned to her face, and she was more animated. Good! Whether it was the decision to pull back from projecting, or the idea of going out with him, she seemed happier.

That realization warmed him. He wanted her happier. He wanted to see that smile on her face.

But he also knew that the last two days had been

exhausting for her, and she'd had a lot of turmoil. He knew she needed to get some rest.

He got up. "I know it's been a couple of long days for you. I'll get going," he said.

She stood up too, and flashed him a smile. "You're right. I'll see you Friday."

"I'm looking forward to it." He retrieved his jacket, then bent down and brushed a tender kiss across her lips.

When he pulled back, he gazed at her for a moment.

He was looking forward to spending time with her this weekend. More than he had looked forward to any date recently—or any date he could recall.

* * *

Sabrina found herself anticipating her official date with Parker as much as she'd looked forward to going to her senior prom with a boy she liked.

She finished her make-up by applying a dark pink lipstick, then spritzed herself with a sexy but subtle cologne, different than her usual everyday fruity scent. She stepped back from her mirror and surveyed the results.

She was wearing a black dress that was flattering to her figure. With it she wore simple black pumps, but the heels were higher than the shoes she usually wore.

She fluffed her wavy dark hair with her fingers, then examined herself one more time.

Her iPod was playing in the background. She'd set it to random selections and a Taylor Swift song was just finishing. There was a brief pause and then she heard the beginning of "Circus."

Ha. She wouldn't mind being the center of Parker's attention. And this time, she wouldn't be putting on any show—projection or otherwise—to get his attention.

It was so nice, she reflected as she picked up her purse, to be dating a man who knew about her ability, and wasn't bothered by it. In fact, if she had to guess, Parker probably admired her ability, since his work was studying psychic abilities in people.

Thursday evening she'd had an "exit" session with Meredith, and had also spoken briefly with Pam. Both understood her desire to take a break from their studies. But both sisters expressed the wish that she come back and work with The Lightning Center when she felt ready. And they both promised to work on helping her control the night projections.

The clock on her cable box read 5:54 when she entered her living room. She sat down on the couch to wait for Parker. The minute she leaned back, she heard footsteps outside followed by her doorbell.

He was early.

She leaped up, eager to see him and start their evening together.

She paused by the iPod and shut it off, then pulled open the door.

Parker stood there, looking more handsome than ever.

"C'mon in," she said.

He was wearing a dark suit. She'd thought he was handsome in a labcoat or casual clothes; in a suit he was devastatingly handsome.

187

"Hi." His eyes swept over her, and the heat in his smile made her melt inside. "You look gorgeous."

"Thank you." His remark had really warmed her up. "You look great too. I'm ready, I just need my coat."

"It got cold out." He stepped inside and she shut the door, then went to take her coat out of the closest, conscious that he watched her every move.

She found it thrilling.

He helped her on with her coat. She left a low light on in the living room and they exited together. Locking the door behind her, she took his offered hand and they went down the stairs to the parking lot.

"How was work today?" she asked lightly, enjoying the feel of his hand securely surrounding hers.

"We're studying a person who can predict earthquakes. We've never had anyone with that ability before at The Center, so it's proving fascinating. Alicia and Tanya are doing research on it, but it's a rare talent. Not much is known about it."

"That does sound exciting," she said as they approached his jeep. "By the way, ask Neal and Alicia if they've seen the latest ESP study that came out of Duke University this week. I think they'll want to read it."

"I'm impressed you've read it already. Yes, Neal saw it and passed it on to Alicia. They're going to give us a report at our next staff meeting."

Once inside his Jeep, she asked if they had any other patients with rare abilities.

He sent her a sideways look. "Astral projection is pretty unusual. Besides you, we've only had one other patient with it. You must have done a lot of research on projecting," he said.

188

"Yes, I did. If you or anyone at The Center wants to see my books and my copies of different articles, I'd be glad to share them."

"Thanks. We might do that."

"I had someone coming in to do research for a paper on ESP today." She heard the excitement in her voice. "Since I've done a lot of research on that myself, I knew the best sources to look at. I found it exhilarating to help him."

"What kind of ESP?" he asked, turning onto the road near the restaurant.

"Precognition. He was doing a report on it."

"What other kinds of research were you doing today?"

She described helping one student find research about New Jersey during the Revolutionary War, and another looking into geological formations in the area. "Of course, with the Sterling Hill Mining Museum in Ogdensburg, there is information available from them," she said.

"We visited that place in elementary school," he said.

"We did too. A lot of schools go there."

They pulled into the restaurant's parking lot, which was almost filled. The place was small but he'd made a reservation, so they were shown to a secluded booth.

They studied the menu, and Sabrina ordered a salad and chicken parmigiana. Parker chose soup instead of a salad and the chicken cacciatore. They also ordered wine to go with their meal.

While they sipped wine and ate their salad and soup, Sabrina was acutely conscious of Parker. This was not the first time she was with him in a social setting. But the times when they'd had dinner at the diner, and at seafood place, they'd still had a doctor/patient relationship. Now there were no tests, no exhaustion after a projecting session, no one peering anxiously at her. Just the time to enjoy each other's company and learn a little more about each other.

She was also conscious of a humming sense of awareness that being with Parker was causing. A kind of heightened sense of perception. Not just any man would make her react this way. It had to be because she both was attracted to, and liked, Parker.

But she'd never been quite this aware of any man, quite this attracted to anyone.

The little flow of excitement through her was a bit unnerving. She found she wasn't as hungry as she expected, even though the food was delicious.

Despite her being acutely aware of Parker, the conversation flowed. She made a conscious effort to relax.

He spoke about how he'd always wanted to be a doctor like his dad; and how Pamela had too. And how, after being struck by lightning, he'd gotten interested in the neurological and medical effects on patients who had the same experiences.

"And Meredith didn't want to study medicine?" she asked, as their main courses were served.

He shook his head. "No. She wasn't sure for a while what she wanted to do. She always kind of looked after us, a typical big sister." He grinned. "But she wasn't interested in medicine. She was, however, interested in The Lightning Center. And she liked helping people so—she decided to go into social work

190

and be our social worker. She ended up getting her doctorate." He said it with pride. "So she's technically a doctor too. Drs. Parker, Pamela, and Meredith Costigan." He grinned.

"Keeping it in the family," she joked. She cut into a piece of her chicken, then chewed it slowly. It was delicious, made with fresh tomato sauce, and spicy.

"Yes. My parents liked the idea." He speared a piece of green pepper. "Our grandfathers helped us set up The Lightning Center and fund it, and we also have some grants for several studies. We started with the staff you see here except for Alicia and the part-timers. We hired her about six months after Neal; and we added the grad students about a year ago when we saw Neal and Alicia had way too much work. We're thinking of hiring one more psychic examiner. Plus, we're expecting at least one more grant, so we'll have plenty of funding."

"That's a pretty big staff," she said, wondering how they managed to pay everyone.

"We have several private investors funding us. One is a billionaire who was himself struck by lightning. He keeps a low profile. I'm not going to use his name, and he has so far only been tested a couple of times. But's he's fascinated by our research. Besides the grants from a couple of medical and psychic foundations—including some big-name ones—there's a couple of corporations which also invested in us, following our work closely."

She could see how proud he was of his family's pioneering center and research.

Sabrina felt like she had known Parker for more than a few weeks. But in addition, she felt that sensual humming that comes when you're with a man you're attracted to. And in Parker's case, she was *very* attracted.

She wanted to touch his hair. To feel his lips firmly against her own. To wrap her arms around his neck…

But she also wanted to know hm better. Know his likes and dislikes, how he felt about things.

"I know you have a lot of pride in The Lightning Center," she said, sipping her mellow white wine. "What gives you the most satisfaction about it?"

He paused, thinking. "I think working with my family for a common goal."

That surprised her. "I thought you would say doing ground-breaking research."

"That's important, too." He picked up his wineglass. "But I don't think I'd be as happy doing research with colleagues who were all mere acquaintances."

"Some of your coworkers must have been acquaintances, once."

"True. And I can tell you, people like Neal who have worked with us for a long time have become like family. But I'm still glad to have my family— especially my sisters—working with me."

"You're very close," she observed.

He drank some wine, then set the glass down with a clink. "Yes, we are."

"I'm surprised none of you are married." She said it lightly, then studied him for his reaction.

"Meredith was. She got divorced a few years ago." He frowned. "The guy was a jerk. He never appreciated her sweet, wonderful personality."

"That's too bad. She's better off without someone like that."

He eyed her. "Just like you're better off without your idiot ex-boyfriend."

"Thanks for that thought." She cut up, then chewed more of her chicken, savoring the delicious cheese melted over it. She appreciated his support of her.

"So how come you never married?" he asked, his eyes meeting hers over his wineglass.

She felt herself flush. "After Devon, I was—reluctant to get involved." She looked out the nearby window, at the lights from the train station shining close by. "I guess I was afraid no one would accept my ability."

"Your talent." He covered her hand with his. His skin was warm against hers. "It is, you know," he added, as she focused on him again.

"Thanks. It's nice to know you understand and respect my abil—my talent." She found it difficult to call it that. "And—what about Pam, and you?"

"What about us?"

"Neither of you ever married." She found herself waiting on edge to hear his answer.

He set his fork down. "Pam came close, once. A guy in medical school. But it ended badly, and I think now she's overly cautious."

She waited.

"As far as me… there was a woman I was very close to, and I thought I was getting serious about her." He frowned. "But—after a while I realized we didn't share the same goals, and she was very selfish. When I broke up with her, she turned on me."

Now Sabrina put her hand over his. "It's okay, you don't have to tell me." She smiled. "In fact, I think I'd prefer not to hear any more about another woman in your life." Because tonight, she wanted to be the only woman he was thinking about.

He responded with a big smile.

She switched the topic to asking about The Lightning Center's building. He told her it had been an empty medical facility for several years when they found it, and they'd reconfigured it to meet their needs.

They finished the meal with coffee and chocolate mousses, which were perfect—sweet and luscious but light.

As they left the restaurant, Parker took her hand and led her to his car. Even that small touch sent a thrill zooming up her arm and straight to her heart. A chilly wind blew but it didn't erase the heat she felt.

They drove back to her condo, chatting about a TV series they both had liked and were contemplating re-watching.

When he pulled into a parking space near her home, she turned to him.

"Want to come in for a drink?" She didn't want the evening to end.

"Sure." He sounded eager.

The brisk wind struck her cheeks as she exited the car.

"Look at the stars," he said quietly.

She looked up. The night was clear, with a partial moon, and the stars sprinkled in the sky glowed brightly. A small wisp of a cloud moved from west to east, making the beautiful night sky look slightly mysterious.

"I was always fascinated by the planets and the stars," she said. "I used to want to float in the night sky, and be able to gaze at the planets up close."

"You've come close to doing that." He said it gravely.

She glanced at him. "Yes, I guess I have. Closer than most people. But—I need to get a handle on those night projections. And get away from doing them for TLC for a while."

He took her hand. "That's understandable. And—for what it's worth—I'm glad." His sentence ended on a fierce note.

She focused on Parker. He regarded her with an intensity that took her breath away. As if it was his greatest wish for her to stop projecting for now. As if he wanted it badly.

Because it left them free to have a "normal," not-professional relationship?

As she gazed into his eyes, wind gusted suddenly.

"Come on," she said lightly, and led him down the path to her condo.

She felt feminine beside his tall frame. They took the stairs to the second floor, where she let him into the condo. Once inside, they shed their coats and she hung them in the coat closet.

"Would you like coffee or tea—something hot—or a glass of wine or a soda? Or I have sherry or a liqueur," she finished. "I love Amaretto and have that; I also have some melon liqueur and Frangelico."

He followed her into the kitchen. "What are you having?"

"Amaretto. It's my favorite." She smiled.

"Then I'll have that too."

She had a couple of Waterford liqueur glasses which she had found at a garage sale and really liked. She took them out, then moved to the cabinet that held her small liquor collection. She found the distinctive Amaretto bottle and poured them each a drink.

She moved back to the living room, Parker following her closely. "Want to watch TV?" she asked.

"I'd rather talk."

"Me too." Her voice came out breathless. She turned on her iPod, programmed it for a jazz mix, and soft jazz music filled the air.

They sat on the couch, cozily close, and sipped their drinks. The almond flavored liquor slid down her throat, sharp and sweet.

She was feeling warm. And yet, as Parker met her gaze, an icy shot of nerves spiked through that warm glow.

Parker faced her, leaning back on the couch, and sipped his drink.

"Were you interested in psychic abilities and phenomena before you were struck by lightning?" he asked, studying her.

"Yes. Yes, I was. I remember reading a book about a girl who had ESP and being fascinated. I then went and found some other books at the library and bookstore." She took another sip of her Amaretto. "What about you?"

"We were struck so young that I knew nothing about ESP at that age," he said. "But I became interested in psychic phenomena once I realized Pam and I could communicate." He smiled. "Plus, everyone in our neighborhood knew Lorna, and I heard my mother talking to her one day about ghosts. I was further intrigued by her experiences." He took another sip of his drink, then set the glass down carefully on one of the coasters on the table. "Like you, I started researching and reading when I was a pre-teen." He leaned back. "I see you have a lot of books here." He waved at her bookcases, at the couple of books on her coffee table. "What's your favorite kind of book to read?"

"I love historical western romances," she answered promptly. "The kind with strong women and brave men. They take place in the American southwest in the late 1800s and they are full of adventure and sometimes mystery. I also like cozy mysteries and my taste in non-fiction is eclectic—of course books on paranormal events and research; books on travel, cooking, astronomy, the weather—all kinds of things." She smiled. "I love to read. How about you?"

"I read a lot of different types of books," he said. "Especially thrillers, espionage, mysteries in fiction; and in non-fiction, like you I read a lot on paranormal abilities and research. I also like other kinds of scientific books. I'm reading one now on volcanoes."

She nodded, and placed her own drink down. They had that love of reading and interest in science in common. She asked a couple of questions about his favorite writers, and he mentioned several she knew of but hadn't read yet.

"Bob Mayer's and Harlan Coben's books just fly off the shelves at the library," she said. Noting he had finished almost his entire drink, she asked "would you like more?"

As she said the words, she leaned forward, extending her hand to pick up the glass.

He caught her hand.

Startled, she looked up at him. What she saw there, shining in his eyes, made her shiver with anticipation.

Desire. Pure desire. *For her.*

CHAPTER IX

The knowledge that Parker wanted her slammed into her, taking her breath away. He squeezed her hand, and warmth rushed through her, like lava from the volcanoes he'd mentioned moments before.

He wanted her… and she wanted him too.

She clutched his hand. "Parker," she whispered, her voice raspy.

"Sabrina, I—" his voice was unsteady. He moved, letting go of her hand, and tugged her into his arms. Bending his head, he captured her lips.

His kiss was firm and left her reeling. She wanted more, wanted him. Her hand moved to his neck, and she felt the springy hair there. She inhaled the masculine aftershave he preferred.

His kiss became harder, more demanding. He pulled her closer and she responded, the kiss igniting, turning frenzied. She clung to him, wanting more. Wanting *him*.

He freed her lips for a moment, and kissed her face, her temple, her chin, then captured her lips again.

She heard a soft moan and realized it was coming from her own throat. Freeing her lips for a moment, she murmured "Parker…"

He bent his forehead to touch hers. "Sabrina… I

want you. I want to make love to you. I have for a while but—now we can. We have no professional relationship any longer. Let me make love to you, sweetheart." He stroked one hand down her cheek. His fingers left a blazing trail where he touched her.

At his words, her insides melted.

"Yes," she whispered.

He stood up, pulling her with him, and bent to kiss her again.

She pulled her mouth away. "Parker, I'm not on the pill right now—I haven't needed to…" Her voice dwindled.

"I have protection." He said it firmly yet softly, and she knew he had thought of it before coming here.

She was glad. "Come here," she whispered, and led the way into her bedroom.

She clicked her night table lamp on low, then turned to face him, kicking off her pumps.

His eyes gleamed as he pulled her close. "Sabrina," he said, his voice a low rumble. "I've wanted you—wanted this—since I met you." And then his lips came down on hers, hard and possessive and demanding.

Thrills cascaded through her body, reaching every limb. She couldn't think, she could only feel as he stroked her hair, then moved his hands down to cup her backside.

She had never thought of that as a sensual move, yet when Parker touched her this way she felt sexy. Desire wound its way through her insides, through every molecule in her body.

She ran her hands along his chest. The muscles were firm beneath her hands. He obviously worked out. As she stroked his chest, she felt the strong and rapid beat of his heart.

She could also feel his hardness pressing against her through her dress. He wanted her as much as she wanted him.

His hands roved over her body. "How do you get out of this dress?" he rasped.

She couldn't help grinning. "I'll do it." She stepped back, and pulled the dress slowly over her head, tossing it on the carpet. Then she pulled off her pantyhose.

She heard his sharply indrawn breath, and turned to meet his eyes. The stark desire there made her knees weak.

She was glad, very glad, that after work she'd taken a quick shower and put on her sexiest blue lace bra and matching bikini.

"You are beautiful," he said simply. "Gorgeous." He brushed his thumbs over her breasts, encased in the sheer lace.

Instantly, her nipples peaked and she caught her breath.

He scooped her up and placed her carefully on the bed. Then he pulled off his suit jacket, kicked off his shoes, and pulled off his tie in a startling sensuous move. She caught her breath. Then he followed her down on the bed.

He pulled her close, nuzzling her, his hands sliding all over her. Everywhere he touched she could feel flames ignite. She did the same, sliding her hands over his shirt, then slowly unbuttoning it. Finally, she tugged it off him.

She eagerly touched his chest. It was warm and

solid, with dark hair, and she could smell the citrusy aftershave even more now. She let her hands glide over him, then returned to his nipples and stroked them.

He groaned. He reached behind her and unfastened her bra, pulling it off, and it went flying.

He bent and took one nipple into his mouth.

She arched, gasping "Parker!" as intense pleasure shot through her.

"You like that?" His voice was husky and masculine, and she felt an ache start deep inside her. An ache that only he could ease.

"Yes…ss…" she said, her voice throaty. He moved to her other nipple, and again she arched, savoring the intense pleasure that shot through her.

She moved her hand downwards, and cupped him. He let out a groan. He was rock hard.

"God, I want you," he said, kissing her face all over.

She fumbled with his belt, and he helped her. Before he slid his pants and boxers off, he paused, and she saw him remove a few foil packets. He placed them on her night stand.

She touched his hardness. It was like silk-covered steel. He sucked in a loud breath as she stroked him, and he groaned her name. "Sabrina."

When she looked up at his face, he was gazing at her with intensity. "You are so beautiful." His voice was hoarse. He reached out, running his hand down her side, lingering by her breasts, then brushing the top of her lacy panties. "So. Beautiful."

She wound her hands around his neck and pulled him down. "Make love to me," she whispered.

201

He slid beside her, moving his hand to the top of her panties, then tugging them down. She wiggled out of them, kicking them off, and then his hand traveled up.

He brushed his fingers upwards, sending a sharp shot of desire through her, and she arched up again.

"Sabrina." It was a mere whisper. He kissed her breasts, then laved one nipple, and inserted a finger where she ached the most.

"Oh!" she gasped, nearly carried away with the delight of his touch. His finger in her core, his mouth on her nipple, was igniting a fire unlike anything she had ever felt. "Parker—Parker…" she felt herself coming close to ecstasy.

He moved back, freeing her breast, and she heard him sheath himself. She reached out and boldly stroked him. He was hot and hard and oh-so-ready.

Bending over her body, he eased himself into her. He was big, so big, but she shifted to feel him closer, as close as possible, as a moan escaped her.

"Sabrina!" As if he couldn't help himself, he plunged forward.

She felt herself spiraling, tightening, as if the only sensation in the whole world was him

inside of her, hot and hard.

Nothing had ever felt like this. No one had ever felt so good. No one in the world.

And as he rocked them both they exploded, meeting his thrusts with her own, screaming out "Parker!" as stars danced beneath her eyelids.

"Sabrina!" It was a guttural, purely male sound, as he followed her to the peak of pleasure. She felt him vibrating within her, his ecstasy matching hers.

Slowly, sweetly, they drifted back to earth.

He pulled her next to him, and at some point he covered them both with her comforter.

Slowly she became aware of her surroundings. His breathing, still heavy. The sound of wind rattling the windows. The warm and moist skin of his chest against her fingers.

"Hmmm…" she murmured, snuggling closer.

"Sabrina… that was… spectacular." He hugged her.

"Wonderful," she murmured.

"Extraordinary." He pulled back slightly, and in the semi-dark she could see his smile.

"Do you want to stay here tonight?" she asked quietly.

"There's no place I'd rather be." He tightened his hold on her, his breath tickling her ear, his cheek against hers.

And his hand began trailing down her side, then up to cup her breast. She smoothed her hand over his chest, then, as he kissed her, pressed her body against his. Her whole body stirred again as desire built inside her.

They made love again, slower this time but just as satisfying. Once again she reached the stars and felt him do the same.

They drifted off to sleep holding each other, and she felt wonderfully content…

Once during the night, Parker awoke, feeling totally satisfied. Sabrina was wrapped around him, snuggled close, and he breathed in her sensual perfume—different and mysterious, not the one she wore every day. Her beautiful body was pressed against him, and he felt the rise and fall of her chest as she slept peacefully.

Making love to her had been extraordinary. It wasn't just that she was gorgeous—there was something about *her* that woke every primitive male instinct he had. He wanted to possess her, to please her, to protect her. To make her scream his name in ecstasy just as she had, again and again. To make her beg for him to fill her, to possess her completely.

She was delicious. Wonderful. *His*.

When he awoke, they made love again, then showered together, laughing. He caught her in the shower and pleasured her until she came apart again, and then she moved over him with her mouth until he could barely stand. His climax was earth-shattering.

As they toweled off, he grinned at her. "I have to stop at the pharmacy and buy more condoms."

"Get a large package," she quipped, smiling wickedly.

He had to go into work for a short time. Luckily, he had a duffle bag in his car with extra clothes. He pulled on his jeans and ran out to get them. Coming back and getting dressed, he watched as Sabrina covered another sexy bra and bikini set—pink this time—with her jeans and a red sweater.

"I want to see this sexy lingerie on you again," he growled, "later. And to spend the day with you. I have to go into the office for a while, but let's spend the afternoon—and evening—together."

"I'd love to." She stretched up to kiss him.

She made them coffee and oatmeal for breakfast. She agreed to meet him at The Lightning Center early in the afternoon.

"And tonight, stay at my home," he said, pulling her onto his lap.

"I'll be glad to." She grinned.

His insides warmed at her closeness. He loved how affectionate she was, how unreserved in his arms. Loved the curves of her body, the silk of her hair.

"I have to work from 12 to 4 on Sunday but I'm free all day today," she murmured.

"That's great." He kissed her again, then sighed. "I know I have to get going." It was already after nine and he had an appointment at ten.

"But I'll see you later," she said sweetly, smiling at him.

When he left, he gave her a resounding kiss, and there was a spring in his step as he walked to his car.

Driving to work, he relived the exciting night he'd spent with Sabrina. Exciting and—something more. Something solid, something big.

As he neared his office, he realized that when he'd made love to her, it had shut out everything else.

He tried not to probe minds unless it was necessary. But sometimes it simply happened that he read someone's thoughts. In this case, he'd been so concentrated on giving Sabrina pleasure—and yeah, getting his own too—that there wasn't room for anything else but his thoughts of Sabrina, of caressing her, of giving her the ultimate ecstasy.

Nothing else had jumped into his mind.

He parked in the back lot, and left his car. Then

he stopped, staring at the building where they studied people with extra-ordinary abilities and talents.

He was one with special talents. And now that he and Sabrina were lovers—no, more than that, they were *romantically involved*—he needed to come clean. To tell her about himself.

He would. Later.

He usually had no problem getting right into his work, but that morning he did. As he glanced over his notes for his exam of a new patient, a teenage boy who had telekinetic abilities, he found himself thinking of Sabrina. Of her gorgeous face and body, her lush breasts, the way she arched toward him as she cried out his name in passion…

He almost groaned. He had better get his mind back to his work or he'd be getting hard all over again.

He managed to concentrate on his new patient. But afterwards, when Pam popped into his office, he saw the look of surprise on her face as she regarded him.

"Parker? You seem unusually happy," she said. She crossed her arms and leaned against the doorway.

Ugh oh. He wasn't doing a good job of shielding his thoughts from his twin. He put up an immediate wall, but from her narrowed eyes he suspected she guessed something of his activities the prior evening. "Pam, Sabrina decided she wants to take a break from our studies for a while. I'll tell everyone on Monday," he said hastily, hoping to distract her.

"I wonder if that's why you seem so happy?"

"I'm just in a good mood." He said it lightly. He didn't want her guessing any further details. "I have the rest of the day off to enjoy, after I finish this report."

She was studying him, as if she knew he was putting up blocks but didn't want to challenge him on it. "I'm positive you'll enjoy the day, Park." She smiled mischievously. "I'm leaving in fifteen minutes. I'm meeting a friend for lunch."

"Have fun." He pretended to refocus on the file in front of him.

"You too." And then she winked at him.

He stared at her.

She was grinning as she left his office and moved on down the hall towards her own.

Sabrina was going to meet him at one thirty. They'd agreed to have lunch separately so he could go over a few items in his files, and he guessed by then everyone else who was there today would have left. Well, maybe not Alicia. She had a tendency to work extra hours on Saturdays. He wasn't sure if it was ambition, a lack of other things to do, or perhaps wanting to get ahead of Neal in research. Maybe a combination of all three.

Meredith, Pamela and Maura all called their goodbyes within the next half hour. The quiet in the center was peaceful. Once he heard Alicia in the hall. He finished his work, got up and wandered into the break room to have something to eat. He knew there was half a pizza there from a few days ago, so he warmed up two slices, and sat down to eat.

Alicia entered the room. "Hey." She poured a cup of coffee and took a sandwich out of the fridge.

"Hey. What are you working on?" he asked.

"Looking over test results from that new kid, Dylan; and creating a new test for him and some others," she said. "I'll probably leave in a little while."

"Me too."

She left the room with her food, and he heard her go back upstairs.

He finished his lunch, threw away his paper plate and recycled his bottle of iced tea. Once back in his office, he put away the file on Dylan.

And suddenly, he got a flash: the image of his friend, Colin.

Colin and he had both majored in pre-med in college, and after their freshman year, had roomed together and become close friends. They'd gone to different medical schools, and Colin had ended up becoming a cardiac specialist in Maryland.

He knew from the image and the feeling he got with it—something he couldn't put into words—that Colin was thinking of him, and wanted to speak to him soon.

Once in a while, he got these spontaneous telepathic messages form people he knew. He would act on it and call Colin now to say hello.

They had a nice conversation, and he promised to come down to see Colin, his wife and their new baby boy. He didn't stay on long because he knew Sabrina would be here soon.

He felt like a teenager, about to see his new girlfriend. He couldn't wait for her to get here.

CHAPTER X

Sabrina found the front door to The Lightning Center unlocked, and she slipped into the empty reception area.

Her heart was beating harder than normal and she recognized the anticipation curling in her body.

She couldn't wait to see Parker—to be held by him, to make love to him again.

He was wonderful. Considerate, bringing her to the heights of passion before he let himself peak, holding her close afterwards and caressing her. And making love to her again. Most men, in her limited experience, didn't have the stamina to make love as soon afterwards as he did.

She wondered if it was because of the electricity that sizzled between them—an uncommon, intense energy that went from her to him and back, that seemed to attach them to each other.

Parker. The perfect lover.

It was quiet inside The Center; almost spooky. She followed the hall to the right towards Parker's office, and saw the open door and light spilling out into the darkened hall.

"Parker?" she said in a hushed voice. Her heart danced with anticipation.

He appeared at once at the doorway, grinning broadly. "Hi, Sabrina." Striding forward, her pulled her into his arms and kissed her.

She kissed him right back. "I'm glad to see you," she said when he stepped back, surveying her.

"Me too," he responded. "C'mon, let me shut down my computer and we can get going. Alicia's still here and she'll finish locking up."

She followed him into his office, where he slid a file onto a holder and then shut down his computer. Picking up his laptop bag, he turned off the light, called goodbye up the stairs to Alicia, who answered, and then went to the front where he locked the door.

They exited from the back, and he drove her to her car in the front.

"I have to stop at the drug store," he said. "You know what for."

She laughed. "I know. I'll follow you there, and then to your house."

It was a short drive to the large chain drugstore. She went inside with him, and they walked to the aisle for "family planning."

First, he picked up a box of the popular brand he had used last night. Then, holding it, he studied a few other kinds, selecting one box called "For Her Pleasure."

Parker turned to her, and waggled his eyebrows.

She felt herself blushing. "You don't need that. You gave me plenty of pleasure last night," she whispered in his ear.

"And I promise to give you more," he vowed. "But it might be fun to try these too. I'll buy both."

"Okay, we'll try them out."

210

His grin was infectious. "I can't wait."

She followed him, her cheeks still hot, and stood on line beside him at the check-out counter.

Once they exited the store, she felt more excitement pouring through her. She was going to Parker's home... to spend time with him. To make love with him.

A delicious thrill wound up her spine at the thought.

She followed him to his house, which was only a couple of miles from the pharmacy. Once there, he let her in with a flourish. "Here we are." He grabbed her cloth duffel.

She entered his house, and as soon as the door was closed, he pulled her into his arms again. "I've been dying to hold you since the moment you walked into TLC. To do more than hold you." His lips met hers in a demanding kiss, and she clung to his shoulders, reveling in it.

When they came up for air, he rasped, "I don't know about you, but I'd love to make love right this minute—"

"Me too," she answered breathlessly.

They raced up the stairs.

Before they reached his bedroom, he was tugging off her sweater and she was pulling off his. They shed their clothes on the way to his bed, pausing only for him to pull down the shade and drop the two boxes of condoms on the night stand. She barely had time to take in the details of the blue bedroom with its navy and gray accents.

"Sabrina—Sabrina—" he breathed, kissing her feverishly, touching her everywhere.

211

"Parker…" she moaned as he tugged gently at her nipple. "Oh…"

By the time they tumbled on the bed they had all their clothes off. Sabrina kissed him feverishly. She wanted him, fast and hard. Parker sheathed himself, then thrust into her.

She cried out, and he did too, as they fell into the abyss of pure pleasure.

They must have dozed for a little while. When they awoke the light was dimmer around the sides of the shades, and Parker touched her gently.

"You're so beautiful. But you're more than that."

"I feel the same about you," she murmured, gliding her hands over his firm chest. "You're gorgeous but so much more than your looks." She slid her body on top of his. "And you're a wonderful lover."

They made love again, slower this time, enjoying every touch, every sensation. She reached the heights several times, marveling at Parker's ability to fulfill her desires so often that she lost count. That had never happened to her before—if she'd had an orgasm, there had been only one. *If* she'd had one.

But their lovemaking was more than that. She knew she'd brought him to the peak many times. But laying in his arms, she felt a unique connection. As if… as if her mind as well as her body was entwined with his.

As if their very souls were touching.

She'd never felt anything so powerful.

It was electric.

She was driving him wild.

Making love had never been so earth-shattering, Parker acknowledged. The pleasure before and after was unbelievable. The desire, the satisfaction—it was like being struck by lightning all over again, the electricity between them was so intense.

But it didn't include the pain of really being struck by lightning. Only blazing excitement and satisfaction. And heightened sensations like he'd never felt before.

He cradled her against him, as their breathing slowed down and returned to normal. She was wearing her more sensual perfume again, and her silky dark hair brushed his neck and chest. He felt complete as he held her, as if they fit together perfectly.

But now he felt that reminder probing his mind. The thought that he had to talk to her.

She moved, and he met her eyes. She smiled.

Remorse rumbled through him. He *had* to tell her.

"Sabrina," he said, weaving his fingers through her hair. "I have to tell you something."

She sat up. "It sounds serious."

He propped himself against the headboard beside her. "Well, it is. It's something I tell very few people. In fact, at the Center, we like to keep our talents to ourselves. We don't want to—influence people."

She raised her eyebrows. "Talents?"

"Yes. Remember, you asked Pam if being struck by lightning had affected her and I? And she told you that we always had some ESP?"

"Yes, I remember." She shifted to look at him directly.

"Well." He swallowed. This was harder than he'd

anticipated. He hoped she wouldn't be disappointed in him. Or mad. "While it's true we always had that twin ESP thing going on, when we were struck, we developed other talents." He cupped her shoulder, feeling her soft skin.

"Go on."

"Pam developed precognition—the ability to sometimes tell events form the future. In fact, when she was a teenager she drew a picture of you and me after a dream about us."

Her eyes widened. "A picture of us?"

"Uh huh. Even though we hadn't met. She said you'd be important to me." He tightened his hand on her shoulder.

She smiled.

"You are," he added emphatically.

"Glad to hear it. What about you? What talent did you develop?"

"Mental telepathy." He sucked in his breath, waiting for the fall out.

"You can read my mind?" She scrambled to sit further from him, her mouth open.

"Sometimes. Not all the time," he hastened to add. "Sometimes it just happens. But I can usually control it. Generally, I don't deliberately try to read people's thoughts—unless there is a real reason to, and I know them well. It's just that sometimes, these thoughts slip into my mind."

She continued to stare at him.

"I've never tried to read yours," he said. "But— do you remember the first night you projected into my home office?"

She nodded.

"Well, I caught your thoughts. You were thinking of me holding you." He touched her on the shoulder again. "That's how I knew you were there. The image came clearly to me."

"I… see." She took a breath. "What about—other times?"

"I've never tried to deliberately read your mind," he said. "And—when we make love, Sabrina, that blocks out all thoughts. All I care about is making you feel wonderful, feeling close to you, making love. That's all."

She gave him a tremulous smile. "Okay. I wish you had told me before, though."

"I'm sorry I didn't." He took her hand and brought it to his lips. "Please don't be mad. None of us tell our clients about our talents."

"But you told me."

"You're not a client. You're my lover. My—" he paused as the enormity of it hit him. "More than that. You're my girlfriend. If you want to be," he finished, searching her face.

"I want to be." She gripped his hand.

Happiness burst inside him. It felt so right, their being together. "That's what I want, too." He kissed her, hard. "I want to be exclusive with you."

"Me too," she whispered. She pulled back to look at him. "I'm glad you told me, Parker."

"And—I might as well tell you more. We're doing tests for a project. We believe that when two people have an ability—any kind of ability—it makes each person's stronger when they're together. That may be why your projections with Pam or me are stronger and clearer than when you project with

215

Meredith, who doesn't have more than the usual ESP, or slightly more."

"That's an exciting hypothesis," she said.

"Yes. And there's one more thing—"

"What?"

He swallowed. This might be the most difficult subject of all. "I should tell you about me and my old girlfriend, Dara—"

She held up her hand. "I don't want to hear about her now. Not when we're in bed together."

"Alright. But I should tell you soon—"

"What am I thinking of right now?" she demanded. A smile lit her face.

He stopped, and looked at her, reaching out with his mind.

She was thinking of making love.

He grinned. "I'll be happy to oblige." He pulled her into his arms.

<hr>

Later, they took a quick shower together, then ordered Chinese food for dinner. Afterwards they decided to watch a movie, and settled on one of Sabrina's favorites, the first Avengers movie.

They enjoyed it. What Parker enjoyed most, though, was holding her in the circle of his arms.

When it finished, they discussed their favorite parts of the movie.

"I love the way they all come together to work as a team," Sabrina declared.

"I agree." He reached over and took her hand. "Let's go to bed."

Her answering smile was all he needed to get his engines up and running. He was hard before they reached the top of the stairs.

And he got even harder when he saw the sexy fire-red nightgown she'd brought to wear. One look at her in it and he was practically salivating.

They made love, and there wasn't one part of her he didn't caress. She came apart several times in his arms, and again when he plunged into her heat. He called out her name when he climaxed, holding her tight, barely conscious of anything but this moment, this woman.

***

Cuddled close beside Parker under the thick comforter, Sabrina recognized she hadn't been this happy in… well, she never remembered feeling quite so happy.

She did reflect on his having an ability. She wasn't surprised, with his strong interest in ESP and other paranormal abilities, that he had one himself. She did wish he'd told her, but understood his reticence.

The fact was, he'd confided in her, which he said he rarely did. She was honored.

She must have slept deeply for a while. But at some point, she became conscious of that rising feeling, of floating on the night air.

She took a quick look around. Parker wasn't in bed. She saw a light under the door of the master bathroom as she floated upwards.

The night was clear, and stars lit the sky. The

moon was partial and beautiful, the air crisp. She looked down at Parker's home.

She drifted over a few houses, not far from his. Then dropped into one of them suddenly.

She was in a bedroom lit only by a dim light. There was a girl—a teenager—sitting on the floor by a bed. She was sniffing, crying quietly.

In her hand she clutched a bottle of pills.

Sabrina's insides tightened. Was she contemplating suicide?

She reached out, trying to call "No!" to the girl.

The girl lifted the bottle of pills and stared at it.

"No!" Sabrina repeated, more forcefully.

The girl suddenly threw the bottle aside and buried her face in her hands.

"It's alright, sweetheart. It's a bad dream."

She recognized Parker's voice nearby. Sabrina reached out to touch the teenager, but as she did she felt Parker's hand grip her own wrist.

"Sabrina… Sabrina… it's alright. It's just a bad dream."

"No," Sabrina said, her voice choked.

"Come back, Sabrina. I'm right here, sweetheart.'

As she heard Parker's words she actually could feel his arm around her, and she felt herself lifting from the girl's room, being pulled back into his home.

She was floating above his house now—above this room. She saw herself, tangled in Parker's arms and his blanket, his face close to hers.

"It's alright Sabrina. I'm here."

She felt his arms around her, his warm breath on her face, inhaled the male scent of him. And realized she was back in her own body.

218

"Parker," she gasped.

He held her tightly. "Shh, Sabrina. It's alright."

"I was—projecting." She struggled to sit up.

He sat up with her, then pulled her close, holding her.

"I thought so." He caressed her hair. "It's okay."

"No, it isn't. I think one of your neighbors is thinking about killing herself." Glancing at the clock on the nightstand, she saw it was 1:09 AM. Briefly, she described the scene she'd witnessed. "When I screamed no, she threw the pills away from her," she finished.

"That sounds like the teenage girl who lives two doors down," Parker said. "Right now, I better call her parents."

"Would you please? I'm worried about her. Did you know I was projecting?" she asked.

He tightened his hold on her. "When I heard you cry out 'no' I thought it was a nightmare… but when you didn't respond when I told you everything was okay, I realized you must be projecting. And I was reaching out to you, to your mind, when I felt confusion and fear. Then you came back."

"Another night projection I couldn't control," she said, and sighed.

"We'll figure out how to help you." He got up. "I'll call her family now. I have to find their phone number."

Sabrina heard him go into the bedroom he used as his home office. She saw light flow into the hall as he flicked the switch. She heard him at his desk, heard him grabbing for the cellphone which was charging there.

After a minute or two she heard him speaking. "Carl? It's Parker Costigan, your neighbor. Listen, I

219

have to tell you—" he went on to describe that his girlfriend had had a dream about Carl's daughter, and the details. "Please check on her," he urged. There was a pause, and then, "you're welcome."

A moment later she heard him plug the phone back in, turn off the light, and return to the bedroom.

"C'mon, sweetheart, let's get some rest. Her father's going to check on her." He climbed in beside her.

"Thanks," she whispered.

His breathing soon became slow and steady, and she knew he'd gone back to sleep quickly. It took her a little longer, but in the warm, safe cocoon of his arms, under the heavy comforter, she soon fell asleep too.

Sunday dawned bright but cold. They made love, showered and had breakfast together. Parker had muffins in the house.

"I wish I didn't have to work today. I'd rather stay here with you," she said.

"At least it's not for the whole day. I'm going to call my neighbor Carl and speak to him again, check and see if he needs a referral or something for his daughter. Then I'm going into the office to go over some files I didn't get to yesterday. How about we meet at five and then have dinner and spend the evening together?"

"That would be great." She smiled.

Before she left, he pulled her into his arms.

"I'll see you later," he promised, and kissed her soundly.

She was humming and her body hummed right along with her voice as she entered her car.

It had been a spectacular weekend—and it wasn't quite over yet.

Parker was in the best mood he'd been in for a long time when he pulled into the back parking lot at The Lightning Center.

He spotted Neal's car immediately.

He knew there was some kind of rivalry between Neal and Alicia. But the fact that they were not only staying late, but working a lot on weekends, was a concern. They were both excellent at what they did and he didn't want them to burn out.

He'd have to talk to his parents on Monday about hiring more help, maybe making Neal, who'd been here the longest, head of the Psychic research and testing team. He already was in charge of the part time students.

That decided, he went upstairs to say hello to Neal, who was busy at the computer, then wandered into his own office.

Once in front of his computer, he tried to concentrate on looking over test results from Friday and Saturday morning.

But Sabrina kept popping into his mind.

She was beautiful. And the most responsive lover he'd ever known. Just picturing her had his dick twitching. He couldn't wait to make love to her again.

Her uncontrolled projection had been disturbing for her—but it may have saved that girl's life.

Instead of calling, he'd knocked on the neighbor's door this morning after Sabrina left for work, but no one answered. He planned to try again later, before he saw Sabrina.

Three times in the next hour he found his mind wandering back to Sabrina, and three times he had to push the thoughts away. If he could review his files now, he'd have more time on Monday, which was going to be full with patients.

He was supposed to meet Sabrina at her home at five. By three he had finished his work, and he drove home to try to contact the neighbors.

Mrs. Burke opened the door when he knocked.

"Hello, Doctor Costigan," she said. "I—thank you for your call last night." Her face was grave.

"Your daughter's ok?"

"Yes. We found the pills in her room, just like your girlfriend dreamed." Like Sabrina's parents, he had attributed her vision to a dream instead of astral projection. Not all his neighbors knew what he did for a living, and he knew dreams were more likely to be accepted by most people than astral projection.

"I wanted to know if there's anything else I can help you with. Do you want my sister—she's a psychiatrist—to refer her to a doctor specializing in teens?"

Mrs. Burke sighed. "We called our minister and got a name from him this morning. Thank you anyway."

"That's good. Well, call me if you need anything else." He turned to go.

"Doctor—thank your girlfriend for us."

He smiled at the woman. "I will."

It was difficult, but Sabrina managed to keep her mind on her work—at least, for most of the afternoon.

Sunday afternoons were often busy with students

doing last-minute research. Today wasn't as busy as usual, though, and she guessed that the warmer, sunny day had a lot of people out pumpkin-picking or attending football games. Two students needed help with fairly simple research, and the rest of the time she was doing routine work, checking on books she was considering for the library.

Her thoughts routinely circled back to Parker. He'd been such a wonderful and considerate lover— always making sure she was satisfied at least once before seeking his own release. Holding her close, whispering words of admiration. And what a body his lab coats had hidden! He had the most masculine chest and shoulders she'd ever touched.

Concern about his neighbor pricked at her mind too. She hoped the girl was going to get help.

She couldn't wait to leave, and hurried out as soon as her shift was over, eager to see Parker.

She'd done her food shopping during the week, and now threw together a chicken and rice casserole, popping it into the oven before he rang her doorbell.

"Hi," she greeted him.

He pulled her into his arms and gave her a loud kiss. "Hi. Mmm… something smells good."

"Dinner," she said. "I figured you might want a home cooked meal."

"You figured right! How soon 'til it's ready?" he asked.

"About an hour. Hungry?" she joked, smiling up at him.

"Not just for food." He waggled his eyebrows. "I have an appetite for something else."

"Tell me about your neighbor."

223

"They called their minister and he gave them the name of a doctor to take her to."

"Whew." She let out a relieved breath.

Before she could say another word, he tightened his hold on her. They were soon shedding their clothes and making quick, intense love. Afterwards they joked around while they dressed, and she finished the dinner preparations.

"Do you like to cook?" he asked, setting silverware on her kitchen table.

"Yes. It's one of my hobbies, but since I live alone, I don't cook a lot for myself. Do you have hobbies?"

"I'm a first-degree black belt in karate."

"Ohh! That's impressive," she said, sliding oven mitts over her hands.

"I only practice about once a week now, since we're so busy at work. Pam has a brown belt. I tease her about being not quite as accomplished as me."

"Does Meredith too?"

"Nope. She was more involved in dance. Pam was too."

Parker asked about her week's schedule. She was off Tuesday. She was planning to touch base with Pam and Meredith and see if they had ideas about her night time projections.

"Although I can't be sorry about last night's," she said, as she placed the casserole on a trivet.

"You may have saved a life. Let's get together Tuesday night, okay? And next weekend—all weekend?"

She was happy that he wanted to spend so much time with her—because she wanted that too. She recognized how important Parker had become to her in a short time.

Later, they watched TV and made love more slowly. Afterwards, they held each other close. As she drifted off to sleep, Sabrina thought again about how very important Parker was to her.

Sometime in the early morning hours, Sabrina found herself moving upwards. She caught a glimpse of her adjacent bathroom, it's light on. Parker must be inside. She went through the roof, then circled her condo area. Slowly she drifted towards Rt. 80—she recognized the highway—but then she veered off into a field.

She saw the flare of lights, and as she drew closer, she could feel heat and smell something burning.

A car was on fire!

"No!" she cried out.

But this time she didn't startle herself awake. She watched, as if she couldn't tear her gaze away, and the fire grew fiercer, with flames licking the cold night air.

Arms were holding her. "Shh," Parker soothed. "It's okay Sabrina, it's a bad dream."

"The fire!" she exclaimed.

"It's alright. Come back to me, sweetheart."

She was suddenly pulled backwards.

She felt a jarring and her bones seemed to rattle as she re-entered her body.

Gasping, she opened her eyes.

Parker must have turned on her night table lamp. She was half sitting up in bed, with his arms around her, holding her close. He stroked her hair and she felt herself tremble against him. His skin was warm and she caught the citrusy scent of his aftershave.

"It's alright, sweetheart." His voice was calming. His body warmed her chilled one.

"I saw—" she gasped. "A car was on fire."

He continued to stroke her hair. "It's okay. I don't know anything about a car," he said softly, "but it's okay. I'm right here."

He pulled her back down and she clutched at him as he covered them both with her comforter.

After a few minutes, her trembling stopped, and she grew sleepy against his vibrating chest, hearing the steady beat of his heart. She felt protected.

Monday proved to be a busy day at work, and it was his day to stay late.

The morning meeting started with his suggestion to get another person on board to help Neal and Alicia. Everyone agreed, especially when his father reported that they had received two grants—one of them unexpected, which there had been a lot of competition for. They would use the same ad they had for Alicia; Neal was in charge and would run the ad and put out feelers in the community of para-psychologists he knew. There was a brief discussion which resulted in Neal being named their head of Paranormal Testing.

After that, they went over several patients. Meredith spoke about meeting with Evan Lassiter later in the week. Then Parker brought up Sabrina.

"She's stressed out, and she decided to stop coming here, at least for a while," he said flatly.

His parents and Maura and Alicia looked

surprised. Neal remained solemn. Of course, Pamela and Meredith already knew.

"Why?" Alicia asked.

"She was so upset after not finding Clarisse. It took a toll on her, mentally and physically," he said. "But she does want Pam and Meredith to come up with ideas to stop her night-time projections." He had shielded his thoughts about that subject when he entered the room. No one knew he was involved with Sabrina, although he was aware that Pam suspected.

He'd observed that the two recent night-time projections Sabrina had experienced had both been when he'd used the bathroom in the middle of the night. Which made him conclude that when he was in bed with her, holding her—as he did when they slept together—he acted as an anchor, holding her in place. Whether it was physical or emotional anchoring was anybody's guess. But he wasn't about to discuss it here.

"At least for now, we need to give her some space," he finished. "But we also need to find out how to help keep her from projecting in her sleep."

Pamela's eyes narrowed, and he realized that she had somehow picked up—whether now or over the weekend—that there was more to his concern than a mere doctor—patient relationship.

He set more mental blocks around his thoughts. "She tells me she's been having more projections during the last week."

"I'd like to hypnotize her at some point if my next idea doesn't work," Pam said. "I do have an idea for something to anchor her. I thought of a stuffed animal, but that seems too childish. So, I looked for a pillow, with textures to help her grip it, and found this." She took out a textured beige pillow from under the table. "At least we can try it."

"That's a great idea," Neal said. There were murmurs of agreement around the table.

"I agree," Parker stated.

"But we should keep studying her and her projections," Neal protested. "She can give us valuable insights. Let's see if we can encourage her to come back."

"If we can help prevent or reduce the night-time projections, then she may agree to do more projections with us," Parker said. But inside he felt a hole in his gut. If she came back, what would happen to *them*? To their relationship? Of course, if they were already involved and she came to TLC, she could be a client... right?

Pam shot him a look. He wondered if she'd somehow managed to sneak into his thoughts and was aware of that last one. He turned to regard Meredith instead of his twin.

They concluded by briefly discussing another patient who was returning this week.

When the meeting ended and Parker pushed his chair back and went to leave, his sister Pam was right beside him.

"What's going on with you and Sabrina?" she asked, her voice pitched low so only he could hear as they left the room.

He glanced at her. "Nothing."

"Come on, Park. I know you. There's something." Her eyes were accusing.

Obviously, he hadn't camouflaged his relationship

with Sabrina completely enough, because his sister suspected something.

He shook his head, casting a glance at his parents, who were speaking to Neal.

Pamela clamped a hand on his arm and practically dragged him down the hall. He let her lead him to his office, where she turned on the light, shut the door, and whirled to face him.

"What is going on?" she demanded.

"Nothing—"

"Don't give me that crap!"

He rocked back in surprise. He rarely heard his sister this angry. Something else must be bothering her.

Was it the discussion about Meredith's upcoming meeting with Dr. Lassiter?

He sighed, and sat down behind his desk. His sister continued to stand.

"Ok," he said, keeping his voice calm, hoping to soothe his twin. "Now that she's not projecting anymore, I feel I can get involved with her. There's no conflict of interest if she's not really my patient."

"Have you told her about Dara?"

"Yes." He met Pam's eyes. "Briefly. Not the complete story, though. She didn't want to discuss it."

"And about your talent?"

"She knows that, too. What are you so annoyed about?" he asked, choosing his words with care. Something was bugging his sister.

"Well, at least you told her the truth. But—what if she uses it against you, Park?" Pam's face was softening. Concern tinged her voice. "I don't want to see you get hurt like you were before. And Sabrina—I

229

like her. I don't want to see her hurt, either." Pam dropped into the chair in front of his desk.

He focused on her. He recognized her familial love for him and her concern for Sabrina. More than for a normal patient. He realized his sister really liked Sabrina.

"I had a dream about Sabrina last night," she said abruptly. "It was disturbing. I think it was a precognition dream."

"What was it about?"

"She was projecting around a house, in a remote area, surrounded by woods." Pam frowned. "She was—she met something truly evil."

"What do you mean?" He leaned forward.

"There were people inside. No, I didn't get a look at them. But they were bad news. And someone outside was doing something to chase her off—casting a spell, maybe." Her frown deepened. "All I know is that there was a sense of evil around all of them. It frightened me."

"Thanks for the warning." He touched his sister's hand lightly, where it lay on his desk. "Did you get a sense of when it will happen—if it does?"

"I think… soon. Not too far in the future," she finished.

"I'll tell Sabrina."

But after she left the room, he mulled over her words.

Had this truly been another precognition dream of Pam's? Would Sabrina really meet someone who was evil?

Of course, he and Pam both knew that sometimes, she simply had bizarre dreams. Like any other human being would. They didn't all come true.

But she seemed particularly disturbed by this one.

CHAPTER XI

Sabrina worked a long 9 AM to 9 PM day on Monday. It was busy at the library, so she had limited opportunities to check her phone. Parker texted her several times, asking how things were going, and she texted back. There was one text that said he was thinking about her and missing her—which made her insides feel all mushy.

Tuesday was a beautiful October day, all golden and warm. She did laundry as she cleaned, then made cupcakes for them to eat. They'd agreed to bring in Chinese food again and she thought the cupcakes would be fun for dessert.

By two o'clock she headed to The Lightning Center to see Pam. Pam had called and asked her to come in "unofficially," as she put it, because she believed she had something which would help with the nightly projections.

"Thank you for coming in," Pam said as Sabrina took a seat in her office. "I know you wanted to take a break from us; but I also know the night-time projections are disturbing you. You know I thought holding something to anchor yourself might be a solution."

"Yes," Sabrina agreed. She didn't want to tell Parker's sister that she'd figured out that when she slept in Parker's arms, she was anchored and didn't project. The only time she projected while they were sleeping together was when he left the bed.

Pam smiled. "I'd like to try this." Turning, she lifted a nubby beige pillow from the credenza behind her desk. She handed it to Sabrina.

Sabrina gripped the pillow. It said "Be Happy!" in dark cursive writing, and had raised tufts in a swirling pattern.

"Before you go to bed each night," Pam said, "tell yourself this is your anchor, a way to stay in one place, in your bed. When you go to bed try holding it lightly. Then, if you feel yourself projecting, try to make yourself hold on tight, repeating to yourself it will help you stay in one place."

"I'll definitely try," Sabrina vowed. Maybe this would work!

She was tempted to visit Parker, but forced herself not to. She didn't want to be one of those super-clingy girlfriends, which guys, in her experience, disliked. At least Devon had.

Once home, she had a couple of hours before Parker came over. When it was close to the time for him to arrive, she hurried to put on more make-up and comb her hair. She was dressed in blue jeans and a pink top with a low neckline. As she spritzed on some perfume, she decided to buy herself a new nightgown. Parker had certainly seemed to like the one she wore over the weekend and she had very few sexy ones. She hadn't needed them in the last few years.

But now she did. The thought of Parker's reaction had her growing hot.

The doorbell rang. He was here!

The minute she opened the door he stepped inside and pulled her into his arms, slamming the door behind him. The zing of his kiss was as sizzling as always, and reverberated down to her toes.

"I missed you," he said, pulling back to regard her.

"Me too." She smiled.

He held up the bag from the Chinese restaurant. "Here it is—shrimp with Chinese vegetables for you and General Tsao's chicken for me. And fried rice for us both."

She'd already set her kitchen table, and they put out the food, talking about work the last few days. She learned that he'd had a jam-packed schedule with a couple of new patients plus testing some of their current ones.

"But no one with the ability to astral project," he said.

"You look a little tired. We should turn in early," she suggested.

He smiled. "I agree." Reaching out, he squeezed her hand. "I'm tired—but not that tired."

She grinned, part of her warming at the thought of his hands on her.

When they went to bed, he brought her to the heights of ecstasy; and he cried out her name in passion. Afterwards they cuddled close, drifting to sleep. Holding on to Parker, she didn't think about the pillow Pam had asked her to use.

On days when Parker came in later, he missed the general morning meeting; but Pam had left him notes from it, which he skimmed. There was a new patient who was able to communicate with animals—that was something they hadn't seen before, and he was looking forward to speaking with her. Another new patient who could see past lives—something they'd only seen once in the last three years. Neal had preliminary test results from Martin which Parker could study during his dinner hour.

He was due to examine Russell, a patient who was returning after being sent to Japan for his job for six months; and Louise, a patient back for her annual check and testing. She'd been one of their first patients, a woman who had strong precognition dreams.

The day passed swiftly, and although thoughts of Sabrina caught him at odd moments, he concentrated on his patients and their fascinating test results. He was tired but satisfied as he sat in his office at 9:15, finishing his notes.

"I'm heading out."

He almost jumped at Meredith's voice. He'd been so absorbed in his notes on Louise that he hadn't heard his sister in his doorway.

"Okay, see you tomorrow," he said.

She was regarding him seriously. Her thoughts came to him without his reaching out. She was thinking of him—and Sabrina. Thinking that they were meant for each other.

He was not ready to discuss his girlfriend with his oldest sister. Their relationship was too new.

"I'm leaving soon," he added, "just as soon as I finish my notes on Louise."

Meredith left, and he also heard Neal call

goodbye. Finally, he finished his work, stretched, and shut down his computer.

He wished he was going to Sabrina's, but they'd agreed that since this was a late day for both of them, they wouldn't see each other tonight.

He *really* wished they were getting together.

As he gathered up his things, he got another flash in his mind. It was so startling that he grabbed for his chair, then abruptly dropped into it.

Dara. What the *hell* was she doing in his head?

He clenched his jaw. He saw, quite vividly, that she was thinking about the day they'd broken up.

Dara was the last person he wanted to think about. He mentally shoved her out of his brain.

He left the center and headed home. As he drove closer, he could see two police cars and an ambulance.

In front of the Burke's house.

His stomach turned to ice.

CHAPTER XII

The doorbell's ring sliced through the quiet of Sabrina's apartment.

Who could be here…? She placed her book on the coffee table and hurried to the door. Maybe it was Parker, missing her?

She looked through the peephole. It was him!

Whipping the door open, she greeted him. "Hi!"

"Hi." He looked weary, and she detected worry in his expression.

"Is everything alright?" she asked as he shut the door behind him. At ten o'clock, it was late for him to drop in. And she sensed it wasn't merely because he wanted to see her. Then, as he turned to face her, she guessed. "That girl—did something happen?"

"Yes." His eyes met hers. "When I got to my street, there was an ambulance in front of her house."

"Oh my God." She sat down abruptly on her couch, suddenly cold despite her comfy flannel pjs.

He sat beside her, his leather jacket still on. "I went right over. Mrs. Burke was crying and so was her husband. It looked like their daughter Vanessa took a bottle of aspirin. They were bringing her to the hospital to pump her stomach, but fortunately she was still breathing."

"Thank God they found her in time." Sabrina found herself clutching her hands together.

"Yes. Her mother noticed the music from her room had stopped and it was too quiet. When she knocked there was no answer, so she went in and found her on the floor. Vanessa wrote a note."

"Do you know why…?" she began.

He took her hand in his. His hand was cold, not the usual temperature. "Apparently her boyfriend broke up with her about a week ago. But that's not all. She was failing a class. And a couple of days ago she heard her parents arguing. It seems Mrs. Burke had found out her husband was having an affair, and she decided to turn the tables on him and have an affair herself. They were talking about a divorce."

"Oh, the poor kid," Sabrina said. "That's a lot to handle."

"Yeah, and her older sister is away at college, and her younger sister is a perfect, straight A student who is popular with everyone. Vanessa may have been kind of floundering anyway." He sighed. "I wish they had taken your first projection more seriously; she had an appointment with a doctor but not for two more weeks. I'm sure Pam would have seen her right away." His frown deepened. "Of course, if we hadn't told them, Mrs. Burke might not have even looked in on Vanessa until it was too late."

Sabrina nodded. "Maybe it's a good thing I projected. Maybe I shouldn't be trying to stop. Maybe I need to go back to The Lightning Center so I can learn how to control them more, be more effective—"

"No," he said.

"No?" She stared at him, her mouth open.

237

"No." He shook his head. He felt like there was a rock in his stomach, and fear enveloped him at her words. This was worse than seeing that ambulance.

If Sabrina returned to the Center—if she was once more a client—then what would happen to them? To their—affair? No, it wasn't merely an affair. It wasn't just a relationship.

It was much more.

He didn't want to lose her. "You should be trying to keep your projections to a minimum. And I hope the pillow will help you to stop doing it at night."

"You don't think I should be projecting?"

"Sabrina, I've seen first-hand how taxing these night-time projections are on you. Not only are you exhausted afterwards—you're upset. More than upset. I think your decision to stop testing last week was wise."

"But I helped someone," she said. "I wasn't able to help Clarisse, but I did help the teen, and the little girl who'd been kidnapped. I always hoped my projections could be used for something good." She stared at him. And then, comprehension burst over her face. "You mean—since you're a doctor there, you wouldn't be able to—see me anymore?"

"I don't know." He grit his teeth. "I'm not sure of the answer, since we got really involved while you *weren't* a client. We have something good here—no, great." The thought of losing her was painful. "I don't want it to end."

"Neither do I." Her voice was shaky.

"But I…" he jumped up. He started to pace. "Sabrina, I want to continue seeing you. That's important to me."

She stood too. "And to me. But if I can help people…"

He couldn't stand it if she called a halt to their seeing each other. Sabrina meant more to him than Dara ever had.

The knot in his gut tightened. Was Sabrina going to initiate an argument, so she could end things between them? Then blame him?

"I think you should continue to take a break. You feel so upset after some of these projections—" he protested.

"I agreed to the break only a week ago," she said slowly. "But this turn of events—the projection into Vanessa's room and the fact that it may have saved her life—is making me look at things differently. I'm rethinking my decision." Her eyes met his, and he saw tears there. "If I can save a life… I was devastated when I couldn't help Clarisse, but—" she paused in front of him. "But—there may be others I can help— like Vanessa."

He reached out and pulled her into his arms.

She burrowed into his embrace.

"You're a wonderful person," he said, his voice strained. "But I don't like seeing how difficult it is for you. I—can't go along with you on this."

"Isn't your job sometimes difficult too?"

"Part of being a doctor," he said slowly, "is doing what you have to, and being compassionate, but still separate enough and objective enough to do your job well."

She nodded. "I guess I need to be more like that—caring but more objective when I do these— these projections."

239

He pulled back to stare at her.

After a moment, he voiced his thoughts. "I'm worried about you."

She placed her hand on his cheek. "It'll be okay." She leaned in and gently kissed him. "Somehow, we'll find a way."

"Sabrina—" he studied her. She was so beautiful, so caring.

Sabrina stared back at Parker. Her insides were twisted into knots, the thought of stopping their relationship—even temporarily—like a punch in her middle.

He pulled her tight against him, dipped his head, and kissed her. The kiss turned harder, more demanding. He broke the kiss, and, sweeping her into his arms without a word, carried her into her bedroom. Thrills rushed through Sabrina like a river gone wild.

He put her down on the bed and slid beside her. His lips returned to hers, fiercely, and he caressed her through her light flannel pajamas.

His demanding kisses and the possessive way he touched her ignited a fire deep inside her. She kissed him back as unrestrainedly, pulling off his jacket as his hands reached under her pajama top to caress her breasts. She gasped at the sheer eroticism as he rapidly pulled off her pajamas, then rolled on top of her, fully clothed. His erection pressed into her. He bent his head, suckling one breast, then the other. Hot desire spiked in her. Wanting had never been so intense, so piercing.

"Parker," she moaned, as her body writhed beneath his.

She scrambled to unbutton his shirt, then pulled it off. He helped her pull off his clothes, until his chest pressed against hers, skin on skin, and she gloried in the heat of it, the male power she felt against her own femininity. All the time they kissed, fiercely and hungrily. "Hurry," she whispered raggedly. She'd never felt such urgent need, so much arousal.

He paused to sheathe himself, then he was perched between her thighs.

"Parker—" she gasped.

He plunged into her.

"Ohh!" There were no words for the feeling he generated in her.

"Sabrina…" it came out as a groan, as he pushed himself to the hilt.

She wrapped her legs around him, and he began that ancient, pulsing rhythm. She joined him, meeting his thrusts, their cries mingling until she saw stars.

"Sabrina!" he called out as he reached the summit.

Slowly, they sank back to earth, until she was conscious of her mattress beneath her, the tangle of the comforter and some clothes, his rapid breathing mixed with her own.

He rolled to the side, taking her with him so his full weight was no longer on her, and wrapped part of the blanket around their legs.

She'd never experienced such passion, such sudden and intense wanting, the desire to have him inside so immediately, so completely. It was as if she'd been struck by lightning all over again—and nothing short of being joined with Parker could complete the need she felt.

His breath was still coming in gasps.

She trailed her fingers down his side, and sighed.

"That was… spectacular." It had never, ever been this good with anyone else.

"Unbelievable," he said at the same moment. He kissed her, tenderly this time. Then held her as if she was something precious, stroking her hair.

Parker held Sabrina, her back to his front, and knew when she slipped into sleep.

Sleep didn't come so easily to him.

Sabrina was thinking of going back to the center. Which would put their relationship at risk.

But more than that… Sabrina was thinking about what she wanted. To project, to help other people.

She wasn't thinking about him. Or his needs. One of which was for her to be safe.

He clenched his teeth. God, was she like Dara? That she could be anything like the selfish woman he'd once cared for was alarming. Was she? He hadn't thought so, but now—

He couldn't help wondering. And being afraid.

Sabrina had said all along she wanted her gift to help others. Was her gift more important than their involvement?

If it was, then it was better that he learned now. Before something happened, before she did a number on him like Dara had.

It was some time before he was able to fall asleep.

He hadn't intended to sleep at Sabrina's apartment tonight, but he couldn't tear himself away from her arms, from her warmth.

He had set his phone to buzz early and wake him. He threw on yesterday's clothes, dashed out to the car for his duffle with his spare clothes, and came back to shower and change completely. Sabrina was still fast asleep.

When he got out of the bathroom, she was awake. She kissed him briefly, then got into the shower. Did that short kiss mean she was thinking of ending their relationship? His stomach felt hollow.

They ate a hurried breakfast, not talking much. He guessed that between their passionate love-making and the emotional evening discussion about whether she was going to keep projecting, she was as confused as him.

"I promise I'll call the hospital and find out how Vanessa's doing," he offered as he left.

"Okay. Thanks."

There was no plan about whether they'd see each other tonight—although they had agreed last weekend that they'd spend this upcoming one together.

He kissed her hard when he left, wanting to linger, but knowing he couldn't.

***

As she watched him stride out the door, Sabrina felt her heart squeezing.

What was going to happen to them? She wanted to keep seeing him. To see what could develop, where this relationship could go. But—she needed to help

243

others. It had been a dream of hers for a long time. She very well might have to go back to The Lightning Center and resume projecting there til she had more of a handle on it.

But—she couldn't imagine her life now, without Parker being a part of it. A huge part.

Her whole being sizzled like it had when she was struck by lightning.

And that's when she knew.

She was in love with Parker!

CHAPTER XIII

His thoughts continued to bounce all over as he drove to the Center. Would they have to stop seeing each other? If Sabrina was anything like Dara, maybe that would be best. But—he wanted to see her.

Needed to. In a short time, she'd become an important part of his life.

For the first time ever, he was five minutes late to the nine o'clock meeting.

His parents were getting coffee, Meredith was chatting with Alicia and Pamela was looking at some notes. Neal was stirring sugar into his coffee. Lorna was texting on her cellphone.

The minute he walked into the room, every face turned to him.

"Sorry I'm late," he said, striding to the coffeemaker.

"Is everything okay, son?" Edward asked. "You're never late."

"Something happened with my neighbor," he said, grabbing a mug and helping himself to the coffee. The rich aroma invigorated him. "I'll tell you about it."

They all took places around the table.

He described, briefly, how Sabrina had projected

and saw his neighbor holding a bottle of pills; how he'd called, and the following day had gone over to warn them; and how the girl had tried to commit suicide anyway. He deliberately blocked out Pam but she was staring at him with narrowed eyes, a look of suspicion on her face. She must have guessed that he'd been with Sabrina at night.

And maybe it was time to confide in his sisters. He could use some advice. And none of his friends who lived nearby, like Kyle, understood completely just how much the Center meant to him; or knew about Dara. And, he suspected, his sisters were aware of his growing feelings for Sabrina.

"I discussed the situation with Sabrina," he said calmly, and took a sip of the bracing coffee. "She was, naturally, very upset."

"How awful," Meredith murmured, as the others around the table agreed.

"Sabrina's thinking now she could have done more; and she wants to resume projecting," he said. "I don't think it's a good idea. I've seen how stressed she gets when things don't go well. I think we should concentrate on helping her control her nightly projections and that's all for now."

Pamela was staring at him accusingly now. He could actually *feel* his twin trying to break down the mental barriers he'd put up.

"I agree, she may need a break," his mother said.

Meredith chimed in. "It may not be the right timing for a break. She may need to work with us a little more. It sounds like that's what she wants."

"Her projections are helping a lot of people," his father remarked.

"It really should be her decision," Alicia pointed out.

Even if it meant parting ways with him? "Of course, it's her decision. I just think she may need some space from her projections." He hadn't meant to speak so harshly, but that's the way it came out.

The others were staring at him.

"I'll talk to her," Pamela said, "and see what she's thinking." She looked at him with a challenge in her eyes.

He didn't want everyone at the table to guess what was going on. "Okay," he agreed, trying to sound casual.

"Next item—" his father began abruptly. "Neal has already gotten a bunch of applications for the new parapsychology examiner and researcher. He and I are interviewing three people later this week."

"Will they be able to start quickly?" Meredith asked.

Neal answered. "That's one of the questions we're going to ask. Next week we'll probably interview a few more possible employees; then narrow it down to the top two, and we'll get the rest of you in on that."

"Anything else?" Edward asked, glancing around the table.

"Yes." Meredith spoke up. "I attempted to see Evan Lassiter yesterday afternoon." She spoke slowly, as if she was the bearer of not-so-good news.

Everyone leaned forward, and Parker found himself gripping the spoon he'd used for his coffee.

"He says"—Meredith took a breath—"that he'll only speak to Pamela." She looked at their sister, a worried expression on her face.

Pamela blanched. And for just a second, her barriers wavered. Parker couldn't help seeing the image in her mind; Evan Lassiter—not his publicity photo—but leaning against a desk, in casual clothes, smiling.

Then a curtain came down, shutting off the picture abruptly, and he knew his sister had hastily put up her blocks again.

But not before he'd seen that image she had of Evan.

She still had some feelings for this guy. He knew it. And he was convinced that not all of her feelings were negative.

He sent her an assessing look.

Pam turned away, and looked instead at Meredith.

"Why does he want to see *me*?" she demanded. Her fingers gripped her iPad tightly.

Meredith shrugged. "I don't know. I asked, but he wouldn't say. He just repeated that he would only talk to you."

Pam muttered something under her breath which sounded suspiciously like "fuck."

Their mother raised her eyebrows.

Everyone was looking at his twin now. Even Neal looked surprised.

"Well, can you meet him, Pam?" his father asked.

She sighed, loudly and unhappily. "I guess, if I have to."

Parker knew it was the last thing she wanted to do. He'd have to see if she'd tell him more another time.

After he spoke to her about his own problem.

As they left the meeting, Parker moved over to Pam. He pitched his voice low. "Can I meet with you and Meredith this morning? It's important."

She met his gaze. "Of course. I don't have an appointment til noon. What about you?"

"My first patient comes in at eleven. Let's talk now."

"Meredith is free now too. I'll get her and we'll meet you in your office."

He proceeded to his office, where he turned on the lights and settled behind his desk. Less than five minutes later his sisters joined him there. Pam shut the door and they took the two seats in front of his desk.

"What's on your mind?" Meredith asked in her gentle voice.

As succinctly as he could, he spilled his guts to his sisters.

They listened, as any good counselors would. Their expressions of understanding and empathy were clear.

"So, I don't want to lose her," he said. "But I'm afraid. What if our client relationship prevents me from seeing her? And what if she wants it that way?"

"I think your telepathic connection to Dara's thoughts are influencing you too much—making you worry more than you should," Meredith stated.

"And there is a work-around," Pamela said. "I agree with Meredith, by the way. Don't let that bitch Dara mess with your head or emotions. That's in the past. Sabrina's not like her."

"What do you suggest?" He recognized the desperate tone in his voice.

Pam shot Meredith a look. He felt that they were

249

communicating on some level. Well, Meredith might not have more than slightly-above-average ESP, but they were sisters. Their connection might not be as strong as his and Pam's, being twins—but it did exist. He knew it.

"Sabrina can come here, but not see you or be tested or treated by you. If she needs more neurological tests, we can send her out for them. And if she's projecting, you know I can easily attach the EEG monitors to her as well as the EKG ones," Pam said.

"That will work," Meredith chimed in. "As far as her being like Dara—I think you're way off base. Do you honestly believe if you broke up with Sabrina she would call someone and accuse you of cheating?"

He focused on his oldest sister. "I hope she's not like Dara. But I haven't known her very long."

"Long enough." Meredith smiled. "You're in love with her, aren't you?"

His mouth dropped open. "In love? "I'm not—"

His sisters were both smiling at him.

"You are," Pam asserted.

He closed his mouth. Was he? In love with Sabrina?

He pushed the thought aside to consider later. "That's not the question now. I like your idea of having Sabrina come without having any interactions with me while she's here."

"I'll put it in motion right away," Meredith said.

He grinned at his sisters. "Thanks, you two. I can always count on you." Just talking with his siblings made him feel one hundred percent better. He stood up, and hugged them one at a time.

"Love ya, Park." Pam said. For a moment, he thought he saw tears in her eyes.

"Love ya," Meredith echoed as she hugged him. When she stepped back, she was smiling broadly. "I think Pam's idea will alleviate the problem of a conflict of interest," she finished.

After they left, he dropped back in his seat.

Was he in love?

He turned the idea over in his mind. He cared about Sabrina. Wanted to be with her all the time. Aside from the sex—which was absolutely the best—he enjoyed her company. Admired her. Could see himself with her for—a long time.

Forever.

It was like that lightning strike years ago. The thought burned into him.

Yeah. He was in love.

CHAPTER XIV

The hours at work dragged. At least today, Sabrina was working a shortened day.

But the disagreement with Parker—plus the mind-blowing sex—had her on edge. She wanted to keep seeing him. But she also wanted to help people. Why was he being so negative?

Her mother had invited her for dinner to celebrate her Aunt Trudy's birthday. Her sister was coming and even her brother was joining them, since he got out of classes early on Thursday. He'd also managed to schedule no classes on Fridays, so she knew he'd be staying over.

When she pulled into the driveway, she saw her brother Joey's car was already there.

Her mother had just started setting the table. Sabrina hugged her, then helped. Aunt Trudy arrived, and then Lindsay entered the house, lugging a pop-up hamper full of laundry.

"The food should be ready in a few minutes," their mom said. "Lindsay, go ahead and throw in a load of wash. Aunt Trudy wanted Italian, so I made lasagna and a salad and garlic bread."

Joey came downstairs and they soon sat down. Joey described the classes he was taking, as they ate, and Lindsay talked about complications on a will she was working on. Aunt Trudy, who was an office manager, spoke about some of the people she worked with. Both Lindsay and Joe had work to do this evening, and Lindsay was going straight to work tomorrow morning. Joey was staying until Sunday, having dinner and going to the movies with local friends while he was in town.

"What's new with you?" her mother asked, focusing on Sabrina.

Sabrina took a breath, then began speaking about the Lightning Center.

Aunt Trudy made a sound of distress when Sabrina started, but after that listened quietly with the others as Sabrina discussed the tests and how they were hoping to help her control her night projections.

"I have helped a few people with my projections, so I don't want to give up projecting entirely," Sabrina concluded. Lindsay nodded, a sympathetic look on her face.

"Oh, Sabrina, you shouldn't let other people know," her aunt said, almost moaning, "even for research."

The time had come to get some answers. Sabrina took a sip of her soda. "Why not?"

Her mom and aunt exchanged glances.

Then her aunt spoke. "I used to—used to—project, sometimes," she began, her voice hesitant as she sat stiffly in her chair. "You know this. It hasn't happened for years. It wasn't nearly as much as you but… I mentioned it to my friend Sharon. Or… the person I thought was my friend. She immediately told one of the popular girls in our gym class, and soon—it was all over

253

the school." She grimaced. "I became—everyone was laughing at me. Everywhere I went for the next few weeks, I heard people laughing, sometimes outright, sometimes behind their hands. Or whispering... that was worse. I heard some of those whispers... she's an idiot... insane... a freak." There were tears in her aunt's eyes. "I wanted to crawl away and die."

"I understand," Sabrina said, sympathetically. "I confided in someone back in school too and they mocked me."

"We told our parents, and they yelled at her and told her to shut up and never speak about it again," Sabrina's mother, Lorraine, added. "Our mother was afraid. She was muttering that it could be the work of the devil."

"How awful," Sabrina said, laying a hand on her aunt's arm.

"Please, please don't tell people about this!" her aunt begged.

"People are different today," Lindsay said, coming to Sabrina's defense. "I don't believe at this point people would make fun of Sabrina—and she's older and can handle it if they do." She sent Sabrina a supportive look.

"That's right," Sabrina said. "And don't forget these are all professionals. Kids did mock me when I was in school—but the people at the Lightning Center are all doctors, social workers and trained professionals. They have seen some very interesting abilities—more unique than mine—people who can predict earthquakes or see ghosts— "

Her mother and Joey looked intrigued. "Ghosts?" Joey asked, helping himself to more garlic bread.

"Yes. There's an older woman there, Lorna, who volunteers. She was struck by lightning as a baby, she was told, and can see spirits of those who have passed. She told me dad and grandpa were nearby the other day." She looked around the table, challenging them to dispute Lorna's observation.

"Did Dad say anything?" her mother asked, a hopeful look on her face.

"Not that she could hear. I didn't hear anything either. Lorna said he was smiling."

Trudy sighed. "These people shouldn't encourage you."

"The policeman I helped to find his friend's daughter, certainly wasn't making fun," Sabrina added. "He was quite grateful."

"Please listen." Her aunt leaned forward earnestly. "No good will come of it if you tell people. For the rest of high school, kids made fun of me and said I was a freak."

"But that was high school—kids do make fun of others, especially those who are a little different," Sabrina pointed out. "They did with me, too. I'm an adult now, and the world is different today." As she said the words, she reflected back on her own experiences. Maybe they weren't quite as terrible as she had thought at the time.

Except, of course, for Devon's horrible reaction. As her boyfriend, he should have been totally supportive. "Besides," she added, "what's ridicule compared to the life of a child? Or the life of anyone, for that matter?"

"It's not *that* different today," her aunt muttered.

"Leave her alone." Her mother stuck up for

255

Sabrina. "I'm beginning to think she's right, Trudy, and we've been keeping this under a rock for too long."

Sabrina turned in her chair to look at her mother.

"That's because she hasn't gone through what I have." Her aunt's voice was more bitter than Sabrina had ever heard it. "Falling in love with Allen, being betrayed—" she sniffed.

Her mom leaned over to give her aunt a swift hug.

"What happened?" Lindsay asked, staring at their aunt.

Aunt Trudy sniffed again, then began. "I was twenty. I met Allen at a party. I was working my first job—I had gone to secretarial school and gotten a good job—and he was about to graduate from college with a degree in political science. He was thinking about grad school or law school." She sniffed again, then grabbed her napkin and wiped her eyes. "I fell in love. Head over heels."

They waited in silence. Even Joey was staring intently at their aunt.

"After we were dating a few months, he introduced me to his widowed mother. He was an only child. One day a few weeks later, he told me she thought there was something strange about me.

"I wanted to come clean, and thought honesty would be important to our relationship. So I told him about—about my projections." Her voice cracked.

"And...?" Sabrina prompted.

"And..." again Trudy sniffled. "He rejected me. Said I was strange, a freak of nature, that something was wrong with me! And if he was going to be a lawyer or have a career as a politician he couldn't be associated with a weirdo like me!" She started to cry.

Sabrina and her mother both went over to hug the distraught woman.

"He missed out on a loving woman," Sabrina's mom said staunchly.

"He's not worth your tears!" Sabrina declared indignantly. "If he could reject you because you're different—because you actually have a power, an ability—then he doesn't deserve you!" As she said the words, it was as if a spotlight suddenly shined in her brain.

He wasn't worth it. He didn't deserve you.

And Sabrina knew, that the same was true of Devon. He had rejected her—and he had not been worth her tears.

She gasped.

Lindsay was staring at her.

"The same is true for me. I deserved someone better than Devon!" she stated.

"I agree," Lindsay seconded. "Anyone who doesn't appreciate you two as you are—well, you're better off without that kind of guy!"

"I agree too," Joey spoke up. "Allen and Devon were definitely jerks."

Trudy wiped her eyes. "You really think so?"

"Yes," Sabrina said, her voice firm. "First-class jerks."

"I—I never married because I never got over him," their aunt confessed.

"Well, you should get over him now," their mother declared, resuming her seat. "I've been telling you he wasn't good enough for you—maybe you'll believe me now? Now that your nieces and nephew are telling you the same thing?"

Trudy stared at her plate. "I really think—he broke up with me because I'm different, I'm—weird. Most people will think the same."

"Not today," Lindsay insisted.

Their aunt looked unconvinced.

"I bet he's not even successful," Lindsay added. "What's his last name?"

"Allen Franks." Aunt Trudy shook her head. "He married about a year later. And he did become a lawyer. He and his wife had three children. The kids are probably grown now."

"I heard a rumor he ended up divorced," their mother said. "You're so much better off without him. I heard he cheated on his wife, and she was supposed to be a nice person. I never told you since the subject of Allen always upset you."

Aunt Trudy looked at their mom. "Really?"

"Really. So much for him being a desirable person." Their mom made a face.

Lindsay grabbed her cellphone from her pocket and began clicking away. "I want to check something." Two minutes later, she said, "Ah ha! I found it. I thought his name sounded familiar." She looked around the room at all of them. "He was disbarred a couple of years ago."

"He was?" Aunt Trudy gasped.

"Yeah. He was caught bribing jurors." Lindsay grimaced. "So, he really isn't such a wonderful person."

"Anyone who could drop you for your abilities is an idiot," Sabrina added, and their brother nodded vigorously.

Their aunt's face was pale. Sabrina wondered if she was rethinking all her reactions from previous years, her dashed hopes and dreams. The bastard had broken her heart—and she had never married. Was she wondering if she had been wrong to cling to her feelings for this man all these years?

She hoped her aunt was adjusting her thoughts, and feelings. It wasn't too late for her to find love!

She didn't voice that thought though. She didn't think Aunt Trudy was ready to hear it.

Their mom switched the conversation and began speaking about a cousin. Later, cleaning up, Sabrina mulled over what she'd learned about her aunt.

She'd been dropped by a boyfriend who didn't believe in her. Just as Sabrina had been dropped by Devon.

But now Sabrina *did* have a boyfriend who believed in her. Who accepted her ability, even if he was afraid it was difficult for her when she used it.

She paused in scooping leftover salad into a container.

Parker believed in her ability. And he was worth fighting for.

Love was worth fighting for.

When she left her mom's house, Sabrina drove directly to Parker's home, less than a mile away.

She'd checked her phone and saw she'd missed a call from him over an hour ago. But she wanted to see him, not just talk on the phone.

The house was dark except for a low glow she

could see through the dining room window. Maybe Parker wasn't home and had left one light on.

She rang the bell. And waited.

After a couple of minutes, she rang it again. No one answered.

Sighing, she headed back to her car.

He might be working late. He could be out with a friend.

Discouraged, she drove home. Once there, she tried calling him. She got voicemail.

Unsure of just how much to say, she simply asked him to call when he had a chance. After a shower, she read for a while, but since he didn't call back, she got into bed and turned off the light.

In the dark, she couldn't keep her thoughts from Parker. He was worth fighting for—but would he want to, or be able to, continue their relationship?

Parker's day had been jam-packed after the conversation with his sisters. He hadn't had a minute to call Sabrina until dinner time. When she didn't answer, he left a brief message, saying he wanted to see her soon, then got back to work.

He was seriously thinking of going straight to Sabrina's home when he finished with notes on the last client around nine. As he shut down his computer, his phone buzzed. It was Mr. Burke.

"Hello, Carl."

"We need help," the man said, "please."

"How can I help you?"

"They want to discharge Vanessa from the

hospital tomorrow. Please, you said you or your sister might be able to help?"

"My sister Pam is a psychiatrist," he said. "I can ask her."

"Can you come over and speak to us? It's really important. The hospital isn't giving us much advice. They keep saying we need to get a psychiatrist to speak to Vanessa. But she doesn't want to talk to anyone. We need help!"

Parker's could hear the anxiety in the man's voice. "Let me see if I can get hold of Pam," he said. "I'll call you back."

He found Pam upstairs, finishing up looking at some test results with Felipe.

"Of course, I'll try to help," she said when he explained the situation.

Within fifteen minutes they'd arrived at the Burke's house. Parker and Pam sat and talked to Vanessa's distraught parents.

They both begged Pam to speak to their daughter, and refer them to someone she thought could help. "You're young and hip," Mr. Burke said. "I think she'd talk to you."

"I can speak to her, maybe get her to open up a little," Pam said. "But then I'd refer her to someone who specializes in teens. I do research, not counseling."

"That would be wonderful," Mrs. Burke said. "The hospital social worker gave us some names but we don't know anything about these people."

By the time Parker and Pam left it was well after ten o'clock. Pam had followed Parker, so she got into her car and left for her condo.

Parker checked his phone. He'd missed a call from Sabrina while they were helping the Burkes.

It sucked that it was so late. Parker drove the short distance to his house down the street, his teeth clenched. He was afraid Sabrina would be sleeping. He didn't want to drop in on her and disturb her rest. She'd mentioned waking up early on Friday because of something going on at the library. But he thought she'd said she might be getting out of work early.

Once inside his house, he dashed up to his home office and checked his office schedule on the shared drive. He had morning meetings, but the afternoon was free.

He was going to go over and talk to Sabrina if he had to haul her out of the library.

⁕──────⁕

Sabrina set the alarm and was up earlier than usual that Friday. Today the library's big, used book sale started, and she had to be at work early.

All through her shower and quick breakfast, she thought about Parker and how they could continue seeing each other. She was not about to give up on a relationship with the best man she'd ever met. A man who knew and accepted her for what she was. Even though he had his own doubts.

And she was going to do her best to remove those uncertainties.

She thought about and rejected several scenarios. Obviously, he couldn't leave his job—The Center was his brainchild, his life's work. But, she wondered, could there be other such places? If there were, she could go to another research facility. Somewhere she could get help and be separate from Parker. She would ask him immediately.

As far as his doubts about her—she would have to try to convince him she was reliable. Could his worries have something to do with his former girlfriend?

She arrived at work by eight fifteen, and by nine o'clock when they opened, the library instantly became flooded with people. There were lots of people heading down to the large conference room in the basement where the books were displayed. There were also the usual college students with papers to research. Sabrina helped find information on everything from tornadoes to the Alamo. When it was her turn to supervise the book sale, she was able to recommend some of her favorite authors to one woman.

She had silenced her phone at work, but when there was a lull she checked it. Parker had texted. *I want to see you. Can we get together later?*

She replied *Yes!* before getting back to work. After that, she kept her phone in the pocket of her pants so she could feel the vibrations when he texted back.

Less than ten minutes later he did, asking if he could come over around one o'clock.

She texted that she was working until two. She wanted to see him as soon as possible, so she suggested he meet her at her condo at a quarter after two.

His response was swift. *Okay!*

She couldn't wait to get home. When she left the library, she drove as fast as she safely could on the rural county road to get to her apartment.

Parker's car was there when she pulled up.

He was out of his jeep before she had turned off her car. He raced over to her. "Sabrina!"

She jumped out, slamming the door behind her, and ran to meet him. He grabbed her and pulled her into a tight embrace.

"Parker," she whispered into his chest.

"God, Sabrina, I missed you."

She looked up at his face. "After only a day and a half?"

"Yes." He kissed her, hard.

"Let's go inside." She disentangled herself and led the way into her condo.

Once they'd shrugged out of their coats, she took Parker's hand and steered him to the couch, where they both dropped down.

"Parker, I—"

"Sabrina—" he started at the same time.

"I want to say something." She held up her hand. "Parker, I want a relationship with you. And I would never expect you to leave The Lightning Center, the achievement you've worked so hard for. So I was thinking, if there's another facility like it, I could go there."

He shook his head. "There isn't."

Disappointment hit her hard, like a punch. She'd been counting on a similar place being out there. "Oh."

"But there is a way." He gripped her hand, his warm one around her colder one. "My sisters suggested I excuse myself from all of your treatments, tests, projections—whatever. That way we won't be in a clinical relationship."

Relief and happiness bubbled up in her. "That will work," she said enthusiastically.

He nodded. "Yes. I think it's a great idea." He raised her hand and kissed it.

"Now, as far as us…" she regarded him. "I know you have some—concerns about me. I can't help thinking it has to do with your former girlfriend." Now she clutched his hand tighter. "Why don't you tell me about her?"

"I guess you, of everyone, have a right to know." He gave a sigh, and dropped her hand. Rising, he began to pace.

"I met Dara in medical school. In our third year, we had a lot of the same classes and we started to date. She was fun to be with, and we seemed to like the same kind of things—music, travel. I thought she shared my hopes to help people, my visions." He frowned.

"At the end of the spring semester, we'd gotten together one night to study for our final exams. She announced she wanted to join her uncle's prestigious—and prosperous—dermatology practice, and she wanted me to also. I protested, reminding her that I wanted to study neurology, and start The Lightning Center." He paced away from her.

Sabrina waited.

He turned to face her again. "She started talking about how much money we could make when her uncle retired. I realized she was not the person I thought she was. She assumed I'd give up my dreams for her. We had a huge fight, and I broke it off. When I left her apartment, she was screaming at me. All I knew was that I was glad I'd learned the truth about her character."

"She sounds like a selfish person," Sabrina said.

"And more concerned about money than helping people, or your dreams."

"Yes. Only I hadn't seen that aspect of her previously. But—there's more. Two days later we had an exam in a class we both took. Afterwards, she called the professor and accused me of cheating on the final. She said that I used telepathy to read the professor's mind during the test to find the answers!"

Sabrina gasped. "What?"

He dropped down beside her on the couch. She could clearly see the agitation in his face, his mouth turned down, his brow furrowed. She wanted to hug him, but knew he wanted to get out the story first.

His phone rang. Parker ignored it, and Sabrina was glad. It was important for them to talk.

"It was a big blow," he said tersely. "Me, cheating? I always got A's because I studied hard. I never used my ability for any nefarious purpose. Never cheated on a test!"

"I know you wouldn't," she declared.

"There was an uproar. I was horrified," he continued. " But after several turbulent days, the tables turned on Dara. No one believed I could possibly read people's minds. So skepticism saved me from any punitive actions. And besides, she had no proof. In the end she looked like a lunatic, and people though she was just being a bitch because we'd broken up."

"She was." Sabrina leaned forward and squeezed his hand. "What happened to her?" She didn't even want to say that woman's name.

"She dropped out of medical school the following semester. The last I heard, Dara had taken a job teaching first aid." He stared at Sabrina. "You know how sometimes I get these flashes—these thoughts—from someone I know? Like when I got the flash from my friend Colin? Well, right before I found out about Vanessa, I got a flash from Dara, for the first time in years."

"That's weird."

"I know, and I pushed her out of my mind. But it brought up the whole thing all over again." He ran his other hand through his hair.

"I'm glad you told me," she said solemnly. "Parker, we should share these things."

"I know. Because I care—"

His phone rang again, and this time, hers buzzed too.

Shit. Just when he was about to say something significant.

He stopped. "Maybe something's going on—"

"Go ahead and answer it." As much as she didn't want an interruption, the fact that both their phones were ringing simultaneously gave her an uneasy feeling.

He slid his out of his pocket. "It's Pam. And before her it was Kyle."

Uh oh. She peeked at hers. "Meredith called me at the same time. They must want to get hold of us both." Her stomach tightened. Something was wrong.

Parker tapped his phone. A moment later he spoke. "Pam? What's going on—"

His eyes widened, and then he met Sabrina's eyes.

"There's an emergency. Kyle needs you."

CHAPTER XV

Parker stared at the woman he loved, his insides icing over.

"Pam says Kyle has been trying to reach me. There's been another kidnapping he needs help with. Not a non-custodial parent—it's more serious than that. And this time, the FBI is also involved."

"The FBI?"

"Yeah. Hold on, Pam, Sabrina's with me." He spoke into the phone, then turned back to Sabrina and focused on her. "They want your help. It's the daughter of a New Jersey Congressman."

"Of course," she said, getting up from the couch.

"She said yes," Parker told his twin. "But Pam—"

"Listen, Park, we have a lot to do." Pam's voice came through the phone in a rush. "I have to call Kyle back and tell him to come here. Tell Sabrina there will be two federal agents with him. And Park—" she stopped.

"Yeah?"

"Remember that evil I told you I dreamed about? That Sabrina would run into?"

He didn't like where this was going. "Yeah, I remember."

"This is it. I know it. She's going to need my support. Even Meredith's."

And not his? He tightened his hand on his cellphone. "Pam—"

"Can you get her here right away? I'll call Merry and Neal's here, so I'm sure he'll help."

He looked at Sabrina, standing up beside him. "Can you get ready quickly?" he whispered.

"Yes." She ran into her bedroom.

He turned his attention back to Pam. "We'll be there as soon as we can." Frustration gave an edge to his voice. "I know this could be life or death, but what lousy timing. Sabrina and I were just having a serious conversation."

"Glad to hear about the conversation. I'm sure it will keep til later. Let me speak to Meredith before she leaves the building. Thank Sabrina for us." She hung up.

Less than ten minutes later they were headed to The Lightning Center in Parker's car. Sabrina had brought her own iPod, telling him she wanted the music it contained. As he turned out of Sabrina's development, he placed his hand on hers. "I'm sorry we didn't finish our discussion," he said.

"I am, too." She angled her body to look at him. "We'll talk after this session."

He brought her hand to his lips and kissed it gently. *I love you.* He heard the words in his head. He opened his mouth, but hesitated. He wasn't quite ready to say them out loud.

"I hope I can help." Sabrina bit her lip.

"If anyone can, you can," he affirmed.

She smiled. "You have so much confidence in me. I hope I live up to it."

"Always. You're a wonderful person, Sabrina, and I'm not just talking about your ability." He left it at that. There would be tine to talk afterwards. He hoped.

They arrived at The Center a few minutes later. Since it was Friday afternoon, he expected few people to be there. They went upstairs, and he found Neal in the computer room, and Pam bustling about the living room area where Sabrina usually projected. She'd put out the white candle.

Alicia appeared from the hall doorway. "I'd like to help."

Pam, Parker and Sabrina turned to her.

"Pam said she was worried about evil she sensed." Alicia held up some kind of leaves. "My sister is Wiccan, and has taught me some spells. I'd like to do a protection spell around Sabrina, to ward off evil."

"Thank you. I appreciate that," Sabrina said, then turned to Pam. "What evil?" She could smell the distinct but appealing scent of basil.

"I had a dream," Pam confessed, looking uncomfortable. "That you were projecting, and ran into something evil."

"I'll deal with it," Sabrina asserted.

"I'll be with you," Pam said. "For support. And to add my psychic strength to yours."

"Let me have a minute to myself," Sabrina said. "It's been an emotional couple of days, and I'd like to clear my head."

"Of course." Pam inclined her head, and Parker followed her out into the hall.

As they did, they heard voices downstairs.

"I'll bring the police up here," Neal said, and scooted to the stairs.

Parker turned to Pam.

"I want to help—"

"No, you can't." She shook her head. "Remember, we said you shouldn't be involved with her treatments, of any kind. She'll have my psychic energy to help her."

No. He was not going to stand by while Sabrina dealt with whatever evil Pam had foreseen.

"Dammit, Pam, this is serious. You sensed evil. This could be dangerous for all we know. We don't know what kind of people—what kind of energy—could be out there."

"But—"

"No way I'm stepping aside." He set his mouth in a hard line. "Sabrina is more important to me than anything else." He took a deep breath. "If necessary, I'll step aside from The Center. She's the most important thing in my life."

CHAPTER XVI

Sabrina sat, trying to think of nothing, trying to relax her muscles. The day had turned gray, and gloomy light filtered in through the windows. Alicia moved quietly around the room. She was waving the basil around, and murmuring softly.

Sabrina gathered that the info that Alicia's sister was Wiccan had been a surprise to everyone at the Center. Not that anyone thought badly about it—everyone here was respectful, and today it was well-accepted as a religion. If Alicia could help in any way, she was grateful.

She wasn't too worried about Pam's dream. She'd met evil people before—like when she'd found the little girl whose mother had taken her away. With Pam's protection, she was sure everything would be fine.

If she could find the girl. She tried not to think of Clarisse.

She heard voices, and Pam peeked in. "Can we start?"

Sabrina nodded.

Pam entered, and behind her was Meredith. "Meredith has her own power. Not ESP, but the power of compassion. I believe she'll be a help."

272

Parker entered. Sabrina raised her eyebrows. "I thought—"

"I'm here to help," Parker said firmly, taking a nearby chair. "Nothing will stop me."

Sabrina noticed the challenging look that passed between him and Pam, then Meredith.

Meredith closed the blinds, then she and Pam also took seats. Pam sat closest to Sabrina, right next to the couch.

"Neal is in the computer room, with Kyle. There are two agents who will wait in the conference room downstairs for any results. We don't want too many people crowding the psychic pathways up here," Pam said.

"I'm joining Neal." Alicia moved out of the corner where she'd been doing who-knows-what. and exited the room, shutting the door behind her.

Pam handed her a photo of the girl, then attached the monitors.

"In case these details help—she was kidnapped while at the mall with her mom and two of her friends," Pamela said. "She—Kayleigh—takes dance and violin lessons and also likes to play soccer."

After watching the Avengers movie again with Parker last week, Sabrina had added the theme music, played over and over, and other numbers from the movie to her iPod. Somehow, the music made her feel strong. And she suspected she was going to need that strength.

Sabrina mentally prepared to commence her search. *You can do this*.

CHAPTER XVII

Sabrina lay back on the couch, smelling the sweet scent of the vanilla candle as well as he underlying basil. She heard the beginning strains of the Avengers theme music. She clutched the photo of the girl in her right hand.

Pam leaned forward and grasped her left hand. Immediately, warmth flowed through her hand and wove its way through her body. She could feel Pam's positive energy.

She glanced at Parker, sitting tensely nearby; and Meredith, also sitting close. Calming waves seemed to move through the room. Perhaps Meredith did have some kind of ability.

"I'm ready." She shut her eyes, willing her body to relax, seeing the girl's photo in her mind's eye.

She pushed herself upwards, lifting to the ceiling. She was through the roof, staring down at The Lightning Center building, the cars in the parking lot.

Slowly she turned. The wind buffeted her as she began to move towards Route 80. She was heading east.

"I'm on Route 80," she murmured. "I'm going east. I have a way to go, I think."

She moved past the Roxbury and Mt. Arlington

exits. She flew over the road, seeing light traffic below. The day was gray and getting darker, and the wind up here was strong. It almost seemed to push her in the direction she wanted to go. "I'm in Parsippany," she said as she recognized exits nearby. "I'm—yes, I'm turning to get on Route 287. North," she added.

She watched the road below her. She was moving swiftly, going through Boonton.

"I'm getting off the highway, onto Rt. 202," she said. After a moment, she added, "I seem to be leaving Boonton. I'm not sure where I am. It's unfamiliar."

She heard a voice nearby murmur something, too low for her to catch, or even be sure who it was.

She scanned the ground for landmarks as she moved. It was a residential area, where clusters of houses met forested areas. Finally, she saw something.

"I can see train tracks," she told the others. "And, I see a firehouse."

"Could you be in Montville?" Pamela asked quietly.

"I don't see any signs, but—maybe that's where I am. I don't know this area," she confessed. "Wait." She could see a street sign on the left. She was turning there. "I'm on Jackson Valley Road. I'm going north."

"You're doing great," Parker whispered.

She continued to move in that direction. Then she felt herself veering off. "I'm on a side street. There's no street sign. I don't know the name."

"That's okay," Meredith soothed.

Sabrina continued further into a thickly wooded area. She was going up a driveway. "I'm approaching a house."

The house she was nearing was a ranch, long and sprawling, on level ground. "It's a one-story home surrounded by trees," she said. "A ranch in the shape of the letter "C" on its side. Spanish style, judging from the tile work around the door and windows." A strange shimmer surrounded the house. "There's— something odd. There's kind of a circle surrounding the house."

"Can you describe it?" Parker's voice was hushed.

She felt herself lowering closer to the ground. "It's wispy, like fog, but shimmering. I'm going to look in the windows to see if I can find the girl." She moved towards the house.

She approached the shimmering area and started to go through—when she was forcefully bounced back.

"What?" she screeched.

"What is it?" Parker sounded far away.

"I don't know. I've never felt anything like it. It was like I got a shock from static electricity. This fog is not letting me go further." She frowned. "It's like— a force field of some kind. A barrier." She put out her hand, and slowly moved forward.

This time, expecting the rebound, she wasn't so shocked. Her hand stopped at the wall of fog as if it was solid. She gave it a push.

"I can't get through!" she cried. She could feel desperation welling up in her. "I'm pushing and pushing and it won't let me go through. And I see it's at the top of the house, too," she added, glancing up. "I can't drop in."

"You need help." Parker's voice was louder now. A chair scraped nearby, coming closer. And then, she felt his hand on her right one.

A jolt of electricity zoomed through her. It was

powerful, and felt as strong as the lightning that had hit her so long ago.

"It could be some kind of protective spell," Pam said. "Sabrina, we'll give you our psychic strength, and help you get through it."

For a moment, Sabrina felt a shot of panic. Would she be able to get through? Then she heard Meredith's calm voice.

"I'm here. We can do this, Sabrina."

Sabrina approached the mist, slower this time. "I'm going to try to get through the barrier now." She hovered for a minute. She could see lights on in several windows, glowing through the dark afternoon. The light outside was fading. She concentrated, hearing the music of The Avengers in the background, smelling the sweet vanilla and basil scents. She clenched her teeth.

Instead of the scents and sounds around her, she narrowed her focus to her body. She felt the energy coursing through her, especially Parker's electric sizzle. Like they were one. The sensation was so strong she could feel it in every muscle.

And then she was concentrating on the wall in front of her.

"Here we go," Sabrina whispered.

She stuck out both her hands, and started to push through the fog.

It resisted for a second. Then, as their combined energy flowed through her, she propelled herself forward. The protective circle began to disintegrate in front of her eyes. Slowly, with the strength of the others behind her, she moved forward.

"I'm—getting through—slowly," she gasped. She

continued to push through the mass. She could feel the snap and crackle of their energies, adding intense power to her own. With one last thrust, she broke through the barrier, and floated over clear ground only yards from the house. "I'm through!" she whispered triumphantly.

"Great." It was Parker again.

"Do you still need our strength?" asked Pam.

"I probably will to get back," Sabrina told them. Her heart was pounding as she drew closer to the house. She felt a lessening of their combined energies, as if they had drawn back.

"Let me see what's up." She approached a large bay window—probably the living room, she guessed. "The living room looks empty." She moved past the front door to the other side. "So does the dining room—there's no furniture in here at all." She slowly circled the building. "Wait—here's a family room. There's someone here, burning something—it smells like incense."

"Be careful. It may be the person who cast the spell," Pam whispered.

The woman, with long, dark hair, was bent over something. "Yes... I'm getting negative vibes from her," Sabrina murmured. She backed away, then continued around. "There's a bedroom. Empty. Here's another." She frowned. A man lay on the bed.

As she observed him, and she drew closer, a horrible sensation smacked her in the head. It was worse than the barrier she'd already encountered. "Oh no!"

"Sabrina! Are you alright?" Parker sounded a million miles away.

278

Coldness enveloped her, from her head to her toes. "It's like the wall, but there's nothing I can see. It's a feeling of pure evil," she said. "This must be what Pam was talking about. This man is bad. Very bad. There are vibrations coming off him that are nasty."

"You should come back now," Parker said emphatically.

"The man seems to be napping." She continued on, smoothly and quietly, hoping no one could sense her own presence or the combined energy of those helping her. Only Parker had ever sensed her inner self during a projection, but the dread welling up inside of her made her cautious. She didn't want to take any chances.

"Here's another bedroom—wait. There's a girl here." She peered into the window. A dark-haired girl was slumped in a corner. "She's sleeping, or maybe crying, in a light blue room. She's looking up. Yes, that's Kayleigh." Relief coursed through her. She pulled herself up so she could ascertain its position. "I'm above the room now. If you were coming up the driveway, it's on the left side of the house, towards the back."

"Good. You've done great," Parker said. She could feel his grip tighten. "C'mon back now."

"I'm sure you've given us enough to go on, Sabrina," Pam added.

A feeling of excitement shot through her. "Do you think they can find her?"

"Yes." That was Meredith's voice.

"Okay." Sabrina rose up. Once again the mass of glittering fog was apparent. "I may need help to get through the barrier again."

"You got it," Pam said.

Her hands outstretched, Sabrina cautiously went forward again, conscious of the energy the others were sharing with her. Especially Parker's. They were all at her back, psychically, pushing her forward. Parker's hand held hers, hard. She felt something else in his hold—something she couldn't stop to define now, but it was more than his psychic energy.

"Come back to us," he urged.

Then, she saw movement below. The dark-haired woman came running out of the house, shouting and waving her hands. Sabrina couldn't hear what she was saying. The psychic wall seemed to shimmy.

Sabrina rushed through it, pushing with all her might. "Help me!" she cried. "I think the woman knows I'm here!"

"I'm here now too," Neal said.

"We're all here!" Parker declared.

Sabrina could actually feel the renewed energy, especially Parker's, the blast and strength of it running through her. She was able to discern the distinct vibrations of each person. Parker's was strongest, like a ray of light.

Their combined strength was enough to push her through the protective shield, out and above it. "I'm away from the house." She hovered for only a second, then turned and sped away.

"If they know I've been here, they may try to move the girl," she gasped. She moved over the narrow road, back onto a wider one. "I'm coming back." She suddenly felt drained, more than usual, and kept her eyes on the road as she followed its twists and turns.

"There's the fire house—and the train tracks—I'm on the county road now". And she could see the town of Boonton. "I'm approaching Rt. 287."

Once she was floating over the highway, she felt herself sagging. She was zapped of energy.

"I hope I have enough energy to get home," she muttered.

"You will." Once again, she heard Parker's voice, felt his hand squeeze her own, and a burst of energy sped through her.

With the extra energy pulsating through her body, she flew over Route 287, turned onto Route 80 going west, and was soon hovering above The Lightning Center. She plunged downwards, back through the roof, the ceiling, and saw herself on the couch. Parker was sitting on the floor beside her, bent towards her, his hand on hers. Behind him sat Pam, her hand on Parker's back; and Meredith sat behind her sister, touching her. Neal had a hand on Meredith's shoulder.

Sabrina felt herself being sucked back into her body, and gave a long, shuddering sigh. "I'm back."

Opening her eyes, she met Parker's gaze in the dim room, and struggled to sit up.

"Easy, take it easy," he said, his hand cupping her arm to support her.

And then everything went black.

CHAPTER XVIII

His heart stuttered when Sabrina collapsed. Parker caught her, and laid her back on the couch. He quickly took her pulse.

"Her pulse is rapid, but not horrible," he reported to the others who converged to surround them. "I think she fainted." He smoothed her thick hair back from her face. Her breathing was faster than he liked.

"I'll get the blood pressure machine." Pam darted to the corner where it was, then returned and placed the cuff on Sabrina's upper arm. Parker held his breath. After a minute, he saw that her blood pressure was lower than normal but not dangerously so. He let out a long breath.

"She's ok, it's just a little low," Pam said. She removed the other monitors on Sabrina's body and head.

"With what she's been through, it's no wonder," Meredith said.

"She could probably use a glass of brandy," Neal said. "I can go up the road to the liquor store if you want."

"That's probably a good idea," Parker agreed. Even an MD knew that some old-fashioned remedies could help.

"I'll go speak to Kyle," Pam murmured, and left the room with Neal.

"I'll get a towel with cold water," Meredith said, and scooted out too.

Parker sat beside Sabrina, holding her hand. "It's okay, sweetheart," he said. "You're safe here. Everything went well."

He waited a minute or two. She didn't stir, and worry pinged inside him. "Sabrina," he said. "Please come back to me."

Meredith re-entered the room. "Here." She thrust a towel at him. One end was cool and wet.

He smoothed it on Sabrina's forehead. His oldest sister left the room again, giving them some space.

He waited. Sabrina's breathing had slowed, but she didn't stir, even with the wet cloth.

"Sabrina, I love you." The words spilled out.

Her eyes popped open. "You love me?" she squeaked, and struggled to sit up.

Relief cascaded through him. "Are you alright? Do you feel okay?" He supported her as she sat up.

"I'm okay," she said breathlessly. "You love me?'

He paused, and realized he'd just laid his heart on the line. "I do." He brought her hand to his lips, and kissed it. "I love you, Sabrina. When you were projecting I was scared. Scared that whatever evil was in that house would be dangerous for you."

"I'm alright." She brought their joined hands to her mouth, and kissed his. "Oh, Parker." Her smile was like a beam of sunshine. "I love you too!"

He gathered her into his arms and kissed her, hard. Happiness shot through him like a lightning bolt.

283

"You're more important to me than the center, than anything," he confessed, gazing into her eyes. "I'm never letting you go."

She brought his head down until their lips were inches apart. "That sounds perfect to me," she whispered, and kissed him.

EPILOGUE

Sabrina placed the last of the books on the appropriate shelf, then stood back.

Deep satisfaction swirled in her. The Lightning Center's library was ready.

She'd left her job at the county to be the new director of TLC's Library of Psychic Research, right here in the building where so much had happened. She'd catalogued and arranged all their media the last three weeks, then added more journals, books and even films she'd found. The expanded library would be put to good use by their growing number of researchers, their clients, and even open, by appointment, to members of the general public who wanted information.

"That's it," she said to their interns, Madison and Felipe, who'd been working with her today.

Madison dusted off her hands. "That's great. It's starting to snow, so I think I'll leave now."

Sabrina glanced out the window. It was a Friday early in December, and she could see snowflakes beginning to meander down. The clock on the wall said 12:15, so the staff would be leaving soon. "Have a good weekend," she said to the interns.

"You too," they both chorused, and left the room.

Sabrina moved to her desk. A photo of her with

Parker, taken in mid-October, perched there. She'd never been so happy. She'd moved in with him in November, and their days were filled with rewarding work, and their nights with love. He was wonderful to her, always considerate, always caring. And she tried to show him every day how much she loved him by doing things to make him happy, too.

Near her desk was a framed certificate of thanks from Congressman Bennett, whose daughter had been rescued the day she'd projected. The kidnappers—a man with a long track record of crimes and his cohort, a woman who was almost as bad—were in jail. The woman had admitted to using dark arts to try to keep them from being found, and had struck a plea deal. The man was awaiting trial.

The opening of the door had Sabrina turning. Parker strode in, grinning.

"Do you like your new space?"

"I love it." She walked over to meet him, and slid her arms around his waist. "I love you."

"I love you too." He moved back, grabbing her hand. "C'mon, I want to show you something."

She let him lead her. In the hallway they passed Alicia with Ashish Singh and Courtney Wallenberg, their two newest researchers. They'd gotten enough grant money to hire two people. They were all on their way out, and called goodbyes.

They went upstairs. Earlier Neal, Meredith, Tanya and Pam had left the building, so she and Parker were alone up here. He brought her to the living room area, then shut the door.

"This is where I first told you I loved you," he said, leading her to the center of the room.

"I'll never forget it. It brought me back to consciousness," she said, smiling up at him. "I heard your words very distinctly."

"So it seems appropriate—" he hesitated. He took her hand.

Her heart began to hammer.

"Yes?" she whispered.

He dropped dramatically to one knee. "Sabrina, I love you. I always will. This feeling between us—it's electric."

"Yes, it is." Her hand trembled.

"Will you make me the happiest man on earth? Will you marry me?"

"Yes!" she shouted. She flung herself into his arms and they toppled to the carpeted floor.

He kissed her soundly. "I love you. I love you."

"I love you," she echoed, kissing him back. She could swear she was floating on air, just like she did when she projected. Only this was a thousand times better.

The love that flowed between them was more powerful than lightning.

THE END

PREVIEW OF
LIGHTNING STRIKES AGAIN

Book 2 in the LIGHTNING STRIKES SERIES

CHAPTER I

Meredith Costigan tried not to think about the fact that her last "assigned" discussion involving The Lightning Center had not been a success. Today she would be talking to Richard Belton, a prospective employee, not to someone who was questioned their mission. She lifted her head, pasting a confident smile on her face as she selected a table in the coffee shop.

At ten thirty in the morning, the coffeeshop wasn't too busy, so they should be able to have a private talk. Silverware clinked and voices echoed through the large room.

Her goal was to convince Richard that the research he could do at The Lightning Center would be more of what he wanted to accomplish, without all the paper-pushing and politics of a university. And that their facilities were just as good—or better.

A dark-haired man entered the coffeeshop. Meredith recognized Dr. Richard Belton immediately from his photo on the university's website.

He was as tall as her brother Parker, who stood 6 feet 2 inches. His hair was brown and slightly wavy. He scanned the room.

She stood up. "Dr. Belton?" She waved him over.

He strode to her table. "I'm Meredith Costigan," she introduced herself, and they shook hands. "It's a pleasure to meet you."

His hand was large, and hers felt surprising feminine against his rougher palm. A frisson of awareness shot through her.

"Ms—I mean, Dr. Costigan. The pleasure is all mine." He smiled, and she got the feeling his words were sincere.

"You don't have to be formal. Meredith is fine. Please sit down. Can I get you coffee?"

"Allow me."

"No, this meeting was my idea. I insist."

He smiled again. "Alright. Just black. And please call me Richard."

She went to get him his coffee and her own with milk and sweetener. When she returned, he was sitting in a relaxed position.

She wished she could feel more relaxed. She'd been keyed up before he entered the building, but now as she sat facing him, she was super aware of this handsome man. And the fact that her heart rate had increased.

Meredith sat, smoothing the skirt of her medium-weight, royal blue colored suit. She wanted to look professional, and back home in New Jersey, it was cold and snowy. So she hadn't wanted to lug out her summer clothes yet. But here in Florida in February, while not exactly hot, the weather was well into the 60s and humid.

She placed her business card on the table as Richard sipped his coffee. The printed card had her name, contact info, and the logo of The Lightning Center in the corner.

"Here's my card, so we can touch base easily," she said.

He took it and studied it for a few moments. The professional photos on his website didn't do him justice, she thought. He was more masculine-looking than she'd expected. He appeared to work out regularly, with muscles evident beneath the simple light blue long-sleeved shirt he wore.

He raised his eyes to meet hers, and again awareness shot through her.

Something she didn't want to feel right now.

"I've read about your Center, and the paranormal research you've been doing," he said. "It's fascinating. Now, tell me—how can I help you?"

"Thank you for agreeing to see me. I know your schedule is busy," she began. "I have a specific reason for coming to Florida." She leaned forward slightly in her chair, trying her best not to appear anxious. "We at The Lightning Center would like to offer you a job."

His eyebrows rose. "A job?"

"Yes." She smiled. "I know you are doing a lot of research here. We offer you the opportunity to do the research you want to, on lightning, through The Lightning Center. There is also the possibility you could consult at the state university. My brother, Parker, has several contacts there. We would like you to coordinate with our studies about which kinds of lightning are more likely to strike people; and which are more likely to develop abilities in people who were struck."

He looked surprised. "Tell me more."

"We will provide you with state-of-the-art equipment, and it's possible that the university can provide you with interns to help with your projects and research. You will have the facilities you want."

"Florida has the most lightning strikes of any state," he said slowly, appearing to mull over what she'd said. "New Jersey doesn't have nearly as many."

"But we do have our share. And that is why," she said emphatically, "I am authorized to offer you the following salary…"

As she named the figure, his eyes grew wide.

The amount they were offering was very generous. She knew for a fact it was more than he made at the university, since public universities had to make that information available. She knew, too, that the college here was not particularly prestigious and while the equipment was supposed to be good, he could accomplish far more working with them.

She voiced her thought. "You can accomplish a lot of ground-breaking research working for us. We've read some of your recent papers which are on line; but we believe you'd have more control over what you research in addition to our requests."

He leaned on the table.

"This salary is generous," he said. "Enough to make me consider it."

"You will even have time for your photography, I'm positive. I've seen your award-winning photos on your website. Those photos are stunning," she added.

"Thank you." She could see he swallowed. "It is tempting. I will consider your offer."

At least he hadn't turned her down.

"Research on whatever aspect of lightning I want?" He drank more coffee.

She sipped hers. "Yes, as long as you can work on our requested studies too."

There was a moment of silence.

"Tell me some more about The Lightning Center," he said abruptly.

Meredith relaxed into her chair. This was the easy part. She had spoken to supporters and groups about the center countless times, since it was dear to her family's hearts.

"The Lightning Center was a long—held dream of my father and brother's," she started. "Years ago, my brother and sister—they're twins—were struck by lightning. They developed some extraordinary abilities—more than just the average communication between twins. My brother and father were eager to research and explore the phenomena of people who were struck by lightning and developed abilities such as ESP. We officially opened The Lightning Center over three years ago with this goal, and it's grown more rapidly than we anticipated. We have doctors like my brother, my father and sister; psychologists; nurses; and social workers like myself all doing research and helping people to control and learn from their abilities."

She leaned forward slightly. "I've read your bio on your website. We know you were struck by lightning, too."

He nodded. "When I was twelve. I was always interested in the weather, but one day I was walking home from school with a friend, and out of nowhere, I was struck. The next thing I knew I was lying on the ground and EMTs were around me."

"Is that when you decided to go into meteorology?" she asked.

"Exactly. I decided I wanted to specialize in studying lightning after that incident." He took a breath. "Your center sounds quite impressive," he stated. "But…"

"But…?" she questioned, leaning forward further. She caught a whiff of his aftershave, fresh and woodsy.

"But… I really do like what I'm doing here." He sat back and folded his arms.

"You can do whatever research you want working with us," she urged. "In addition to ours. And, it's possible our studies could enhance your research. Plus," she added, pulling out what she felt was her winning card, even though it was early in the game, "we know you're originally from Oradell, New Jersey. You'll be much closer to your family working for us." She gave him a big smile.

"That is true," he said, thoughtfully. He paused.

Please, please, she thought. It was important to the Center that they have a solid scientist on board for this lightning research. Someone known in the field. It could add so much to their knowledge—not to mention the prestige. They were careful about hiring people with solid reputations and credentials; he was no exception.

And it was important to her, very important, that she be the one to successfully bring Richard on board.

"Well," he leaned back. "I will definitely consider this offer. It's too generous not to. By the way," he said, switching gears, "where do you get your funding?"

"That's a good question. My father and grandfather put a lot of money away early on for this center. And, we have several companies and private investors—including a billionaire who wishes to remain nameless, who was struck by lightning. We also have obtained quite a few grants for our research on mental telepathy and other abilities. Several universities are following our studies closely."

"And have you made any interesting discoveries?" he challenged.

"Yes." She said it proudly.

"For instance…?" he probed.

"For instance, we are working with a young woman who was doing astral projections. She could deliberately do it during the day; but at night she was projecting when she didn't want to, unable to control it," Meredith described. "We're helping her control her ability while improving it." The woman was her future sister-in-law Sabrina, who was engaged to Parker.

"Fascinating." The way he said it reminded her of Mr. Spock in the original Star Trek reruns.

"Yes, it is," she agreed. "We're finding a great deal of variety in the abilities people have acquired after being struck by lightning. They've developed ESP, pre-cognitive dreams, the ability to predict earthquakes—it is fascinating, and I'm proud to be a part of it."

"It does sound intriguing," he said, and she caught a wistful note in his voice. "But I really do like my job here"

"I believe you would like working with us just as much," Meredith stated in a firm tone. "Plus, our building has a flat roof." She turned the iPad around so he could observe the photo of their center. She also slid a folder out of the protective case, placing it in front of him.

"The roof is perfect for placing your equipment. We also have some land in the back. We can finish clearing it, and you can use it to set up some

295

equipment there, too, if you wish," she continued enthusiastically. "We can add a storage shed there too. We've already spoken to the zoning office in town. Besides, Parker said that the University has space you can use for any really large equipment if you do some consulting for them." She sent him a smile.

After much practicing, she had developed better than average ESP. She could sense now that he was torn—between the familiar and comfortable, and the exciting but unknown. He'd have to pack up and move, which was always a hassle. But she wouldn't think about any negatives. And she tried not to dwell on how handsome he looked sitting across from her.

She changed tactics, hoping a little flattery would help. "I've seen your photographs on your website. They're wonderful," she said sincerely. "Some of the best I've ever seen of lightning."

"Thank you. I've won a few awards."

"I'm not surprised." She smiled again. "You'd have plenty of opportunities to continue your photography, along with your research. We offer you a very flexible schedule." She pushed the folder over to him.

"As long as you put in approximately thirty-five hours a week—we are open to a flexible schedule. We would require meetings—probably once a week, unless something urgent came up. Again, we would work around your preferred schedule."

He tapped his finger on the table.

"Why me?" he asked.

That was easy. "You're one of the foremost researchers on the meteorology of lightning. We're the premier researchers on the effects of lightning on people—especially the unusual effects, although we're conducted some basic studies of medical effects too," she said. She lifted her cup and sipped some of her sweet brew. "And the fact that you were struck by lightning will probably enhance our unusual research."

"Did you consider Anderson or Paulus?" he asked, mentioning two well-known scientists in the field.

"Anderson is getting ready to retire," she answered, glad her family had looked into a number of people and she could answer this question. "He's in his sixties. Paulus has been in New Mexico for 20 some odd years. He has a family and seems pretty ensconced there. You have only been here for four years. We were hoping you might want to come back to New Jersey."

He didn't answer, just regarded her.

"I don't know," he said. "When you set up this meeting with me, I thought you wanted to discuss some specific research or ask me some questions. I never considered you'd offer me a job."

"Well, please consider it," she urged. "You'd be working on cutting-edge research with us." She knew many less well-known scientists would be beating a path to their door looking for work if they knew it was available. But they wanted him.

Her brother Parker had felt especially that with his credentials, Richard was perfect for the job.

She asked in a congenial voice, "do you have any other questions?"

He picked up the folder, leafing through the sheaf of papers inside. Then his eyes met hers, and she felt that little zing of alertness again.

It wasn't just that he was an attractive man. There was something else there—some current, *some spark,* that seemed to ping between them.

297

He stared at her a moment. "It's a generous offer."

She knew they were open to negotiate further, if he wanted more days off or something similar. But she wanted to reserve that for later. She knew she was a good negotiator—that's why they sent her on these kinds of meetings. She usually got what they wanted.

Except, of course, for one time…

She would *not* dwell on that failure right now. *Please, please,* consider it, Richard! she thought. She gave him a wide smile, and met his eyes, willing him to say yes.

"Well…" he began. He paused. "Could I come up for a visit and view your facilities? Maybe meet some of the other researchers and check out the university?"

A ray of warmth seemed to stream within her. "Of course!" she assured him. "We can pay for your flight and hotel, too." She was positive she'd have no problem clearing that particular expense with the others. Heck, if it meant he'd come on board she'd pay for it herself. "When would you like to come up?"

He thought for a moment. He pulled his cellphone out of his pocket and swiped it, probably checking his calendar.

"I have a long weekend off in ten days," he said. "I could come up Thursday night, visit the Center on Friday, then return here on Sunday or Monday."

"That would be perfect." She wanted to exit on a good note. "Let us know the time you want to arrive and we can make all the arrangements. I'll be in Florida for the remainder of today and tomorrow if you have any further questions." Because they had thought he might want a second meeting with her. Now, it seemed that wouldn't be happening immediately. She could use the day to relax, maybe curl up with a good mystery by the hotel's indoor pool.

"I appreciate the offer." He drained his coffee cup.

"Please call me if you have any questions," she finished.

"I will." He stood and extended his hand.

She stood up, and took his hand, another zing of electricity shooting through her.

"It's been a pleasure," she said.

"The same here." He smiled. "I'll give your offer serious consideration."

She was almost five feet six inches, but at six two or more, he still towered over her. She felt, oddly, small and feminine next to him as she tilted her head to look up.

Their eyes met again, and in such close proximity, she could appreciate the deepness of his brown eyes.

"May I take these papers with me to read them over?"

"Of course," she answered.

They stared at each other for a long moment. With another smile she finished, "I'll speak to you soon!"

"Goodbye, Meredith," he said, smiling back, then he departed.

Suddenly, her legs felt weak, as if she'd run a marathon.

She dropped back into her chair, taking a deep breath. She needed water. That was it. She was probably dehydrated from the plane ride last night and staying in a dry hotel, perhaps from the unaccustomed warmer Florida air.

She finished her coffee, packed up her iPad and stuffed it in its case, then went to buy a bottle of water.

She was a little perturbed by her reaction to him.

She'd met plenty of handsome guys. But Richard's good looks didn't explain the zing—the jolt of electricity—she felt near him. A zing she hadn't been prepared for.

A sensation she had not felt for a very, very long time.

As she left with her water bottle and iPad, the warm and damp Florida air surrounded her. She got into her rented car.

The coffeeshop was close to the university, which was why she'd picked it. It was only a five-minute drive to the chain hotel where she was staying.

The fact that Richard was considering their offer, and had expressed interest in coming to see The Lightning Center in person, was a very good sign.

She returned to the hotel. Once in her room, she kicked off her pumps and glanced at her cellphone, which she'd turned to silent for the interview.

She had a text from her sister Pam. She'd texted: "I had a funny dream last night. Call me after the interview and let me know how it went."

Smiling, she slid out of her suit and got into jeans and a long-sleeved T-shirt. Flopping down on a chair, she punched in Pam's cell phone number.

Her sister picked up on the second ring. "Hi Mer!"

"Hi," Meredith responded, leaning back in the big chair.

"So, what happened with Dr. Belton?"

Meredith described her meeting with the scientist. She recounted his questions, his hesitancy, and her responses.

Then Pamela asked a surprising question. "Is he as handsome as he looks on his facebook photo?"

"You checked him on facebook?" Why was she

surprised? Her psychiatrist sister was, after all, a woman. A curious one.

"Yes. Didn't you? So… is he?"

"Actually, he looks better than his professional photo on his website. But…" a sudden suspicion hit her. "Whoa, Pam. Don't go there," she warned.

"Why not?" her younger sister challenged.

"You know why. I am *not* interested in romance," Meredith replied firmly.

"Everyone's interested in romance. You're human, aren't you?" her sister responded.

"Last time I looked. Seriously, don't even think about it." She certainly tried not to. Since her marriage to Curtis had fallen apart, she was cautious around men. Especially handsome men. And she was determined to keep any relationships strictly casual.

"I'll tell you about the dream I had last night," Pam said, "when you return. He *was* working for us in my dream."

"That's a good sign!" Meredith said, glad to change the subject. "And your dreams come true about 95% of the time."

"If they're precognitive dreams," Pam said. "Sometimes my dreams are just plain silly, like everyone else's. The other day I dreamed I was in an airplane with grandma and she was flying the plane!"

"You should psychoanalyze that one," Meredith said, laughing.

They spoke for a few more minutes, and then Pam told her she had a patient coming soon, and they ended the call.

Meredith stood up. It was almost lunchtime, and she'd had only a quick, small breakfast before meeting

Richard. Time to get lunch and forget about Richard Belton—at least for a few hours.

Richard returned to his office at the university, and sat down at his desk He had two journal articles he wanted to read before his next class.

There was another copy of *National Snoop* sitting on his desk. Probably placed there by one of the secretaries, or even a student who may have dropped in. Since he shared this office with two other professors, people came and went all the time.

He sighed, and tossed this copy in the trash.

Just what he needed. *Not.*

Last week that rag had come out with their annual "Ten Sexiest Scientists" poll. He'd been astounded when the department's main secretary had handed him a copy with his photo plastered on the page. Sexy scientists? That was not something he wanted to be known for! He wanted to be respected for his knowledge of, and research on, lightning. To be one of the top scientists in this meteorological field. Not to be thought of as a handsome or sexy scientist.

His name—and a photo of him in casual clothing—had been listed along with nine other people, including a Japanese micro-biologist and Norwegian oceanographer.

He'd been popular in school and had had his share of girlfriends over the years. Even a fiancé, though that hadn't lasted. But he wanted to be respected for his brain.

He came from a smart and successful family. He did not want to be known for his looks!

He sighed again. At least the people at The Lightning Center wanted him for his knowledge and experience.

He turned away from his desk and stared at one of his lightning photographs which hung on the wall. He found himself thinking about Meredith Costigan.

The woman was gorgeous. There was no other word for her. She had wavy red hair that reached her shoulders and looked like silk. He'd had to fight the urge to reach out and grasp a curl between his fingers. Her eyes were a bright, arresting green. Her skin was creamy and fair. Although she wore a conservative suit, her slim body gave hints of curves beneath the prim outfit. And her legs… when she stood, he'd glimpsed long legs in her simple black heels. Legs that seemed to go on forever. Legs that could wrap around a man. His mouth almost watered.

He'd always been partial to redheads. Meredith was a prime example of a gorgeous redhead.

And her aura—which he was fortunate to read around most people—was a beautiful one. Turquoise, a healing color, but brighter than most. Edged with gold, he thought, but that wasn't totally clear.

And something else. It was spiked in one area with pink.

He recognized when auras showed red that the person could be feeling desire, or passion. He'd been in plenty of situations with women where that had been mutual, and he'd seen the red before going to bed with that woman. The pink was unusual, though, and hadn't suffused her whole aura.

Suppressed desire? he wondered.

He rarely shared his ability to see auras with anyone.

But, he supposed, if he did take this job, he'd have to reveal his ability to the staff of The Lightning Center.

At least the people there would take his talent seriously. No one would doubt him or mock him. No scientists working on paranormal abilities would think this was garbage, as some non-paranormal researchers did.

No, there they would understand and respect his ability. Meredith and her family worked with this kind of thing constantly. It was their mission to study abilities.

And that in itself made the job offer even more intriguing.

He was already looking forward to seeing Meredith again.

And he would. He'd be up in New Jersey soon.

The job offer had been surprising. He'd thought she was coming to consult with him. He'd read about the work The Lightning Center was doing, and knew they'd partnered with different researchers in the past. When she'd ask to meet with him, he'd supposed they had a specific question, or area they needed help researching. He'd thought perhaps he might obtain a consulting job from them.

He hadn't thought about being offered a full-time job.

And what a job! The salary was way above what he was making. And the prestige of possibly consulting with the local state university wouldn't hurt either. Of course, he knew some of his colleagues thought the work that The Lightning Center was doing was everything from unusual to downright weird. But with his own talent, their work on the paranormal didn't faze him. In fact, it made it extra intriguing.

He fought an impulse to get up and do a tribal dance of triumph.

He could be back in New Jersey! His brother, his best friend Tony, and his parents all knew he missed his family and friends, and the change of seasons.

But the tried and true was here. He had a good position.

On the other hand, The Lightning Center could be an exciting opportunity. And the salary was very, very tempting.

He wondered what their policy was on co-workers dating.

Ms.—Dr. Meredith—Costigan was a temptation as well. Working in close proximity to the beautiful and intriguing social worker could be a nice perk if he took the job.

He would see her soon.

Maybe, sooner than expected.

He reached for his cell phone.

Meredith was returning to her room after lunch at the hotel when her phone buzzed.

The phone number showing on the display was Richard Belton's.

"Meredith Costigan," She answered automatically, walking down the quiet hall to her room.

"Hello Meredith."

At his masculine tone, warmth rushed through her. Had he decided to take their offer?

"Hi," she said, while unlocking her door.

"I'm considering your offer," he said, as if he

knew what she'd been thinking. "In the meantime, I was wondering… would you like to have dinner with me tonight? You said you weren't flying back immediately, correct?"

She entered the room and shut the door behind her, as her heart speeded up. That same zing pierced her. Would he take the job? She wanted him to, for more than the obvious reasons—

Damn. Was Pam correct? Did she find him so attractive she wanted to know him better? "I'm here for a couple of days," she answered. "Do you have more questions for me?" As soon as the words left her mouth, she wanted to kick herself. Of course it was business.

"This is social," he answered immediately.

Surprise wove through her. She sucked in a breath, hoping he couldn't hear it. "Okay. I'd enjoy having dinner with you." She tried to sound both professional and friendly, but not too eager. She wasn't sure she succeeded at that.

"Great. Which hotel are you staying at?"

She named the big chain hotel on the main road near the college.

"You're right nearby. Can I pick you up at six?"

"That's perfect." *Get a grip*, she told herself. *This may be social, but it's really about getting him to accept the job offer. Nothing else.*

"Do you like Italian food?"

"I love it," she responded. "I'll see you then."

"Okay. See you soon."

He clicked off, and she slowly put her cell phone back in the pocket of her jeans.

She stared at her suitcase. It wasn't really a date,

she reassured herself. This could be an opportunity to impress him some more with The Lightning Center's achievements.

But it sounded like a date.

She shook her head. She'd been struck by love—like others were struck by lightning—once before, with Curtis. But love probably wouldn't strike her again. She didn't even want to think about it happening, after her bad marriage to Curtis.

So, she'd treat this as more of a business meeting, an opportunity to simply get to know Richard better in case they became colleagues.

She'd been about to change and go to the pool, but now she glanced at her wardrobe. Except for the suit she wore this morning, another business outfit in case of a second meeting, pajamas and a swimsuit, all she'd brought for the trip were jeans and T shirts.

But if she was going out with Richard—she needed something nicer.

She'd passed a small shopping center on her way from the coffeeshop to her hotel, not even a mile away. She'd noticed that it contained a store she liked, so she grabbed her purse and headed out. She was going shopping.

Meredith smoothed her hands over the long lemon-yellow top with silver and black swirls that she'd bought and was wearing over new black leggings. She looked slim and taller in the outfit, and she knew she'd be able to wear it again. Black sandals she'd brought from home completed her outfit, and she'd even painted her toenails bright pink. Dangly silver earrings she'd bought at the store completed her outfit.

She picked up her sturdy black shoulder bag and left her room. She was on the first floor, so it was a short walk down the corridor to the lobby.

As she approached the center of the lobby, she saw a dark blue Jeep through the glass doors. It pulled up, and Richard got out.

She went to meet him.

He was wearing the pale blue shirt he'd worn earlier, but he'd rolled up the sleeves and ditched the tie. He smiled as she approached.

Whoa. He looked even better than he had earlier. Casual Richard was even more potent that business—attired Richard.

"Hi," he greeted her.

"Hi." She smiled.

"This restaurant is a favorite of mine," he said, opening the car door for her. "It's close by. I eat there often."

As he drove, she asked him what had originally gotten him interested in meteorology.

"I was always interested in the weather," he said. "I went to Cornell and studied Meteorology, then came back to New Jersey, to Rutgers, for my doctorate. And, as I mentioned, once I had been struck by lightning, I became even more fascinated, especially with lightning and thunderstorms," he continued, swinging into a small shopping plaza.

"You were never interested in broadcast meteorology?" she asked.

"No. I was more interested in the science behind the broadcasts," he said, pulling into a parking space.

He glanced at her, and she got a whiff of his aftershave again, the same as this morning's, but stronger. She wondered if he had recently applied it. He had an odd expression on his face, one she couldn't read. "I want to be known for my knowledge, my research, not as a TV personality who looks good for the cameras."

There was a slight edge to his voice, which she didn't understand, and wondered about.

The restaurant turned out to be casual, and homey-feeling, with a mural of a Tuscany landscape and sunset on the wall. The hostess, a woman in her fifties, nodded at Richard as if she was familiar with him, and led them to a small table in a corner. It felt secluded, and intimate.

They sat across from each other, and she picked up a menu. She could smell the delectable aromas of garlic and spices.

"What about your career?" he asked, barely glancing at the menu.

"About my career?"

"Yes. What made you go into your field?" He gazed at her.

"Well… I always liked helping people. I didn't think I wanted to be a teacher, or study medicine like my parents," she began slowly. "Still, I wanted to make a difference. And with my family creating the Lightning Center, it just seemed natural that I should work there, counseling and helping people."

"Were you struck by lightning?" he probed.

She shook her head. "No, but as I mentioned, my brother and sister were. They're twins," she continued, seeing how closely he listened. "When they were around four, we were all playing outside and my mom

309

was out too, keeping an eye on us. It was a sunny summer day, and Parker and Pam were grappling with a toy in the sandbox—I think some kind of shovel—and out of nowhere, lightning zig-zagged and hit the shovel, traveling to them both." She shuddered. "Of course my mom called an ambulance. She's a nurse, and checked them over while we waited. My dad—he's a doctor—met us at the hospital. They seemed fine at the time. They were checked out thoroughly."

"At the time?"

"Well, here's the thing." She paused as their waitress approached. The young woman eyed Richard, then asked if they'd decided on their meals. Richard ordered the chicken cacciatore, with minestrone soup. Meredith opted for the chicken parmigiana and a salad. They both ordered white wine.

"Please continue," he urged when the waitress left.

"Well, we'd always observed that Pamela and Parker could communicate without words. It's very common among twins," she said. "They would look at each other, get up and walk over to the same room. Or they'd finish each other's sentences. But after they were struck, it became more pronounced. And as they grew older, they both admitted they could often tell what the other was thinking about."

"So their—twin ESP, or whatever it's called, became stronger?" he asked.

The waitress returned with their fresh-smelling Italian bread and glasses of wine. Meredith reached for the bread and broke off a warm, crusty piece. The scent made her mouth water. She hadn't had a snack today after lunch, and she realized she was hungry.

"It wasn't only that." She bit into the crunchy

310

bread. She chewed, then swallowed as Richard watched her. "They each developed other—abilities."

"Such as…?"

"Pamela began to have precognitive dreams—dreams about the future." She reached for her wine glass and took a sip.

"And did these events come true?"

"Many did." She grinned, thinking about Parker and Sabrina, her soon-to-be-sister-in-law. "For example, she dreamed once about Parker and a woman who would be important to him. Someone he would love." She knew she had a silly, sappy smile on her face which she couldn't help. She loved Parker's and Sabrina's story. "Then he met Sabrina—the woman in the picture—and he did fall in love with her. They're engaged now."

"That's fascinating," he said. "Congratulations to them. But… I'm a little skeptical. Maybe if she described the woman in her dream, your brother was looking for someone who matched that description?"

"I don't believe so. He wasn't really looking for a girlfriend—or life partner—when he met Sabrina." Meredith shook her head. "The dream happened many years ago, when Pam was a teenager. She drew a picture of the woman—Pam's a good artist—and when she walked into our center, Parker recognized her at once. As did Pam and I."

"Hmm…" He reached for his wineglass and drank. "And your brother—does he have an ability too?"

"Yes. He can often tell what someone is thinking—if not the exact content, at least the topic," Meredith said. "Mental telepathy."

He stared at her. "Wow."

"It's what really got us started wondering about

311

people struck by lightning," she continued. "My parents began to do some research, and found that many others who were struck by lightning developed unusual abilities. Then, when Parker got older, he became determined to start a center where these people could be studied and get help either managing their abilities, or with counseling if they needed it. Our whole family got on board. Including my grandfather. And his family had a good deal of money to fund it, plus we got a good number of grants." She smiled proudly. "It seemed natural for Pam and I to decide to work there too."

He grinned. "Keeping it in the family. I guess," he added as the waitress returned with his soup and her salad. "Do you have any meteorologists in the family?"

"No, I'm afraid not." She sprinkled some of the French dressing from a little cup onto her salad. She could smell the spices and tomatoes as she sat across from him. "Although I think the field is a fascinating one. Did you ever want to do any of that storm chasing they talk about on the Weather Channel? I do like to watch that channel every morning," she added. She lifted a forkful of salad and took a bite. The vegetables were fresh and the dressing flavorful.

"I went with a couple of friends twice," he said. "And although the storms were exciting, I found I was more interested in thunder and lightning—especially lightning—than in tornadoes and wind."

She nodded. "And so you specialized?"

"Yes."

She asked him about his storm-chasing experiences, and as they ate their main courses, he described some of his adventures, trying to out run storms while still getting some readings on their equipment. "There was one time," he admitted, "the tornado got so close, we were really afraid we wouldn't outrun it. I remember wondering if I'd ever hang out with my brother again."

"That must have been scary," she said softly. "How did you feel after being struck by lightning?"

"Dazed. I remember a split second of pain, and then waking up with people around me. They brought me to a hospital, but I was okay." Except for the ability he developed shortly afterward. He'd started seeing auras within a week.

"One of my friends at college was struck by lightning as a kid, also," he told her. "Chris told me about it. He was hit, and ended up on the ground."

"Was he hurt?"

"No, just a shock. They checked him over and he was fine. And," he added, regarding her, "he didn't have any after-effects. No ESP or anything."

"Not everyone does," she stated.

Their eyes met, and she felt that little tremor move up her spine. Again.

"Tell me about your family," she said.

"You know I grew up in Oradell, New Jersey. I have an older brother who's a lawyer, and went into our dad's law practice. My dad kind of wanted me to do the same."

"You were never interested in law?" she asked. She bit into her chicken. The dish was spicy and delicious.

"Mildly. But the weather is what really fascinated me, and so my parents realized that I was committed to studying science, and they were ok with that. My mom is a C.P.A., and I think she was secretly disappointed neither my brother nor I ended up in that field." He smiled.

"Well, with a doctor father and a mother who's a nurse, and two siblings who are doctors, I'm the oddball in my family too," Meredith said.

"You don't look very odd to me," he said quietly.

That now-familiar shimmer of awareness moved up her again. She smiled, then bent her head to eat some more of the tasty chicken.

Sometimes she *had* felt a little like the oddball in her family. Or... more like the one who wasn't outstanding in some way, the one who faded into the background.

Her parents both came from well-to-do families. Growing up in Mountain Lakes, where they both had been raised, they were products of rich and professional parents. That in itself was not so unusual in their community. Her father's father had been a well-known pediatrician, his wife a poet with a solid reputation. Her mother's father had been a New York stock-broker who made a lot of money, and his wife a lawyer—something that was fairly uncommon for women in her generation.

But her parents had had twins, which while not totally unusual, was still something people remarked on. As a child she heard people talk about "the twins" often, as if they were an unusual breed. She loved her siblings, and her parents tried hard not to show any favoritism to any of their kids. But the twins had gotten a lot of attention when they'd been out in public. And they had both been so cute. She could remember feeling maternal towards them, at three years their senior, and admiring how cute and funny they could be.

"Meredith?"

She whipped back to the present, wondering if she'd missed something Richard had said. "Yes?"

"You seemed lost in thought."

"Oh, I was a little. I was just thinking back to when the twins were young. I did sometimes feel like the odd man out. Especially when the twins got struck by lightning! Everyone made such a fuss… I remember thinking on more than one occasion that I wished I was the one who'd been hit by lightning."

"Some people get seriously hurt, even die," he said.

She twirled some spaghetti around her fork. "I know. And my mother would say, 'Meredith, don't wish misfortune on yourself,' when I mentioned it years later. But—I was a kid, not quite eight, when it happened. I was jealous." She shrugged.

"That sounds normal," he pointed out.

"I know it is," she agreed. "My brother and sister were twins so they already got noticed; suddenly they were involved in an unusual event. Of course, later, when we noticed their abilities…" she trailed off.

"Later… what?" he asked, sipping more wine.

She met his look. "I'd wished I had some psychic ability, too," she confessed. "But, as you said, that kind of envy is perfectly normal." She knew it—but it had never changed her desire to actually *have* an ability.

He looked at her, and she found herself wondering if somehow he sensed what she was feeling—the yearning to have a special ability of her own, just like her brother and sister.

315

"I think everyone would like to have something special about them," he said.

"Although, if you dig into the surface, most people do have a talent or something that sets them apart," she said.

"Yes, that's true. My brother actually has a good singing voice."

"What talent do you have?" she questioned.

He grinned. "Besides my photography during storms, I'm also a black belt in karate."

"Wow! That's impressive, she said. "What made you study karate?"

"I was the nerdiest kid in my class, and people teased me," he said slowly. "Karate meant I could defend myself if needed, and one time when someone tried to call me names and slug me, I was able to flip him. It never happened again, and the other students respected me after that." He grinned.

"Good for you." She asked him about martial arts, and they spoke while finishing their main courses.

She was full, so she declined dessert, but he had a tortoni and they both lingered over coffee.

It struck her that she was enjoying his company a lot. She hoped he would come to work for them, because she also thought he would be an asset to their group.

They left the restaurant. The night had grown somewhat chilly. Stars twinkled in the sky, where thin wisps of clouds hurried past the moon.

When they reached his jeep, he unlocked the door and opened it for her. Standing close, he met her gaze.

Electrifying energy seemed to leap between them. His face was close, so close—all he had to do was bend his head and his lips would meet hers. She could smell his aftershave, hear his breathing. A wave of warmth from his skin caressed her face. A shimmer of longing swept through her, surprising in its intensity, and she had the desire to reach out and touch his face. She fought it.

The moment stretched out.

Then she stepped back. She didn't want this. Certainly not with a potential co-worker.

He moved an instant after she did, stepping back also.

"Thanks," she said, and hastily climbed into the car before she could say or do something she shouldn't. She snapped on her seatbelt as he went around the front of the car, emotions colliding with in her.

She'd *wanted* Richard to bend his head and kiss her. Wanted it with a surprising intensity.

He climbed into the car, and started the engine.

She was silent, feeling awkward from what had almost happened—and her tumultuous response.

"So... I'll see you in a couple of weeks," he said, as if nothing much had occurred.

That was a guy for you. The moment had meant nothing to him. He probably had barely noticed the chemistry between them, and hopefully was totally unaware of any reaction, any longing, on her part.

She relaxed a tiny bit. "Yes. I'm glad you'll take a look at our facility." She kept her voice even.

He agreed to let her know what flight he'd like to take, and she offered to make the arrangements for him to stay at one of the local hotels. They discussed the details of his travel as he drove back to her hotel.

317

When he pulled up there, he jumped out of the car and opened the door on her side, helping her exit.

She turned to face him and extended her hand. "Thanks for dinner, Richard. I'll see you in a few weeks." She managed to keep her tone friendly and sincere without a hint of anything else.

He grasped her hand. "See you soon."

"I'm glad you're considering our offer," she added.

He nodded. "Thank you."

He went back to his car, and she entered the hotel lobby.

Turning, she watched as he pulled away, and then turned onto the main road.

She sighed, and walked back to her room.

Well. That had been an interesting dinner.

Richard was a pleasant person, and obviously intelligent. She had enjoyed his company.

And she'd felt something she hadn't felt for a long, long, time.

Pure desire.

Nothing more complicated than that, she assured herself.

She absolutely didn't want to feel anything else. Her life was finally nice and peaceful. No exciting highs, no terrible lows. She didn't have to worry about Curtis and his hang-ups anymore.

And she wanted it to remain that way.

Richard Belton was not going to change anything.

A FEW WORDS ABOUT THE AUTHOR

Roni Denholtz is the award-winning author of 20 romance novels and novellas; 9 children's books; and over a hundred short stories and articles. She lives in beautiful northwest New Jersey with her husband and adopted dog.

She has volunteered with school organizations, her local animal shelter, and served as President of New Jersey Romance Writers. She collects girls' series books like the Nancy Drew mysteries. She enjoys traveling, photography, and most of all, reading!

ALSO BY RONI DENHOLTZ

Made in United States
North Haven, CT
26 February 2025